A Kingdom of Madness

To Hilary –
With my many thanks
for all you have done that
allowed me to move forward
with this project.
All best,
Linda

A KINGDOM OF MADNESS

LINDA LEVY

Library of Congress Control Number:		2010906931
ISBN:	Hardcover	978-1-4535-0098-9
	Softcover	978-1-4535-0097-2
	Ebook	978-1-4535-0158-0

It is my fondest hope that the characters in this novel seem real. However, this is a work of fiction, and they are not. I have either imagined or used fictitiously all names, characters, incidents and settings. Any resemblance to actual persons, alive or otherwise, or to events or locales, is completely coincidental.

This book was printed in the United States of America.

Xlibris Corporation
1-888-795-4274
www.Xlibris.com
48580

For Dory

CHAPTER ONE

It was a warm May evening in 1969 when Spec Davis left the grim apartment complex in Philadelphia for the last time and headed for the New Jersey Pine Barrens to visit his father. He stopped twice to ask for directions as he drove his pickup along the flat, two-lane road that cut through a desolate landscape of scraggly, crooked pine trees.

He turned onto an unmarked road, paved but rutted, and partly covered with the sandy soil that was everywhere. Almost immediately another pickup approached from the opposite direction, and he pulled over to let it pass. The driver gave a quick wave without looking at Spec.

He continued for a mile or so, swerved to avoid a dog with three legs, and saw that the road had widened. He passed a car without wheels on concrete blocks, a house held up by several long lengths of timber, another with broken aluminum chairs out front, and Spec assumed he was "entering Hardwick." It was barely an hour since he'd left the city.

Hardwick was a tiny pocket of civilization. It looked unreal to Spec, like a movie set, and he half-wondered if it had been moved here from someplace else.

He drove by a laundromat, a post office, and the Hardwick Market, yellow plastic lining its windows to keep the sun from fading labels on the cans and jars inside. Then he pulled into the gas station to fill his pickup and find out how to get to the house by the Hardwick River. The attendant, who stood talking with a group of men, continued the conversation as he walked over to help Spec. There was no complimentary windshield washing.

Spec paid for the gas and received change, too much, it turned out. He handed the extra bills back to the attendant, who stared at them as Spec drove away.

The "Davis place" was another mile out of town. It seemed to Spec that the unpainted, weathered wood houses he passed had sprung from the bleak terrain. There weren't any lawns or flowers, only trees apparently struggling to stay alive. Through the open windows and screen doors he could hear voices, music, and, from one house, loud arguing, but no one was outside on this mild evening.

Even with the directions Spec missed his father's driveway, partially hidden in the overgrowth. He started to shift into reverse but thought better of it and parked by the side of the road. He reached into the pocket of his flannel shirt, took a Camel from the pack, and held the cigarette between his teeth while he fumbled for a match. Then he lit the cigarette, hands cupped, protecting it from a wind that wasn't there. As he inhaled he sank low in the seat, hugging his down vest and shivering. His feet were cold, although he wore wool socks and insulated boots. Spec pulled the visor of his cap over his eyes. He was aware of his jeans against his bent knees, felt the pull of the cloth. He put his hand to his cheek and slowly rubbed the stubble as he puffed the cigarette and watched the languorous smoke.

"Everything okay, son?"

Spec sat up and repositioned his cap. He had not heard the car pull alongside, and now an elderly man was rolling down his window as he spoke.

"Anything I can do for you? You're not from around here, am I right?"

The questions came too quickly for Spec to break in with an answer.

"Thanks for stopping, but there's no problem here," he said at last, aware of the irony.

The man chuckled. "I get it, I get it. Sometimes I drive off for a while, get hold of myself, then head on back to Olive. Need the break, know what I mean? Gets to be an awful lot over the years."

He chuckled again and pulled away.

Spec's heart was pounding and his palms were damp as he stubbed out his cigarette in the ashtray. Then he yanked the ashtray free, emptied it onto the road, and jammed it back with such force that it bent and wouldn't go back in.

"Okay, housework's done," muttered Spec, before starting the truck and navigating his way into the driveway. He turned off the motor and waited a minute before opening the door. Then he jumped out, grabbing the bag of clothes next to him, and started toward the house. He turned abruptly and tossed the bag into the truck's flatbed.

The house was more substantial than the others Spec had seen in Hardwick. If those had "just happened," this structure had not, with its cedar shingles, high windows, stone steps, paneled wood door.

And here he was, knocking on his father's door and wondering if Davis would recognize him as the six-year-old boy he'd been the last time they'd seen each other. Spec had not called to say he was coming. He happened to know his father had no telephone, but he wasn't at all sure he would have called anyway. What would I have said? he wondered, as he waited for someone to come to the door. Pretty hard to know where to plunge in. For all the old man knows, I jumped off a highway overpass, or slit my wrists, or "accidentally" overdosed in a motel somewhere. A lot can happen in twenty years.

He listened for footsteps, but he heard only the high and low pitches of peepers and tree frogs in chorus, and the long, resonant hoots of an owl. Then the sound of television chatter wafted on a breeze, and Spec knew that Dr. Leslie Davis was at home. The door was unlocked, and he let himself in.

He walked into a large room, apparently the only real room in the house. The air was stale, and there was so much furniture that, with its exposed rafters, the place looked like a warehouse. High above the chaos, two large Oriental rugs were draped over the railing of a narrow balcony. He saw that two of the balcony spindles were broken off at the bottom, splintered, as if someone had rolled a bowling ball through them.

"Hello? Who's there?"

The voice came from across the room, by the television set. It was a smooth voice, the corners rounded. Spec hadn't remembered that.

"Sir?" he said.

That's one thing I sure as hell remember, he thought. Like talking to a goddamn superior in the military.

"It's me, Leslie." He shuddered.

"Ah. I see your mother's little nickname didn't stick after all. Spectacles indeed."

Davis was speaking in a low voice, and Spec wasn't sure if his father was by himself or was speaking for the benefit of another visitor.

"Come over here, boy. Let me see you," he said, louder this time.

Spec picked his way around the furniture and over toward the black leather wingback chair where Davis sat.

"Sit down."

Without turning off the television, Davis gestured in the direction of a chair identical to his, piled with books and newspapers that Spec moved to the floor. He lowered himself into the chair and looked at his father, who was at this moment quietly appraising him.

His father seemed old, tired, not the vigorous man Spec remembered, whose wedding photograph sat on the table by his mother's bed. He saw now how similar they were. He had not expected to be looking at an older version of himself, minus the horn-rimmed glasses. They had the same thin nose, deep brown, hooded eyes, square jaw, cleft chin. Davis's hair, once dark blonde like Spec's, was gray and thin and looked as though patting it with his hand would do instead of combing, although Davis had not done even that. He wore a T-shirt and khakis, neither very clean, Spec noticed. His feet were bare, and they, too, needed washing.

"So. What brings you to a God-forsaken place like Hardwick?"

Cuts right to the chase, thought Spec. No foreplay, no bullshit, no nothing. It was not precisely the warm welcome he now saw he had foolishly envisioned: Great to see you, son. How've you been? I think about you. What are you up to these days? Instead it was, "What brings you to a God-forsaken place like Hardwick?"

Spec resettled himself in the chair before answering the question. He almost said, Okay, here goes. I have no idea what to do with my life, so I'm looking for advice from a complete stranger. Oh, and as far as work is concerned, inertia seems to be my motivating force.

"I was just, um, passing through." He sounded to himself like someone in an old cowboy movie who was delivering his line unconvincingly.

Wanting to avoid the silence that was already threatening to grab hold, Spec asked, "Where did all this stuff come from?"

Davis looked around, as if to see what Spec was talking about.

"Ah, yes. My mother, your grandmother, died last year, and I thought it would be simpler to have everything shipped here."

Did you know that your wife also died last year? Spec almost blurted out. He was shocked to feel such instant anger, and he was afraid of saying something that would end this little reunion before it began.

Spec forced his attention to his grandmother's furniture and was surprised at its calming effect. He thought of the house in Philadelphia, where he and his mother had eaten Sunday lunches. He had loved the big, stone house, the enormous front hall, the terrace in back that overlooked formal flower gardens with a fountain in their center. Two of the upstairs bedrooms opened onto tiny, wisteria-covered, crescent-shaped balconies, little smiles of wrought iron that looked out over the terrace and the gardens. Spec used to stand on the balconies and pretend he lived in that house.

He could feel Davis's eyes on him as he walked around. He recognized many pieces of furniture, now streaked and dusty and marred by deep scratches, not polished the way they'd been when servants were in charge. Spec thought of the heavy velvet draperies that were replaced with flowered chintz in summer, an effort to bring light into a house surrounded by tall, old trees. He thought of the ticking of the grandfather clock, the only sound he could hear when he stood alone in her living room, a small boy holding his breath. Here stood the clock, but silent, and the buffet server with the silver tea service, tarnished black, piled on top, and, he assumed, the silver flatware still in the drawers. Stacks of paintings lay on the pedestal dining table that seated twelve for Thanksgiving dinner without adding a leaf. The room was a mass of chests and chairs and lamps. The furniture arrangement was random, and Spec pictured a gigantic child playing with the pieces, even as he used to imagine that same child playing checkers on the great squares of black and white marble that formed the front hall floor of his grandmother's house.

He opened a large, intricately carved ivory box to find two handguns lying on a red satin cushion. He turned to his father, who had been watching him all this time.

"Guns? You keep guns?"

Spec was incredulous, although he didn't know why. For all he knew, Davis was head of the local chapter of the National Rifle Association.

"Well, yes, just a revolver, really. And a pistol. Then, of course, I have my father's shotgun. I don't use it, but I keep it oiled, loaded, and ready to go, just in case."

Seeing the look on Spec's face, he laughed a short, explosive laugh and continued, "Don't worry. It's up on that shelf"—he gestured in the direction of the front door—"and won't cause any accidents or anything like that."

Davis turned to the box containing the guns. "You see the older one there? The revolver? With the longer barrel?"

Spec held it up gingerly, somehow expecting it to fire even if he did not touch the trigger.

"That's the one," said Davis, nodding. "I bought it for protection after someone tried to break into my office when I was working late at the hospital, back in Philadelphia. Whenever I could get away, I'd come down here and practice shooting targets with it. Cans and bottles, that sort of thing. I actually came to like it. Target shooting, I mean."

Spec noticed that, when his father became excited, saliva gathered in one corner of his mouth, and he left it there.

"So I had the gun modified for that, took it to a gunsmith, who reduced the pressure necessary to pull the trigger. That's what you want to do, you know, just apply gentle pressure."

The thought flitted across Spec's mind that, in their first conversation, they were discussing guns. He hated guns. Then there was the smooth, creamy voice that didn't seem to fit the subject. He wondered if his disapproval showed, but if it did, Davis ignored it.

"The pistol I use for plinking. I like walking through the woods, maybe seeing a woodchuck or a rabbit, and saying, 'Can I hit it?'"

He paused, and Spec thought this might be his cue to ask a gun-related question, but Davis continued.

"Did I ever tell you I had a sort of love affair with falconry when I was in college?"

He didn't wait for an answer. Spec was thinking that it would've made a hell of a bedtime story for a little kid. And what did that have to do with guns?

As if reading his mind, Davis went on.

"I had a hawk. What a beauty! It could take down a victim more efficiently than any gun you'll ever see, and nearly as fast. A hawk will kill for sport, you know, if it's not hungry. Just squeezes the life out of some unlucky creature."

Spec didn't like the course the conversation was taking. He put the gun back in the box, closed the lid gently, and made his way to the other side of the room. He was examining a chess table with a delicately inlaid ivory board and wondering if the pieces were around so he could challenge Davis to a game, when a slight rustle made him look up, directly into the eyes of a young woman.

She smiled a timid, tentative smile, held it in place longer than seemed natural to Spec, then let it slide away. She patted her thick, dark hair and adjusted the elastic that held it back at the nape of her neck, smoothed the print cotton jumper she wore over what appeared to be a man's undershirt, and patted her hair again. Even with her loose-fitting clothing, she was very noticeably pregnant. In a piece of a second, Spec felt his world shift course.

Davis, who had come up behind Spec, now walked past him and stood beside the woman. He put his arm around her shoulders, a gesture at once awkward and proprietary.

"Frances, this is Leslie, my son."

Frances glanced at Davis, then turned again to Spec, who realized that until this moment she did not know he existed. He looked at the two of them standing together, his father and this woman who was probably a good thirty years younger. For an instant he saw them as a snapshot, a bizarre parody of a happy couple.

Frances ducked out from under Davis's arm, then moved some papers off a chair and drew it over to a small, round table covered with dust. She looked embarrassed and began to brush off the surface with her hand. She kept her head down as if hoping that somehow, miraculously, no one would see her at work. Then she looked up.

"Can I get you some iced tea?"

He nodded, thinking she sounded more like a waitress than a hostess, and she disappeared into the kitchen. They heard her washing out a glass and breaking up a tray of recalcitrant ice cubes in the sink. After a rather long time, during which Spec and his father stood together in silence, she came back carrying a glass and a small pot of pink geraniums well past their peak. She set the pot in the middle of the table, gestured for Spec to sit down, and, when he did, handed him the tea. The glass was wet, and Spec placed his other hand under it to keep it from slipping to the floor. Frances went back into the kitchen and this time came back with a saucer, flowered and chipped, which she placed in front of Spec. He put his glass down but the indentation in the saucer kept the glass from resting level, so he held it and sipped, one sip after another, his hands turning cold, while Frances and Davis watched him drink.

There was the sound of a child whimpering, and Frances, without excusing herself, disappeared upstairs. Spec and his father waited without speaking, while Spec sat at the table and Davis stood several feet away. In a few minutes Frances returned with one child in her arms and another clinging to her skirt. They wore only diapers. Spec rose as she approached, a long-forgotten courtesy. Frances looked at him, and then quickly lowered her eyes.

"This is Miles," she said, touching the dark hair of the stocky little boy peeking from behind her. She made no effort to force him forward. "Miles is just two. And this," Frances attempted to transfer the weight to one hip, but the child clung to her neck and made it impossible, "is Thomas. He was born on Miles's first birthday. May first."

She glanced at Davis. She combed Thomas's fine, black hair with her fingers and kissed him lightly on the cheek. Nodding toward her stomach, she added,

"And this next one is due in June, so that will make them all just about a year apart. 1967, 1968, 1969."

Her voice had a singsong quality, her own private nursery rhyme.

"He delivers them here at home," said Frances proudly, speaking to Spec but looking at Davis. She didn't believe, would never believe, that he'd had another life before theirs together. She was already pretending that Spec was just an ordinary visitor.

Spec stared at Miles, then Thomas, then again at Miles, who reminded Spec of pictures he'd seen of himself when he was young. He could hardly breathe, and he felt himself furiously fighting back tears that seemed to have been accumulating for decades. He started to speak but nothing came out, so he cleared his throat and tried again.

"Hello, Miles and Thomas. I'm Leslie. Your brother."

Your brother. Never in this lifetime did Spec think he would utter those words.

"Brother" caught Miles's attention. He had recently been introduced to the notion that Thomas was his brother. Now he no longer hid behind his mother but moved next to her, looking openly at Spec, a baffled expression on his face. Spec wanted to pick up the boy and try to explain it all to him, tell him that he, too, was confused, and maybe they could try to understand this thing together. But he did not reach for the child, and he said nothing.

"Well," said Spec, after a long moment. "Well, I'd better take off. Got a long way to go."

No one asked where it might be that he was going, or urged him to stay. "Be seeing you guys," he said to the little boys.

"Good-bye, Leslie," said Davis.

"Thanks for the iced tea, Frances."

She smiled her tentative smile in response.

Spec found his way to the door and went out quietly, his last view that of Frances and the children, who partially obscured the sight of his father.

CHAPTER TWO

Spec backed out of the driveway and parked in the spot he had left just a short time before. He didn't trust himself at the wheel with his shaking hands. He sat on them and slid down in the seat, staring at the windshield, at the dried arcs of dirt left by the wipers. He was breathing quickly, as if he had run a good distance. He waited for the breathing to slow, but it didn't. Instead he began to tremble and his teeth were chattering. He wondered if he was having a heart attack.

He freed his hands and clasped them behind his neck, pulling his head forward. His watch ticked loudly in his ear.

All at once Spec grabbed the door handle, pushed open the door, and stumbled out. He fell against the truck and leaned on his elbows with his hands over his ears.

An insect lit on his trembling wrist, made its way across, and flew away.

Without warning Spec's knees buckled and he collapsed, like something deflating. In slow motion he curled up, feeling exposed, naked. After a long moment he stretched out and eased himself underneath the truck.

He lay on his back with his eyes closed, trying not to think. He ran his fingers over the sandy soil, felt a stone under his shoulder. The wind had come up, and he concentrated on the sound it made as it brushed past Hardwick. But then, without warning, he found himself falling through memory.

He was nine years old, the only boy in his class who wore glasses. The only boy without a father. Even now Spec could picture his friends' fathers, men who walked into their houses every evening, set down their briefcases, and asked how school was today. The fathers and sons went fishing together, tossed around a football in the backyard, worked on their stamp or coin collections. Sometimes they invited Spec to a baseball game, but he knew their real fun began after he'd been dropped off at home. Lying underneath his truck, he felt the envy moving in, taking control, as it had for all the years.

Today was different, though. There was envy, yes, but there was also rage so fierce he felt his face contort. And there was resentment, and longing. And there was heartbreak, as his heart folded into itself until it crumbled.

Tears collected behind Spec's glasses before running down his temples and into the dirt. He doubted he could survive this monstrous wrath that had, at its core, ineffable sadness.

A long time passed before Spec maneuvered his way out from under the truck and got back behind the wheel. His mind and his body didn't seem to fit together anymore, and he had the sensation that he could no longer contain the jumble of feelings. He thought of the small, inadequate closet back at the apartment, crammed full with more left over, and no place to put it.

That night Spec slept at a rest stop popular with long-distance truckers, his head on the old sleeping bag he kept in the cab. He woke frequently, wondering whether he had really seen his father.

He dreamed he was at Billy Jason's house. He knew it was Billy's, because they were in his kitchen, and Spec saw the little pots of plastic flowers his mother kept on the windowsill over the sink. The cuckoo clock announced that it was six o'clock, just as Billy's father entered the kitchen. Billy ran to him and was scooped up and lifted high enough so he could touch the ceiling.

"Hi, Mr. Jason," said Spec.

But the man ignored him and said to Billy, "Want to go to the Phillies game tonight?"

"Sure, Dad! Can Spec come?"

The man turned to look at Spec, seeming to notice him for the first time. And Spec saw that it was not Mr. Jason at all, but his own father.

Early the next morning Spec headed north for Kings Island, a small, egg-shaped piece of land connected by a causeway to mainland Massachusetts. He had taken a gas-station map of Massachusetts, the state he'd wanted to visit since he'd learned to spell it in grade school, spread it on the table, closed his eyes and stabbed it with his finger. It landed on Kings Island. Spec loaded the dice somewhat by making certain his finger veered to the right in order to ensure he would be near the ocean. Lucky I didn't go more to the east, he thought, or I'd be living on a boat.

On that misty day Spec drove over the deserted Kings Island causeway, a wide, two-lane road with generous shoulders. It occurred to him that, if he hadn't been paying attention, he wouldn't have known this was an island, where the terrain rose and fell in graceful waves that reflected its glacial beginnings. He arrived at a T-intersection and debated whether to go left to Fair Haven or right to Quarter Harbor. Then he laughed out loud. What the hell, he thought. What's the rush? If this is where I'm going to live, might as well check out the whole place.

He turned left without signaling and realized he was testing. Would some cop show up and give him a ticket? But no, no cops, and he headed towards town. The hilly road flattened out as he entered Fair Haven.

Spec had not anticipated the flurry of activity, but then he remembered Memorial Day was on the way, and that's when things start to pop at beach resorts. Memorial Day to Labor Day. After that, the place would pretty much go to sleep until next spring. He was reminded of *Brigadoon,* the senior play he didn't bother trying out for. He thought of his classmates in their Scottish dress, playing villagers whose town came to life for only one day every hundred years.

People were painting their storefronts and hanging signs. Nothing like Hardwick, he thought, as he drove through town, passing Rose's Bed and Breakfast, a souvenir shop with T-shirts in the window, a book store, a grocery store, a couple of restaurants, a movie theater, and a number of colorful Victorian houses with elaborate gingerbread trim in perfect repair. Man, thought Spec, these guys must spend their lives painting. Or, more likely, getting somebody else to do it for them.

When he arrived at the marina, he parked his truck and got out. He'd made just one quick stop on the ride up here, and it felt good to stretch his legs as he walked along the pier, looking at the yachts that were being put in the water. "Our Children's Inheritance," Spec smiled as he read to himself, and then "Four French Chairs." Must mean something to somebody, he thought.

In his truck again, Spec went back the way he had come, back to the sign for Quarter Harbor. He drove through woods until the land opened wide in a panorama of beach grass and dunes; beyond, the sand stretched out to meet the sea. The sun hit the water and silvered it like an old photograph.

In the six hours it had taken him to reach Kings Island, he hadn't once turned on the radio, his head so full that he didn't need the company. Now what he needed, he realized, was a drink. But instead of a bar he passed a small hospital, hardly more than an infirmary, and then a diner a short distance beyond. He was beginning to think he was out of luck when, just outside Quarter Harbor, he saw Kings Tavern waiting for him.

The parking lot was almost full. Spec swung into a space at the far end and walked across the uneven pavement to the tavern. Facing him as he entered the dim, smoke-filled space was a horseshoe-shaped bar surrounded by red vinyl stools; bits of stuffing peeked through peeling strips. Behind the bar a board listed "Daily Lunch Specials," a selection that, Spec guessed, was a never-changing one. The tavern also featured a jukebox, a dartboard, the requisite pinball machines ("Amazon Women" and "Space Creatures"), and a pool table in the back. Small signs hung on the wall, next to a Miller clock and slightly askew: "You don't have to be crazy to work here, but it helps"; "Of all the things I've lost, I miss my mind the most"; and "There's no business like *show* business," under a drawing of a buxom, bikini-clad female.

On either side of the room were wooden tables and chairs occupied by the boisterous, joking, lunchtime crowd. Spec found a seat at the end of the bar, where he sat alone with his beer and his cheesesteak with onions. He felt distant and separate, the way he had in high school before he was "discovered" by the girls, when they giggled that he looked like James Dean and told him his glasses were sexy.

Spec was happy to be left alone. He didn't want to have to make small talk, something he disliked and did poorly. He planned to get the lay of the land, then see about meeting some people and finding himself a job. But not today. He ate the cheesesteak, finished it off with a couple of cigarettes and three shots of bourbon, and by the time the place emptied out, there was nothing he wanted to do but sleep. He drove a short way until he found a dirt road that led to the beach. No one would be patrolling yet, not before Memorial Day, and he parked the pickup as he had the night before, lay down on the seat with his head on the sleeping bag, and went to sleep. The truck would be his home for the next year and a half.

CHAPTER THREE

After Frances and the children went to bed, Davis sat for a long time in his black chair, puffing on his pipe. He had been stunned to see Spec. He couldn't get over how much the boy looked the way he himself had looked at that age and wondered if he was as popular with the ladies as Davis had been. He remembered Spec as a child, a quiet, tentative observer with few friends, always anxious to keep out of trouble. Well, until he was six, anyway. Davis didn't know after that.

His brow furrowed slightly as he recalled the morning he'd walked out.

"What time will you be home?" his wife had asked.

"I won't be home for dinner."

"A meeting?"

"No. No meeting. I won't be home at all anymore."

In the slowest of slow motion, her face seemed to break into pieces. She didn't cry, just closed her eyes and turned away with a soft moan. He watched as she bent her head. Her whole body seemed to follow, curving forward, and he thought she might fall, but she didn't. He took out his white handkerchief, shook it open, and started to offer it to her. But there were no tears to dry, so he folded it neatly along the creases and put it back in his pocket.

He left then, drove off with his belongings in the trunk, where he'd packed them during the night.

What the hell, Davis thought now. There's no point in going back. I had to do it, simple as that. I had a career to build, didn't I? How could I do that with a family dragging me down?

Without that family, he could concentrate on becoming Chief of Medicine at Philadelphia Founders Hospital. Concentrate he did, for years, and he positioned himself perfectly to be Chief. He was a shoo-in. He prepared his remarks for when the announcement came, choosing his words with care. He was—not exactly grateful, because he had only himself to thank. He was gratified. Yes, gratified was the word, all right. He was gratified as hell.

One minute a shoo-in and the next minute out on his ear, big-shot to has-been so fast his head was still spinning more than two years later. He replayed once again the scene that brought them here. "How the mighty have fallen," he whispered.

It was November 2, 1966, Frances's twenty-first birthday and precisely four months after they met. They were eating dinner at a small, out-of-the-way Italian restaurant Davis had heard about. The evening had not started well. As soon as they sat down, Frances proudly displayed her newly-pierced ears, a birthday present to herself. Davis thought the custom barbaric, a self-mutilation, and he felt that Frances had betrayed him by not consulting him first, a nagging thought that stayed with him throughout the evening. But this was her birthday, and he kept his thoughts to himself as he regarded Frances, who was wearing her best dress, thin and flowered and altogether unsuitable for the chilly night. She had on her Add-A-Pearl necklace that, Davis suspected, she wore only on very special occasions, and he was slightly uncomfortable that she considered this such an occasion. She wasn't wearing her glasses, another sign that Frances, somewhat near-sighted, wanted to look her best tonight.

They shared a bottle of wine, the bottom half of which was encased in straw, and whose clone sat on the table with a lighted candle stuck in the neck. Davis ordered for the two of them, the same chicken dish for each, and a single order of spaghetti, which they shared. Much to his irritation, both chicken and spaghetti were covered with the same red sauce, and the "green salad" that came with the meal was nothing more than iceberg lettuce drowning in cheap, bottled dressing. Frances seemed not to notice, certainly not to mind, and she made murmuring sounds of pleasure. She chattered about the surprise party she was organizing for a co-worker's birthday, and Davis listened quietly.

While the dishes were being cleared they sat in silence, watching the busboy pick up the two dinner plates and hold them in one hand, fanned out like cards, then stack them with the salad plates, the butter plates, the butter dish and the bread basket, and carry them off. He saw that Frances had become so mesmerized she seemed sorry to see him leave.

When she spoke again, Frances had let her voice drop. Whenever she had something important to say, she spoke softly, so softly that Davis frequently had to ask her to repeat what she'd said. But this time, although she spoke in her near-whisper, he didn't have to ask her to say it again.

"Les, I think I might be pregnant."

Davis said nothing. He took a sip of wine, set the glass down carefully, and touched the linen napkin to his lips.

"Les, I . . ."

"I heard you the first time," said Davis, his tone sharper than he had intended. He remembered the failed condom immediately.

"How far along are you?"

"Well, I'm not really sure, I'm not all that regular, you know, but I think it's probably about three months."

"Three months! Why did you wait so long to say anything?"

"Well, you've—you've been so busy now that it looks like you really are going to be department chief and everything, I remember you said being named Chief was going to be the best Christmas present you could have, and that 1967 was going to start off with a bang, you said, and I just didn't think I should bother you, that's all."

"All right, all right," said Davis, trying to keep his thoughts well ahead of his words. "We'll take care of it right away."

"What do you mean, 'take care of it'?"

"Well, we'll test you, see if you kill a rabbit. Which you probably will." He was aware that this attempt at levity was not successful. "And we'll check you with an X-ray, find out what things look like in there, and then, I'll do, you know, an abortion."

"But Les, how could I? The Church . . ."

"Screw the Church! What do you think something like this would do to my chances at the hospital? All I need is to have everyone saying that Les Davis has a little bastard on the way, whose mummy is easily young enough to be his daughter. No thanks."

It took Davis a moment to realize that Frances was crying. It turned out that she cried, like she said important things, extremely quietly.

Unless he looked directly at her, which he hadn't during his "screw the Church" speech, he couldn't tell. Now he saw that her head was down, and that she had her napkin, stained with tomato sauce, up to her eyes. Her shoulders were shaking, and her thick, dark hair fell forward like a shield. Davis was afraid to touch her, knew he had to keep his distance in order to concentrate. He couldn't think of anything to say, but then he saw she was trying to talk, through the tears and the napkin.

"I can't hear you, Frances," said Davis.

She took the napkin away and looked at him, her large eyes still wet, her makeup running. "Will you marry me?" she said again.

"Marry you! Marry you?" Davis was taken aback, but not so taken aback that he didn't see this was the perfect solution. "Of course I'll marry you. I'd love to marry you! But Frances, you must understand. We can have another baby later, but not now, not this baby. Please. We'll get married after I'm named Chief. What do you say?"

Davis didn't want to use the word "abortion" again for fear of risking a repeat performance. He disliked the idea that he had to plead with her, had to get her permission to allow his life to continue as he had so carefully planned it, but there wasn't much he could do about that. She said nothing more, but Davis was quite sure, and extremely relieved, that he saw a tentative smile appear on her thin, lipstick-smeared lips.

For a long time, Davis's dreams were drenched in blood. He had never seen so much blood. He had not told Frances the X-ray had revealed small but perfectly formed twins, two tiny fetuses that had caused all the bleeding. She had hemorrhaged, and he had not counted on that. He was working blind, relying on instinct to tell him when the job was done, feeling his way, looking for not one but two fetuses, blood everywhere, as he'd never thought it could be. He'd had to give her a transfusion.

Frances had been in terrible, desperate pain. She stuffed a towel in her mouth to stop herself from screaming, but then she didn't know where she was or what was happening to her, and violent, searing shrieks escaped from her. Frances, who had whispered a prayer of forgiveness before he began, had ended the night with hoarse cries that sounded barely human. And then she was still, so still he thought he had lost her. Then the sobbing, louder and louder, moaning and wailing. Nothing he could say would soothe her. She was soaked with blood and perspiration and tears. For the briefest moment the sight overcame him. He turned away and took a long, deep breath and let it out slowly. When he turned back he knew for certain that, if he'd had it to do over again, he would have proceeded exactly the same way.

Davis shifted in the black chair, put his head back, and puffed on his pipe. He closed his eyes and there was Frances in her thin dress and her Add-A-Pearl necklace, but in his imagination there was no Italian restaurant. Instead they were dining at Pour Deux, an elegant French place, drinking champagne and celebrating his appointment at the hospital.

"Let's finish up and get out of here," said Frances in a throaty, slightly drunken voice. "I'll show you something special when we get back to your place. I'm ready if you are!"

Davis imagined his pleasure at her bold sexuality, brought on by the champagne. The truth was they had a passionate relationship, but she wasn't this vocal about it. Still, she had phoned him that first time—she, a secretary in the hospital admissions office. "The new girl" was how she identified herself when she called, unaware that he knew exactly who Frances Taylor was. She didn't quite say "Hello, handsome," but it was close. He remembered his shock in bed that night when he discovered she was a virgin. He'd assumed she did this all the time, but no, and he was pleased. Flattered, too. She was very attractive, if less well-endowed than he would have liked, and here he was, an ex-swimmer who still had his looks, he had to admit, but whose muscle had turned to fat, which didn't seem to matter to her.

He made her laugh, and that made them both happy. She loved the way he bought two extra movie tickets so they could keep empty the seats in front of them, particularly amusing on a busy Saturday night when couple after couple tried to sit there, and he pulled out the four ticket stubs. Four tickets. Four seats.

And she made him laugh, although it was usually unintentional. He chuckled even now, thinking how she used to keep a special dustpan and brush on the nightstand, the better to get rid of the crumbs from one of their wine, cheese, and cracker snacks in bed.

She felt so small against him, so good. Sometimes he wore a big, loose sweater, just so there was room for her to snuggle under it and next to him. There was nothing like it.

Davis opened his eyes. He must have been crazy to think he could have kept the abortion quiet. He'd thought he was safe, taking Frances in late at night when there was not much activity in that part of the hospital. And then there had been the assurances from the staff that no, of course they wouldn't say anything.

It had blown up in his face. In late December, after Frances had had time to rest, after he'd wrapped things up at the hospital, they had come down here.

It wasn't until mid-January that Frances had realized what Davis already knew; she was still pregnant.

"It didn't work, did it?" she'd asked.

"No," Davis had replied. "It didn't." Shit, he remembered saying to himself. It was twins, and I only got one of them.

He had deserved to be Department Chief; he'd earned it. Even now he could feel the familiar anger starting to churn. He knew life wasn't fair. It was his father's explanation for everything: Davis's young brother drowning, his mother's tendency to stop talking for days at a time. Davis had added some things of his own that weren't fair: his father's brutal temper, and his unshakeable conviction that birthday celebrations were nonsense.

Isn't there a statute of limitations on this "life isn't fair" business? he thought now. Christ, I've paid and paid and paid. Just one job. That was all I asked. Just that one goddamn job. Instead I was banished.

Davis knew this was an overstatement, but in fact he had been asked to leave the hospital, and he did so as his disbelief turned to a toxic brew of embarrassment, humiliation and fury. He knew it would be all but impossible to find another job, but he didn't want one anyway. He'd promised himself he would never write another prescription. He'd make up a story, tell people he wasn't allowed to write prescriptions outside of Pennsylvania. Yes, that would do it. People will believe anything if you say it with authority, and he could certainly do that. He was good at that, as a matter of fact, because he'd actually had a voice of authority for a long time.

Now here he was in Hardwick, New Jersey, sixty miles but light years away from Philadelphia and his beloved Academy of Music. "The City of Brotherly Love," thought Davis bitterly. Whoever came up with that one must still be laughing. The city had spit him out and he had landed in the Pine Barrens, for Christ's sake. He shook his head ruefully. Davis knew the guidebooks described the area as "unspoiled," with its million acres sitting atop a trillion gallon aquifer of pure water. There's a fine line between "unspoiled" and "desolate," mused Davis, to whom the smug pretentiousness sounded like some loony travel brochure.

But the place was well named, he had to admit. It sure as hell was barren, devoid of anything worth seeing, knowing, having. He'd never expected to be living in a house he'd bought strictly as an investment, either. Davis knew perfectly well that some people would think it was charming, with its wide plank pine floors, kitchen cupboards with leaded glass panes, antique bathtub, and riverside setting. But he despised the house, despised the fact that it was located in a town whose idea of culture was a community sing.

Davis stretched in his chair and sighed deeply. His pipe was cold, and he laid it on the plate that he used as an ashtray. He got to his feet, and, knowing he wouldn't be able to sleep, took a flashlight and made his way out to the car. It was a second-hand station wagon that he'd acquired by trading in his much newer sedan. "I won't have any use for a fancy car down here," Davis had told the salesman. "Even up, all right with you?" The man hadn't put up an argument.

He drove slowly through the moonless night. He never failed to notice how few hills there were in this part of the world. And on this road, none at all. In town he turned right, continued past the antique shop that was never open despite the "back at noon" sign, and parked in front of the Hardwick Market. When Davis and Frances arrived on that frigid January day more than two years before, the Hardwick Market was their first stop.

The market was run the old-fashioned way, and Davis was captivated as he watched the clerk fill orders by using a long-handled hook to take items off the highest shelves behind the counter, or go to the metal bins that lined the walls, then ring up the sale on a crank-handled cash register. An overworked coffee grinder kept the air redolent of fresh coffee.

The back of the grocery opened into Sally Bea's Shoppe, a cramped and crowded, windowless place that smelled strongly of cats and sold a little of everything, all of it piled haphazardly on shelves and stuffed into display racks. "And I'll throw in the dust for nothing!" Sally Bea would chuckle. From the Sears Roebuck catalogue that lay on the counter she would special order anything she didn't stock. Her customers appreciated Sally Bea's advice ("Now those pants run slim, so they'll fit little Bobby real good!"), and the corners of the catalogue pages curled and nestled together from frequent use.

She was the postmistress as well, and she donned a green eyeshade when anyone needed to buy a stamp. She was a thin, stooped-over little woman, as faded as the crepe paper she sold, with skin very like it, too. She wore lace-collared, flowered dresses that buttoned up the front and hung away from her body, having kept the shape of a younger, plumper Sally Bea.

Sally Bea never changed her prices. "Why would I go and do a fool thing like that?" she would ask in her shrill voice. "Everybody knows what they are and so do I. I'd never remember how much anything cost, now, would I, sonny?" her name for males of any age, as "sister" was for females.

While Davis was buying food, Frances wandered into Sally Bea's and introduced herself as Frances Davis, adding, "My husband is in the grocery store." There. She'd said it, and she hadn't even stumbled over the word. Besides, by the time people started nosing around, they really would be husband and wife, so this wasn't a lie, Frances thought, more like an exaggeration.

"He's doing the marketing!" Sally Bea exclaimed, smiling at Frances. "Well, I say! Times do change, don't they? Must be nice to have a hubby who does all those little household-y things. Takes some of the burden off you. Now *my* husband, God rest his soul, why he used to say he didn't even know where I kept the kitchen! Used to ask me, 'Where are the spoons?' like I moved them around all the time!

"Say, sister, you ought to join us over at the Garden Club. We meet once a month. Kind of nice. Be a good way for you to meet some of the folks here in town."

But later, when Frances told Davis about the invitation, he said no, he wanted her at home. Privately, he suspected there was already enough gossip circulating, and he was quite sure Frances was too naive to keep from fueling the fires if she mixed with members of the community.

Within minutes of their departure, Sally Bea and Eldon, her brother and owner of the market, were comparing notes, she talking about the "young slip of a thing" who'd come into the shop while her husband was buying groceries, he talking about the "much older guy with the fancy duds," who seemed to be her husband. Then the shopkeepers wondered aloud if the strange couple was "a bit closer related than husband and wife." It wouldn't be the first time they'd seen that, after all.

Startled to find that his eyes had filled with tears, Davis shook his head gently, not enough to make the tears fall, just enough to send them back where they came from. Then he turned the car around and headed for the place he reluctantly called home, the cedar-shingled house that stood alone by the river.

CHAPTER FOUR

Frances lay in bed thinking how she didn't like to sleep alone, but that it seemed to be happening more and more often these days. She was afraid of losing Davis, who was a good man, for the most part anyway. And he took care of her. Not like her mother, who got herself pregnant twice, left the "results," as Frances had come to think of herself and Stuart, with their widowed Gran, and never looked back. Frances loved Gran, but she hated her too, with her "standards," and her manners, and her perfect house.

"Just nod and smile and do whatever you want, Sis," Stuart would urge her. "That's what I do." But she couldn't do that. If she lived there, she simply had to obey Gran, and it made her miserable. And so Frances left for secretarial school and a one-room apartment shared with a girl she hardly knew. Gran told her if she left, she shouldn't bother coming back.

For some months Frances dated immature men with bad haircuts and cheap after shave, who pawed at her in the back seat of their cars. And then she met Davis, with his custom-tailored suits and shirts.

But Frances was worried. She had really let the house go, just couldn't keep up with everything. It all started to go downhill when his mother's furniture arrived. Davis wasn't happy with her housekeeping or with anything these days, and the thought of his displeasure made her mouth go suddenly dry. Frances felt scared, scared he would leave them. She almost wouldn't blame him. It would make perfect sense. What did she have to offer? The only thing she could do was type, and they didn't even have a typewriter. She and the children held him back. If it weren't for them—well, her—he'd be at Philadelphia Founders, like he wanted. And then what would happen to her and the children? Where would they go? How would she get money to take care of them?

Frances was overwhelmed with a sense of panic so strong it turned her stomach, and she knew she was going to vomit. She got out of bed and tiptoed quickly down the stairs to the first floor, then made her way to the only bathroom in the house. The warped door didn't close all the way, and she was afraid of waking Davis. It smelled bad in there, and Frances vomited before she could get to the toilet.

"Why can't I get things under control?" she moaned as she wiped the floor. "I used to be so good at it! I kept this place spic and span!"

She went back upstairs and climbed into bed, thinking of the house as it used to be, before chaos moved in and defeated her, when Miles was growing inside her and she prayed each night that Davis would be happy with the baby she loved already.

The pregnancy seemed to give her energy, and every day she had a project. She wanted things to be sparkling clean, just in case Gran relented and came to visit. Frances thought of Gran's own cleaning projects, which reminded her of the housework scene in *Snow White*, the only movie the two ever saw together. And then she *was* Snow

White, her favorite character in her favorite Disney movie, whistling while she worked, although hers was a tuneless, breathy whistle. As for the words, she sang them with forced enthusiasm (*"Put on that grin and start right in / To whistle loud and long"*).

On her hands and knees she waxed and polished the floors upstairs. The space was small on the second story, just two tiny bedrooms off the balcony that hung over the main room. Davis had promised to fix the balcony's broken spindles. Then she continued downstairs (*"When there's too much to do / Don't let it bother you"*), after which she washed windows throughout the house until her arm was sore, even asking Davis to drive her to Shoreline to buy a ladder and a long-handled cleaning device so she could reach the tops of the tall, narrow windows. Davis was glad to oblige. His fondest hope was that the strenuous, unaccustomed activity would result in a miscarriage. Maybe nature would succeed where he had failed.

Frances scrubbed the bathroom floor and fixtures, scratched the chrome faucets with steel wool in her ardor, and used most of a can of cleanser to dim the orange stains in the bathtub (*"Forget your troubles, try to be / Just like the cheerful chickadee"*). She washed and waxed the kitchen floor, scoured the marble counters, waxed the cupboards and shined the badly tarnished brass knobs. Then she lined the cupboard shelves with pink perfumed shelf paper from Sally Bea's Shoppe. When there was nothing more to clean, Frances ordered curtains for the bedrooms, kitchen and bathroom from the Sears catalogue at the shop. "Buy white, sister," Sally Bea said. "You can't go wrong. Stays looking fresh and goes just fine with everything, a real decorator's dream."

Davis's admiring comments gave Frances more energy than ever, and while she waited for the curtains to arrive, she started all over again. She worked feverishly (*Snow White* was going faster now, too fast for her to keep up), stripping from the floors and cabinets the wax she'd applied a few days before, pulling out the shelf paper, until one day Davis came into the living room where she had set up the ladder and started again on the windows. He helped her down and said quietly, "All right, Frances. It's finished now."

As Frances lay in bed, unable to sleep, images came unbidden, images of that terrible night when Davis tried to tear her baby from her. She watched from a distance as she always did, a black and white film being shown in the sort of dark, filthy theater that would feature pornographic movies.

Once more Frances got out of bed, this time to take a garment bag from the closet in the other bedroom. She unzipped it and took out her wedding dress. She held the crushed netting against herself in the dark, the dress she would wear one day when they finally got married, as Davis had promised her.

For her wedding Frances had had her heart set on a traditional white dress, and the place to find it in Philadelphia, she'd heard from more than one bride who worked with her at the hospital, was the Brides Forever Discount House.

The store, a great, cavernous affair, was a converted automobile showroom. With the exception of a mat at the door, the scratched, linoleum floor was bare. Its dull finish did not reflect the utilitarian fluorescent fixtures overhead, which were the source of a great deal of unflattering light. Tall, metal pipe racks supported hundreds of billowing white dresses restrained by transparent zippered bags.

A small, white-haired saleswoman approached. Her face, powdered an unnatural shade of pink, was set off by bright red lipstick that she had applied as if she imagined her lips to be fuller than they were. She wore a dark blue knit dress with a gold belt that circled a waist no longer there. Her black leather lace-up shoes with their thick heels made a clunking sound as she walked across the linoleum floor. She had a tape measure draped around her neck, an oblong pin that said "Mrs. Sweeney" affixed to her bosom, and an expression of welcome on her face.

"What can I do for you, dear?" she asked.

"I want to look at a wedding dress," replied Frances, even as she regretted saying the obvious.

"Of course, of course," laughed Mrs. Sweeney, and led Frances to one of the two chairs that faced a desk piled high with order forms and fabric samples. "You've come to the right place! What precisely are we looking for?"

Mrs. Sweeney seated herself across from Frances and shifted a pile of samples to one side.

"Something not too—not too expensive," said Frances awkwardly.

"Then why don't we take a look at the discontinued rack, dear? We have lots of lovely things that we discount beyond the usual we give on every garment we sell. Then of course we offer a generous lay-away plan."

Frances, who had that comfortable feeling she always had when she knew someone competent was in charge, followed Mrs. Sweeney to the back of the store, past several customers trying on dresses as their mothers looked on, two generations reflected in the huge, three-way mirrors that divided one dressing area from the next. At each station, by the mother-of-the-bride's chair, was a small table with a stack of brides' magazines and a turquoise glass bowl filled with too-brightly-colored plastic flowers. One of the mothers was helping herself to coffee, pouring it into a cardboard cup.

They came to a long rack with a hand-lettered sign overhead that read "Bargains! Bargains! Bargains!"

"Now let's see," said Mrs. Sweeney. You'd be about a size 2, I think." Deftly she whipped the tape measure off her neck and slipped it around Frances's small bosom, her waist and her hips.

"Yes, definitely a 2. A perfect 2, in fact! Oh, you'll have a nice selection, my dear, a nice selection indeed."

At the far left end of the rack, a white plastic square with a black "2" peeked above the dresses.

"We have . . ." Mrs. Sweeney counted under her breath, "five dresses for you to try. Let me take them out one at a time, and if you like what you see, we'll put it on." She took down the first dress and removed it from the plastic cover.

"Oh, it's beautiful! I love it!"

Mrs. Sweeney chuckled. "That's just the first, dearie. Also it's white, and I think something in ivory might be softer for you."

She showed the other dresses to Frances, who nodded enthusiastically at each, but when she saw the last one, Frances breathed, *"That's* my favorite!"

"It is beautiful, isn't it? And ivory, too. Let's try it on."

Carrying the dress over both arms, Mrs. Sweeney led Frances to a small dressing room whose cloth walls billowed slightly as they entered. In one corner was a white wooden post with large hooks screwed into it. Here she hung the dress and began opening the long row of tiny covered buttons that marched down the back.

Frances slipped out of her loafers, took off her slacks and sweater, and laid them over a metal chair, the single piece of furniture in the space. She stood before the mirror as Mrs. Sweeney stepped up onto a stool and lowered the voluminous dress over Frances's head, then stepped down and went to work on the buttons.

"Oh, it's simply gorgeous on you! What do you think?"

"It's about the most beautiful dress I ever saw in my whole life," said Frances, fingering the tiny pearls that adorned the bodice. "I guess I look like a bride, don't I?" She stroked the scooped neckline with her fingertips.

"Yes, dear, you do."

Mrs. Sweeney adjusted the sleeve so the lace point-on-hand was properly positioned. Then she swooped down upon the long stretch of material and swept it expertly into her arms.

"You see? The train forms a bustle for dancing at your reception, after the ceremony. Naturally the dress will need to be shortened, and the sleeves are a bit too long," she said, frowning slightly, "but of course we take care of all the alterations right here. We also sell lovely headpieces."

She pulled Frances's hair back and up.

"Beautiful," she murmured.

It occurred to Frances to ask the price.

Mrs. Sweeney, seeing the look on her face when she heard the figure, said, "I'm afraid these discontinued pieces are the least expensive items we have."

She avoided Frances's eyes, busying herself by unfastening the buttons. Then she had a thought.

"You know, dear, there is a dress in the back that was sent to us by a new manufacturer who is hoping we'll sell his line. To be perfectly honest, it's not up to our standards, but I could give you a good price, and I know it's your size. I remember because it was so small. Generally the samples are larger. But let's get you out of this first."

Frances looked at herself once more in the mirror. She sighed, raised her arms, and the saleswoman, on her little stool again, lifted the dress up and off. Then she went to the back room to get the sample dress.

"Now," said Mrs. Sweeney when she returned, "it's white, not ivory, but I think it just might do." She showed Frances the price tag, said, "We'll take another twenty percent off of that," and held it up to her. There were no little pearls, and the buttons down the back were just for show, covering the zipper. But there were appliquéd flowers, and the top and sleeves were lace, noted Frances to herself.

"Can I try it on?" she asked, touching the bows at the shoulder.

The lace was hard and it scratched when she moved, but Frances discovered that if she held herself very still, she barely noticed it. She patted the layered ruffled skirt. It was perfect.

"I think you can get away without alterations and save some money," Mrs. Sweeney was saying. "If you get a pair of those spiky heels I see the young girls wearing, you'll be all set. You really look very nice, dearie."

Mrs. Sweeny slipped off the dress with care, conscious of the stiff lace and the marks it was making on Frances's fair skin. She zipped it into a silver Brides Forever dress bag while Frances looked on, thinking that, now that it was hidden away in the bag, she could pretend it was the dress with the real buttons.

She made the first payment and calculated that it would be paid off in no time if, after she took out money for rent and food, she turned the rest of her paycheck over to Brides Forever.

On the day she went to make the final payment, Frances decided against having the dress sent to her apartment. She watched while it was taken out of its bag and stuffed with tissue paper to hold its shape before being packed in a box. She was glad to see the zippered bag had been folded and put in with the dress.

Frances took the large, unwieldy package home on the bus, and that night she showed the dress to Davis. She had kept it a surprise, intending to model it, but she was so excited that she simply pulled it from the box and held it up to herself. Beaming, she watched him expectantly.

Davis stared at the dress that, stuffed with tissue paper, looked to him like a decapitated bride. My God, he thought, what were you thinking? Aloud, he sighed and said, "Frances, Frances, why would you want to go and spend all your money on some stiff, cheap lace?"

Frances wouldn't let herself cry.

"Well, I think it's beautiful," she whispered, aware that sobs would interfere with anything else she tried to say.

She comforted herself with the thought that Davis was just nervous because the vote on the department head would be coming up in a few days. He'd feel better after that, and then they could start making plans for their wedding.

It was February, over a month since Davis and Frances had moved to Hardwick. They hadn't mentioned marriage—or rather, she hadn't brought up the subject—since their discussion in the restaurant, when Frances told Davis she was pregnant. But this evening, as they ate the overcooked pot roast meal she had spent the day preparing, at last she spoke.

"You know, Les, this would be a good time for us to get married, with the baby coming and all." She realized she was speaking too fast and tried to slow herself down. "I know you don't want a church wedding, but I'll bet there's a justice of the peace or something around here, and we could have a nice affair. Quiet, but nice."

She didn't mention the wedding dress. If she was going to wear it before they became parents, she didn't have much time. It wouldn't fit if they waited too long, and, as it was, she would have to have it altered.

Davis didn't answer right away, and Frances wasn't sure he'd been listening to her. She wished he would look at her, give her his complete attention the way he used to. These days, even when he did manage to look at her, she could see his eyes were unfocused. And so, because she could not return his gaze, she spoke to the air, as her glance flitted around the room with no place to land.

At length he pulled his chair closer to the table and said, "You know this isn't a good time for me, Frances. I have a great deal on my mind. We'll talk about it some other time."

Frances swallowed deliberately and made herself change the subject. She couldn't allow herself to be upset. Happy mothers have happy babies, she had read in a magazine, and more than anything in the world she wanted to have a happy baby. Besides, she reminded herself, breathing deeply and stroking her stomach, there were years and years ahead when she and Davis could get married. She forced the idea to the back of her mind, felt herself pushing it farther and farther away. Then she covered it up and smoothed it over, the way she used to do with the wax that the dentist gave her to put on her braces ("charity braces" the nuns called them), tiny little pieces of wax that kept the wires from making her bleed.

"I make good rice," she announced proudly, as her fork probed the perfect, separate grains of the single successful aspect of the meal.

Davis looked at her, then down at his plate. She glanced at him and knew what he was thinking: So? What's so hard about making rice?

But she was wrong. He hadn't even heard her.

While she washed the dinner dishes, Frances closed her eyes and saw herself with Davis dancing at their wedding, and a rush of wind filled the long dress and lifted her high in the air, higher than she had ever been before, and she smiled as she floated gently, ever so gently, above Davis, above everyone.

Frances had never stolen anything in her life. "Thou shalt not steal," one of the "Top Ten," as Stuart used to call them. She knew all the Commandments, thanks to Gran.

But the next day in the laundromat, while she waited for the washing machine to finish, she noticed that *Bride's Magazine* was lying next to the familiar, well-worn copies of *Life, Look,* and *National Geographic.*

Frances glanced around. There were no other customers. Miss Alice, whose job it was to make change from the Chock Full o' Nuts coffee can by her side, sat in the back as she always did, wearing her black coat and reading her movie magazines.

Frances perched on the edge of a folding chair and stared at the big, bright-yellow word "Bride's," then at the bride who looked serenely happy to be in her lace-covered dress, her long white gloves, happy to be wearing white flowers in her hair. The cover promised articles on the perfect hairdo, wedding etiquette, "What Makes a Good Marriage?" and "How to Make Friends in a New Community."

Frances's heart was beating fast. It seemed to know before she did what she was about to do—which was to scoop up the magazine along with the laundry when it came out of the dryer, and push everything into the pillowcase that doubled as a laundry bag.

This isn't really stealing, she reasoned, sneaking a look at Miss Alice. Just about everybody who comes in here has already had a wedding, or else they aren't going to have one. Besides, who wants the old August/ September issue in the middle of winter?

Frances walked home hugging the laundry to her chest. Finding the magazine just sitting there waiting for her was kind of a sign that she and Davis would have their wedding after all, she thought. She could feel the magazine inside the bag, and she smiled to herself.

Davis was out for one of his walks when Frances got home. She went upstairs and sat on the bed next to the bag of clothes and flipped through the magazine, looking at the pictures of dresses, veils, china, crystal, sterling silver. "Being a beautiful woman is a profound responsibility," warned Elizabeth Arden.

She read the advertisements for a "telephone starter set," a Princess phone for the bedroom, wall phone for the kitchen, melodic bell chime to announce visitors.

When she heard the front door open, she slipped the magazine between the mattress and box spring, and when Davis appeared in the doorway, she turned from the clothes she was folding and gave him her best smile.

The only scissors Sally Bea sold were blunt-end children's scissors, so they, and a jar of paste, were all Frances had for the project she planned. She got the idea from their unit on the States in fifth grade—tiny Rhode Island for her, because she felt sorry for it. All the children took empty cereal boxes and stood them on their desks, as they'd been instructed to do. Then they cut off the top, bottom and one side, leaving the front, back and the other side intact. It looked like a book with no pages. Then they were free to cover every surface however they wanted, turning a cereal box into a representation of the chosen state. Frances had drawn pictures of Rhode Island's main products (hay, eggs, textiles, she remembered, and how hard it was to draw textiles) and pasted on the Rhode Island-related pictures she got by writing to the Chamber of Commerce.

Whenever Frances found herself alone in the house, she worked on her wedding project, cutting out pictures of brides, gowns, veils, and headdresses, and pasting them in place. The scissors were not designed for such detailed work, and she frowned as she settled for ragged, irregular edges. She took her time cutting out both of the bottles featured in a Taylor Champagne ad, hoping this was another sign that Frances Taylor would soon become Frances Davis.

Already she was planning a second box, this to be covered with the photographs of china place settings, crystal stemware, and actual-size silver knives, forks, spoons. She would get some proper scissors.

When the box was completely covered, Frances began to read the magazine. She had made sure she didn't cut anything away from the articles about what makes a happy marriage, and how to be at home in a new community.

Six brides talked frankly about their marriages, about the importance of communication and compromise. "Marriage is very enjoyable if you can just relax and be yourself," said Anne, one of the brides, and Frances felt her stomach tighten.

To be at home in a new community you had to plan ahead, go to the library, get the local paper, write to the Chamber of Commerce about organizations to join and activities to enjoy. "The most important thing to unpack is the right attitude," she read, and was advised to invite people over if they do not invite you first.

Frances closed her eyes and tried to imagine the house clean and bright and welcoming, with polished furniture and long draperies and flower arrangements. She was unsuccessful, but she kept her eyes closed for a long time anyway.

A few days later she slipped her hand under the mattress but couldn't feel the magazine or the cardboard. She got down on her knees and lifted the edge of the mattress as high as she could but they weren't there. She heard something and looked up to see Davis watching her.

"In the woodstove," he said curtly. "I didn't think you needed them anymore."

CHAPTER FIVE

More than two years later, Frances thought about that cereal box every time she bought cereal for the boys, and she had to buy some today. As usual, she would do her errand now, first thing in the morning. Davis didn't like to be awakened, and it wasn't easy to keep the children quiet,

Frances pushed the big double stroller Sally Bea had given her into town.

"Used, but who cares? It's yours if you want it. Has this extra little seat you'll need when you've got the three," she'd said.

Frances had jumped at it. She didn't give Davis a chance to object, just brought it home.

When they arrived at the Hardwick Market and Sally Bea's Shoppe on this warm morning, Frances took the boys out of the stroller. Carrying Thomas and holding Miles by the hand, she made her way up the three creaking, uneven wooden steps to the porch. Two men were rocking slowly in faded green chairs, and they nodded to Frances as she walked by.

She let go of Miles's hand and opened the door, and as she did so, a bell tinkled overhead. Immediately Sally Bea emerged from her shop to see who had come into the market.

"Well, hello, hello, hello!" she chirped. "Out for a little fresh air, are we?"

"Yes, we are, thanks to you. Where would we be without you, Sally Bea?"

"Certainly not here in town, that's for sure, what with your not being a driver. Am I right? Or am I right?"

She led the way into her shop.

"Sister," said Sally Bea, as she brushed past a display of fly swatters, "I've been thinking, and thinking doesn't come easy to me!" she chortled. Then, "You could use a friend. Everybody needs at least one, and so far as I can see, you are lacking in that department." She pronounced it "De. Part. Ment." And she introduced her to Dorothy Turner.

"Dorothy's an old friend of mine. Moved into town from Philly some years back. She's an artist, paints real pretty pictures, sunsets and like that. You two will like each other a whole lot."

Frances glanced at the tall, heavyset woman standing next to Sally Bea. She wore large glasses and a faint smile. Gray hair fell to her shoulders, and enormous hoop earrings tapped the collar of her loose-fitting work shirt. Her hands, stuffed into the pockets of her jeans, came free now, ready to shake hands if that seemed appropriate. But Frances, panic-stricken, simply looked from Dorothy back to Sally Bea.

"Dorothy's had herself some mighty bad times," Sally Bea continued. "Got through them, though. Now she's got a reputation for being good at listening to other folks' troubles."

What Sally Bea didn't say was that Dorothy had escaped a husband who had nearly killed her, and that she'd promised whatever heavenly power might or might not have been responsible for saving her life that she would return the favor. Anyone she could help, she did help. And according to Sally Bea, Frances was a good candidate for her assistance.

"Yes, indeed, Dorothy's a real good listener," Sally Bea was saying now. "And sister, I think you have a lot to say!"

"Oh, no, no—I don't—I can't—" protested Frances.

Sally Bea cut her off.

"I know all about it." She turned to Dorothy, who was gathering her hair into a ponytail. "Hubby doesn't want her down to the Garden Club," she said, raising her eyebrows meaningfully. She turned back to Frances. "This is just between us, sister. You walk to town pretty much on schedule, I'd say, come in the morning most days. If Dorothy happened to be in the shop then, having her coffee, well, no reason on earth why you two couldn't catch a quick chat while I watch the kiddies, and nobody would be the wiser. You hear me?"

Frances turned pale. She took the boys outside, put them into the stroller, and returned home without the cereal she'd intended to buy.

The next day Dorothy was there, and the next day, and the next, standing by the magazine rack, flipping through a magazine, glancing up and smiling at Frances, who didn't so much as smile back. But then one day Frances abruptly walked over to Dorothy and began to tell her how sad she was, how much she missed her grandmother, how Davis thought it best if she stayed in Hardwick rather than travel all the way to Philadelphia, how her brother, Stuart, came to visit sometimes but she was impossibly unhappy when he left. Before she knew it she was sobbing so hard she couldn't speak, Dorothy's strong, plump arms were around her, and she disappeared into the embrace.

The real estate agent who had sold Davis his house called to say that a barn on the adjacent property had come on the market. "It will flesh out your estate quite nicely," was how she'd put it, and Davis thought what the hell, why not, I'll have more woods for plinking, and bought it without mentioning it to Frances. She was always worrying about money, would they have enough, would they run out, how would they educate the children, and on and on and on. It was easier not to say anything. Besides, he had plenty of money from his successful years, although it wouldn't last forever, he knew.

The following day, while Frances and the boys were in town, Davis went to inspect his new acquisition. He was familiar enough with the property but had not actually been in the barn, which was just visible from the house.

He stepped outside and, finding it not as warm as he expected for this May morning, went back for the tweed sport coat he continued to use. He pulled it on over his T-shirt and walked down the road.

They certainly use the word "barn" loosely enough, thought Davis, as he glimpsed the long, low building through the trees. You'd think a barn would have a silo next to it. Not that he'd ever seen a silo on the property, but still.

For several minutes Davis struggled unsuccessfully with the door, at once certain that it must be locked and mystified because there was no keyhole. Then, realizing a sound hovering in the air was that of wood being chopped, he began to think in terms of getting help. He followed the road in the direction of the sound, and in a short while he came to a small cabin he'd passed frequently. This was the first time he'd seen anyone outside. The sinewy body of the man with the axe impressed Davis, who didn't understand how anyone could be wearing only jeans and a T-shirt on this cool morning. As he got closer, however, he saw it was not a shirt at all, but a collection of tattoos so extensive that no area was left uncovered, all the tattoos neatly arranged in the overall shape of a T-shirt. He also saw that the man was a great deal older than he had looked from a distance, as if a camera filter had been taken away. Davis couldn't help wondering if the large brass belt buckle was as cold against the man's bare stomach as it looked to be.

"Hi, neighbor," said Davis, who was slowly realizing that he probably should know this man, since he lived nearby. Then again, he wasn't much for socializing. The only people he knew in Hardwick were shopkeepers.

The man continued to chop wood.

"Hi, neighbor," said Davis again, louder this time. It crossed his mind that the wood chopper might be hard of hearing.

"I heard you the first time, buster," said the man, his voice clouded by years of heavy cigarette smoking; a cigarette dangled from his lips even now. "What do you want?" he continued, without missing a swipe of his axe. He had not looked up from his work.

"Well, I—I—"

"Out with it, young fellow!" bellowed the man, who put down his axe, laughing heartily and enjoying his little joke, and clapped his visitor so hard on the back that Davis stumbled forward before catching his balance.

Davis knew this would be a good time to smile, but all he could manage was a grimace as he put out his hand.

"Les Davis," he said, sensing that "Les" might be more acceptable to a half-naked man chopping timber in the cold than would "Leslie."

"Hank," said the man, gripping Davis's hand with such force that Davis could feel his bones rub against each other, and he had to bite his tongue to keep from exclaiming in pain. So preoccupied was Davis that not until later did he realize he had no idea whether or not Hank had another name.

"Got a door seems to be stuck shut. Having a little trouble getting the thing open." Davis listened to himself talk and marveled at the way he was trying to adapt his speech to something this man could connect with. It did not occur to him that such a speech pattern had little in common with his sport coat. "I'm just down the road apiece." Apiece? Davis hadn't known the word was in his vocabulary.

"Let's get going then!" said Hank enthusiastically.

As they walked back down the road in silence, Davis glanced sidelong at Hank, at the deeply wrinkled skin that evidently retained its ruddy color throughout the year. Folds, thought Davis. More like folds than wrinkles, really. He had never seen anything like it. And his neck. The veins had quieted and no longer looked like lengths of rubber tubing, as they had when Hank was exerting himself. Out of the corner of his eye he saw Hank light a new cigarette with the butt of the one he'd been smoking.

When they reached the building, Hank turned and pushed his shoulder against the door, which gave way so readily that he practically fell inside. "This some kind of prank, mister?"

Davis searched Hank's face for a hint that he was joking again, but there was none. He decided to drop the pretense of being a Hardwick native.

"Sorry. I'm only a doctor from Philadelphia, with no visible muscles. I apologize."

"Forget it," said Hank, softening. "Say, maybe me and you can make a trade. I got a blister or something on my foot. Mind taking a look?"

Without waiting for an answer, he dropped to the hard ground and removed a heavy work boot encrusted with dried mud, and a heel-less, dark gray sock that was stiff with age and filth. He held his leg up with both hands so Davis could see the underside of his foot. Davis stooped over to look.

"Yes, you're quite right. It was a blister, but now it's an infection," he said, peering at the unwashed sole but not touching it. "Unfortunately, being a Pennsylvania-licensed physician, I can't write prescriptions in New Jersey." Davis paused, almost expecting Hank to call him on it. As if this man on the ground before him would know that indeed he could write prescriptions if he wanted to.

Davis continued, "You need to begin taking an antibiotic as soon as possible. I suggest you get yourself to the emergency room down in Shoreline. And be sure to continue the medication until it's all gone. That's extremely important."

"Thanks, Doc. I had an idea that might be in the cards, but hey, I'm not about to drive an hour for nothing."

"This certainly isn't for nothing," Davis reassured him. "Otherwise you might . . ." Davis was on the verge of giving the worst case scenario but decided against it, "be uncomfortable," he finished lamely.

Hank, thanking Davis over and over again, pulled on his sock and boot. Then, gesturing with his head at the house next door, he said, "So you're the guy who lives here. Been a couple of years, right? Had enough of the big city, I guess."

"Yes, I'm here with my—wife and two boys. And a baby on the way."

"Been pretty busy, huh? Well, guess I'll be meeting the missus and the kiddies one of these days. Now I better be getting back to my axe. Be seeing you."

Hank put out his hand, but Davis, anxious to avoid another bone-crunching handshake, was already thumping the man's arm in a friendly gesture that had the advantage of keeping his own right hand occupied. Hank smiled, a wide grin that revealed the absence of a number of essential teeth, and headed back to his cabin. Davis watched him go, then turned and entered the barn.

The space felt so immense in its emptiness that Davis, with the heavy odor of damp wood in his nostrils, had the sensation he was still outdoors, but that night had descended off schedule, the way it does during an eclipse. Thanks to the small pieces of light that found their way through cracks in the lumber, he could see that the entire building was a single outsized room, a bowling alley for a giant. At the far end was a pair of doors so massive that, Davis was sure, an eighteen-wheeler could drive in with plenty of room to spare. Indeed, the expanse was such that he could easily see any number of vehicles parked in here.

The place might make Davis some money at that.

CHAPTER SIX

The idea was beautiful in its simplicity, thought Davis. The barn would become a garage for car repairs, maybe even be called "The Barn." He'd have the best mechanic and make it the place to go. At the very least, he said to himself, I'll have a reason to get up in the morning besides stand around looking at the river.

He asked Hank to help with the construction, which would involve an office as well as a garage. Hank would act as foreman, hire the help, and outfit the shop with the necessary equipment—hoists, auto dollies, hydraulic jacks, air compressors, and the like—as well as put in windows and light fixtures.

Hank was on board right away. It just so happened that Johnny Johnson, "the best in the business," in Hank's opinion, had made some bad investments and wound up losing his shop. He'd be the perfect occupant. And Hank knew of plenty of locals who would be delighted to get involved in the construction project.

Jobs were not easy to come by, and word quickly got around that the "Philadelphia Doc" was paying pretty decent wages to anyone who cared to lend a hand. In addition, they got free medical advice. They asked about their aching backs, their children's excessive weight gain, their wives' painful menstrual periods. Always he listened patiently and gave them his opinion in language they could understand. When it was simply advice, they didn't try to pay. But when they came with a broken arm to set or a boil to lance and Davis wouldn't charge them, they reappeared with payment of whatever sort they could manage: eggs, potatoes, a hand-knit sweater.

Late one Saturday afternoon, when Davis was inside the garage making lists of materials used so far, over the sound of hammering he heard a truck pull up. He went out to show the driver where to put his delivery and saw it wasn't a delivery at all. It was a station wagon, and one Davis didn't recognize. He stood by the door to the office and watched while five men in their late twenties climbed out.

It took Davis a minute to realize that, without a white coat among them, these were residents from Philadelphia Founders Hospital. And they had come to see him. Two years since he'd left, but that didn't matter. They hadn't forgotten him, and that was the important thing.

There was an awkward moment when Davis felt like throwing his arms around each of his boys and hugging them all, but instead he put his left hand in his pocket and settled for being a sort of one-man receiving line, as they filed past and shook his hand.

"Good to see you, sir."

"Hope we're not intruding."

"We miss you at the hospital."

"It's not the same without you."

"Sorry we couldn't get here sooner."

Davis smiled his "Mona Lisa smile," as it was known back at the hospital, not quite a smile but better than nothing.

"Come into the house, for Christ's sake!" he said.

Davis, a troop leader with his Boy Scouts, led them inside and over to the leather chairs by the woodstove. He sat down and gestured for the men to sit as well. Where, he didn't say, so they moved the piles of books, papers and journals aside and sat on the floor. As Davis lit his pipe, he glanced up to see Frances in the kitchen doorway.

"Come, Frances. As long as the children are napping, I'd like you to meet some friends of mine."

The news had flown around the hospital that Frances Taylor had accompanied Leslie Davis, M.D., to Hardwick, New Jersey. No one, however, knew about the conditions they were living in. The residents, embarrassed, rose as she came over, uncertain as to protocol. Frances's arms remained folded against her stomach while Davis made the introductions. Her head was tipped to one side, and she looked confused.

"Do you want some tea?" she asked.

The men looked at each other and then at Frances, shaking their heads and declining in a murmur.

"Well, then," she said, and went back to the kitchen. She could hear them telling him about the hospital, first low voices, one at a time, then overlapping as they got louder, then boisterous laughter, but they quieted whenever Davis spoke. She heard him describe the garage and the plans he had, and she hoped they were as impressed as she was. He told about his walks in the woods, his plinking. Then he talked about the hawk he kept when he was in college. Frances hadn't known about the hawk.

"I loved that hawk, but I had to give him back to the wild when I went to medical school. No more time for such pleasures. But now I have a gun. I guess you could say I've graduated."

He chuckled, and the men joined in.

The conversation didn't stop until the men reluctantly got up and bid their good-byes. As they agreed in the car on the way back to the hospital, it was great to see the Doc again, they were glad they'd finally decided to do it, but what the hell was going on with the house?

It was the first of many trips that Founders residents made to Hardwick, and when they were no longer residents, those who stayed on at the hospital continued to visit. Every few months the station wagon arrived carrying whoever was able to get away that day, and they stayed for hours. They sat on the floor and listened to Davis expound on a variety of subjects, all in exchange for simply bringing news from the hospital. Then he would pose a medical or ethical problem. Is routine tonsillectomy advisable? Will artificial hearts amount to anything? Will the future of cancer treatment include multiple drugs administered simultaneously? The problem would be hotly debated as he puffed on his pipe and the residents went through packs of cigarettes. Finally one of the visitors would say, "We really have to be getting back," which was code for, "If I don't get something to eat, I'm going to pass out right here," and the cue to leave. Nothing had been offered since that first day when Frances asked if they wanted tea.

It was during one particular visit that Frances began to see their life from Davis's perspective. Up until that moment she had considered them a family that had moved away from the city and settled in the country. Now it dawned on her that, foolishly, she had assumed Davis thought the same.

Conversation had turned to the practice of medicine in rural areas, and Frances listened as she stood by the kitchen sink.

"I've got a drive-in medical practice going here, for Christ's sake," Davis was saying. "They might as well be ordering hamburgers. Folks honk the horn, and out I go with my stethoscope and blood pressure cuff."

They laughed, and Frances could feel her face flush in embarrassment at her own self-deception. She touched her hot cheeks, then took her hands away.

Davis continued.

"They can't pay, of course. Not that I could bring myself to charge them anyway. They don't have two nickels to rub together, but they're good people, proud people, and Jesus, do they love me! They really do.

"Most of what I do is either preventive or deluxe first aid. I don't know that I actually consider myself a medical man at this point. It's more like being in the salvage business."

Tears were spilling down her cheeks before Frances realized she was crying. She didn't know Davis at all.

A moment when she was a secretary in hospital admissions came to her, a shred of remembered conversation. She was in the ladies room, and two women from the typing pool came in and began applying their makeup. They thought they were alone. She could hear their voices change pitch as they leaned forward into the mirror. She heard hair spray being forced from the can, a great deal of hair spray, and the smell, or the conversation, drifted into her stall and made her lightheaded.

"Everybody calls him 'the Doctor,'" one was saying, "like there's only one, or something. Like he's God's own doctor."

"Yeah," said the other, "and then every once in a while somebody'll go to the complete other extreme and say 'Doc Davis.' Doc Davis!

Like they're on friendly terms with the guy! Must be some kind of act. Nobody, and I mean nobody, is on friendly terms with Leslie Davis, and everyone knows it. Or should, anyway."

Frances thought of how she'd lowered the toilet seat quietly and sat with her head between her legs until the feeling of faintness that came over her had passed.

And now, here in the kitchen, the feeling came over her again. She sat on the floor, pressed herself against the cabinet door, and hung her head between her bent knees. Dear Lord, she prayed, please, please don't make me have to go into the bathroom and be sick. Please don't let them see me like this.

She felt ridiculous and mortified and frightened. What kind of a wife was she, that she hadn't known Davis no longer thought of himself as a doctor? The words "deluxe first aid" and "salvage business" crawled over her.

Frances ran the fingers of one hand lightly over her forehead, the way Gran used to do while saying softly, "This will take care's creases away."

When she awoke, the house was still. The children were asleep and Davis had gone upstairs to bed. She rose stiffly from the floor and went up to join him.

CHAPTER SEVEN

When Spec first arrived on Kings Island, still dazed by the discovery that his father had another life and another family, the island was preparing for the summer season. The countdown to Memorial Day Weekend was everywhere in evidence in Fair Haven, as shop owners and innkeepers applied a fresh coat of white paint to their establishments. The garden club put pots of red geraniums along the brick sidewalks, and scraped and painted the dark green park benches that sat under the trees in the tiny town square. A banner announcing the Memorial Day Parade stretched high across Main Street. Kings Hardware replaced the post office as the town's social center, and it was there that word from the Chamber of Commerce spread rapidly: rentals were up, and 1969 had the makings of a very good year.

Spec Davis knew none of this. As he would later confess, he pretty much sat things out, living as he was in his truck. He spent his time drinking at the tavern, or sleeping, and often not being able to remember much of anything about the previous day. When he needed money for liquor, or for gas, or for the little food that he ate, he did a few days' work stocking shelves at Joe's Market. Joe, like the cops who let him park off the road and sleep it off, sympathized with Spec. After all, which of them on this island hadn't had a bit of a drinking problem at one time or another? Joe was glad to give him work when he asked for it, admired him for wanting to work, and always managed to find something for him to do, even at the height of the season when the snot-nosed college kids were falling all over themselves for the privilege of unloading crates from a truck. He liked Spec, and when the weather turned cold, he insisted Spec sleep in the market's back room.

Spec had never thought he'd be living in a truck, but the pickup certainly had that "lived-in" look, he told himself. The floor and seat were littered with pint bottles and beer cans and sticky orange juice cartons, and with crushed chips and cookies. Between the perfunctory cleanings when Spec used his arm to sweep out layers of debris, he stamped into submission the half-empty tins of beans and tuna fish, and the small boxes of dry cereal, bent and broken.

When he could no longer stand the feel of himself in his clothes, Spec visited the public showers down by the dock, washing his clothes without taking them off. If cleanliness is next to godliness, he thought in one of his more lucid moments, I'm damned both ways. He hated his life.

During the second summer, Spec began going to the movies on rainy days, when the films ran continuously during the afternoon and through the evening in an effort to keep vacationing beachgoers from complaining that they had nothing to do all day. He took his bottle into the comforting darkness, where he drank and dozed, then awoke, watched for a while, and drank and dozed again until finally around midnight, Bart, the ticket-taker, shook his shoulder and said come on, Spec, everybody's gone and we have to close up now.

Then it all changed.

Twice a week Spec bought the Island Times and read through it, trying to see how and where he might find his way into this community. It was a rainy Saturday morning in August when Spec went to the diner in Quarter Harbor, paid for his coffee and newspaper, and found an empty booth so he could read in peace before buying his bourbon and heading for the movie theater. Looks like it'll rain all day again, thought Spec, not without some degree of anticipation. He noticed the ashtray at his booth had been emptied, which meant he couldn't scrounge butts and tape them together to make a serviceable cigarette.

His eye flicked over the news. McDonald's was looking to come to Kings Island and forces were lining up for and against the effort, year-'rounders in favor of eating out cheap, and summer residents opposed to having "their island" contaminated by fast food. A 50-pound seal was found injured and was sent to the aquarium in Boston. Dixon Decorators was having a "pre-end-of-season sale." Mr. and Mrs. Theodore Andrews of San Francisco were visiting her brother and sister-in-law, Dr. and Mrs. Edward Castle, of Fair Haven and Tuxedo Park, New York. John Turner, a retired electrician, died while visiting his daughter in Florida. A wildflower walk would leave the Nature Center at eight o'clock Monday morning. A tennis tournament would be held at the community courts the following weekend. Sailboat races were scheduled for Wednesday, with a rain date on Thursday. Tonight there was a free organ concert at the church, after which Gracie Harper would show slides of her trip to Nepal. Local artists were invited to submit their work for the juried Labor Day show at the Stony Ridge Gallery.

In Police Notes, Spec discovered that a television set was stolen from the Fair Haven home of Charles Wilson, and that a Springer

Spaniel was struck by a hit-and-run driver. The dog was taken to a veterinarian in Boston. Spec wondered if it had gone to Boston with the seal.

He read on: "The Rescue Squad responded to an emergency call from Island Cinema at 1:41 P.M. yesterday. Spec Davis, 27, was taken unconscious to Kings General Hospital. Davis, who had regained consciousness upon reaching the hospital, was treated and released."

Spec re-read the three sentences, then removed his glasses, cleaned them, and put them back on. He read the words again. Holy shit, he said to himself. Holy, holy shit. He turned back to page one and checked the date, thinking he might be so screwed up that today was really April first, and one of his drinking buddies from the tavern had arranged for this joke to be played on him. He looked in another paper and another and another to make sure this was in every paper, not just the one he had happened to buy. He glanced around the diner, expecting to see everyone staring at him, but no, they were eating their eggs-over-easy and their sausage links and their hash browns, same as always. Deverna saw him looking around and smiled from behind the counter.

"Life goes on, eh, Spec?" she said, pulling up the starched handkerchief that emerged from her uniform pocket like a flower arrangement, then adjusting the hairnet that covered the puff of her orange-red hair.

"Yeah. Right," said Spec, unable to force a laugh. He appreciated her effort, but she didn't know the half of it, that he had absolutely no recollection of any of this, not even when it was staring at him from page five of Island Times. He remembered Bart walking him out to the truck last night around midnight, asking if he was sure he was okay. It hadn't struck him as odd at the time, but it sure as hell did now, Spec realized. Goddamned odd. Went from the theater to the hospital and back to the theater, and he didn't remember a damn thing about any of it? Christ Almighty. He decided to skip the movies today, rain or no rain. From the bottle in his pocket he poured a slug into his coffee to steady himself, and waited until a decent hour before heading over to the tavern.

Sam was showing the ropes to a young woman he introduced as Trudy Payton. "Things are busy," Sam explained, "and I could use some help. Besides," he added, lowering his voice and speaking into Spec's ear as if divulging privileged information, "I'm not getting any younger."

Spec looked at Trudy, with her long, light hair and pretty, shining face, her bright smile, and the bluest eyes he'd ever seen. She wore an embroidered vest, tight-fitting jeans, and a wide leather belt around her small waist. He found himself repugnant. He left without having said so much as hello.

For a long time he sat in his truck, gazing into the oversized mirror that jutted off the door and thinking Jesus, I look like Santa Claus out of uniform. A little younger, maybe, and a shitload thinner, but that's about it. Except for the fact that I'm also losing my mind.

At the showers he borrowed a towel as usual, removed his grimy clothes, then soaped himself and let the hot water run over him. Spec faced upward into it, bowed his head, and let it slide down his neck and shoulders. He took a long time shaving the beard and moustache. He considered getting a haircut but decided he wasn't ready for that, so he washed his hair, smoothed it down, and tied it back. Having dressed in the mostly clean shirt and jeans he had found in the rear of his truck, he rummaged in his knapsack until he found eye drops. He gazed skyward, expertly dripping in the liquid that would, for the time being, clear the redness from his eyes.

Spec was never sure whether or not Trudy recognized him as the slovenly, hirsute individual who had stopped by earlier that day. She didn't bring it up and neither did he. He knew only that he wanted to spend time with her, have a conversation, and drinking gave him that excuse.

In the days that followed, Spec found it easy to talk about himself, but Trudy preferred to chat about inconsequential things. She liked the trusting atmosphere of Kings Island and the fact that people never locked their doors; she couldn't see why the townspeople had voted to drop the apostrophe from "King's" to make it "Kings" Island.

"So what was it like, being an only child?" asked Trudy one quiet afternoon. She stood behind the bar. Spec sat on a stool in front of her.

She continued, "There were so many of us that we had to fight to get a decent place at the dinner table, so's there would be something left on the platter by the time it came around."

"Different set of problems. Completely different," said Spec. "There were only the two of us, my mother and me. After the split."

He closed his eyes and saw her. The gray hair, the thin, unpainted lips, the unfashionable clothes too big for her slender frame. He looked at Trudy.

"One morning I went down for breakfast and she was crying. Stirring the oatmeal and crying. I asked her where he was, and she didn't say anything. Just kept stirring the oatmeal. I was six."

"Oh, Spec. Did you have any idea it would happen?"

"I don't know. Does any kid really, deep down, think it will? I mean, I used to hear them at night, when I was in bed. He'd be talking pretty loud and she—I'm pretty sure she was crying. Then I'd fall asleep and kind of forget about it by the next morning."

Trudy examined her fingernails. "My parents have stayed together. I never see them, but they're together. And I don't think they're even happy. Families. You can have them. Besides, I wouldn't wish this world on any kid.

"When I turned ten, I was beside myself. Double digits and all that. I had asked for a new bike, but there was no chance of that, much too expensive. I couldn't wait to find out what I'd get instead. Ten! A really important birthday, right? Nobody said anything at breakfast, and I thought they were planning a surprise party. I went to school looking extra, extra nice, so when I got home I would be looking my best and I'd act all surprised. Turned out the surprise was on me. No party, no presents, no cake. They forgot, that's all. The day disappeared like all the others."

Spec leaned forward on his stool.

"Jesus, Trudy. That's pretty bad. My mother never forgot my birthday, but she sure screwed up sometimes. 'I didn't have anybody else to practice on,' she used to say. I remember on my seventh birthday, all my buddies were there. Billy, Joe, Eddie, Moose, everybody. So we're waiting for the cake to come in, and I'm all excited, and in comes my mother. But she's not doing that slow, cake-carrying walk, where you try to keep the candles from going out. Oh, no. She comes rushing in and tells us she forgot to buy candles. The guys just kind of left after that. Don't ask me why we didn't eat the damn cake anyway. It's not like those little bits of dripped wax taste so good on icing or anything.

"I said before that we had different problems, and we did, but we had money problems, too. Difference is, my mother would have walked in front of a bus before she'd discuss them with me. She saved every goddamn cent, including pennies she found in the street, so I could be a 'college boy.'"

"Didn't your father help out? Send money?"

"For a while. Then he kind of stopped, and she was too proud to go after him. They were still married, too, never got divorced. 'Don't worry,' she used to say, 'we can manage just fine. And some day you'll make something of yourself. I'll be so proud.' So what do I make of myself? The king of minimum wage. For that, she read the newspaper in the library so she wouldn't have to buy it. Ate her breakfast in the car so she wouldn't wake me when she left for work. Me, on the pull-out couch. Oh, I'm sure she's looking down at me right this minute and is proud as hell."

He banged the counter with his fist.

Trudy put her hand over his. After a minute she said softly,

"What was her name?"

"Emily," said Spec.

"Emily," repeated Trudy. "That's a beautiful name."

Every day Spec promised himself he would sit and have one drink, two at the most, so he could enjoy Trudy's company, but all too frequently he awoke the following morning in his truck, parked in some remote place he didn't remember driving to, and he knew he had failed himself again.

"Where do you live?" she asked one particularly slow day.

"Come on, I'll show you," he said, as he waved to Sam and helped her on with her coat before leading the way to the truck. He opened her door, then leaned in ahead of her and brushed as much of the debris onto the floor and under the seats as he could. Inside the truck they sat in silence for several minutes, while Trudy waited for Spec to start the motor. Finally she spoke.

"Here?" said Trudy.

"Yeah," Spec answered. "No place like home."

Spec had wanted to sleep with her then and there, right in the truck, had wanted to take her to bed since he'd first met her. But he was embarrassed that he had so little to offer, and hadn't said anything. He couldn't believe it when Trudy suggested one day that he come home with her after she got off work that evening. Two weeks later, she asked him to move in with her.

"You make me feel good all over," she told him, "and I don't just mean in bed."

Spec felt the same way, but he couldn't bring himself to say so.

Home was a one-room, unheated fishing shack that Trudy had arranged to use over the winter at no charge. "External plumbing," she said, laughing and pointing to the pump and the outhouse that were shared by a dozen shacks in the summer but were theirs alone at this time of year. The shacks were grouped in a semicircle at the edge of a bluff high above the harbor, like so many board members waiting for the chairman to arrive. In order to reach the shacks it was necessary to follow a long, winding dirt road up a berry bush-covered hill to the crest, then use the steep, rickety wooden steps that led down the other side, to the rear of the shacks.

Theirs had been built from so many scraps of lumber that Spec dubbed it the "Nail Palace," for the inordinate number of nails that had been called into service. The room, which Spec paced off at about sixteen by twenty feet, had at one end a tiny, wood-burning stove, and at the other, a crumbling foam mattress on a plywood platform. In the center of the front wall was the only window, a disproportionately large one. Outside dangled a rusted thermometer that consistently, mockingly, read seventy-four degrees. The kitchen sink was a metal basin on top of two crates that sat under the window. The crates had been turned on their sides and stacked, making shelves to hold the few eating and cooking utensils. Next to the crates was a small ice chest, their refrigerator. Two mismatched folding chairs and a card table, its plastic top dried and cracking, stood nearby. A leftover piece of the flat, industrial grade, olive green carpeting Sam had used at the tavern covered the center of the floor. At night, light came from a kerosene lantern.

When Spec moved in, Trudy set about making the place more cheerful. Using a worn yellow-and-white striped sheet she bought at the church rummage sale, she made a curtain for the window by tacking up a length of rope and stitching the fabric over it. She tacked another rope around the crates under the basin and hung more sheeting there, hiding the cookware from view. There was not quite enough left for the proper tablecloth she wanted to make, but she hemmed what she had, creating what amounted to a large, square placemat, almost the size of the table.

That winter was unusually cold, and because the fire in the stove went out during the night, Spec and Trudy awoke to a frigid house whose windows were coated with ice on the inside. But Trudy kept her sense of humor. She kept Spec's, too, as he often told her.

"I had opaque glass installed," she teased. "For privacy." And she snuggled close to him under the mound of borrowed quilts and blankets.

When they found the dishwater frozen around the dishes left in the sink the previous night, she hung a picture she had torn from a magazine showing an ultra-modern kitchen, dishwasher in the foreground.

Each day while Trudy was at the tavern, Spec chopped wood. Sam had taken down a number of large trees on his property and said to Spec, "Haul it away and it's yours!" He couldn't have done it without the help of a friend who had a log trailer.

By the end of the day Spec had begun to take nips to calm his trembling hands, and most often, when Trudy arrived home, he was sleeping a sleep so profound she couldn't awaken him. She would drive up in her old white sedan, whose every day threatened to be its last, and if she saw smoke coming out of the chimney, she knew the house would be warm and Spec would be awake. But generally there was no smoke, and she would find him passed out in bed, the scent of liquor strong in the air. She would light the stove and sit next to it cross-legged on the floor, hugging her coat around her until the shack had heated up enough for her to take it off.

On one of Spec's good evenings they sat at the card table eating dinner, feeling the warmth of the woodstove on which Trudy had prepared their scallops in cream, when Spec said quietly, "Marry me."

By the light of the lantern, he watched something come over her face.

"Marry you! Why would you want me to marry you? You hardly know me!"

"I know enough. Just marry me." Then, as if he thought everything would change by the addition of the magic word, as his mother always called it, he added, "Please."

"Oh, you know enough, do you?" Her voice was rising. "Do you know my father drank like you do? Except he got violent? Forgot himself and beat my mother?"

Trudy hurled the words at Spec. She took a deep, shuddering breath and was silent for a moment, and then she spoke softly.

"The next day he'd be astonished at the way she looked, he'd ask where she'd been, what had happened to her to cause the black eyes and the bruises and the God knows what else. And he'd ask about the smell of urine all over the house that was his doing, he urinated wherever he happened to be. My mother never told him, either. She'd make things up, make excuses for him. She didn't want to embarrass him."

"Did he get you and the other kids too?"

The words were out of Spec's mouth before he'd had a chance to censor them. Trudy looked away.

"I'll stop drinking, but—marry me. Please." He couldn't help saying it again.

"It wouldn't work." Trudy had turned to face him. "I can't tell you how often my father promised he'd stop drinking. He'd cry and kneel down in front of my mother, put his arms around her waist and sob and sob, saying he'd change, things would be different, he'd never do it again he swore to God. And my mother would stroke his head and touch his cheek and I'd know she trusted him and she forgave him, and I'd also know nothing would be different. Not ever."

"Trudy, I'm not your father," said Spec, his voice catching in his throat.

He got up from the table and picked up his knapsack. While Trudy watched, he reached into one of his boots by the bed, pulled out a pint bottle, and dropped it into the knapsack. He took another from behind the woodpile, and still another from the pocket of the heavy jacket hanging from the back of his chair and put them into the knapsack along with the first.

"Okay, that's it. No, wait a minute. One more." This time he flicked aside the curtain under the basin, picked up the deep blue bottle of "antacid" that he kept on the lower shelf, and deposited it, too, in the knapsack.

Without putting on his jacket, Spec went out into the cold, and Trudy could hear his crunching footsteps as he walked across the frozen grass to the edge of the bluff, where the land dropped down to the harbor. She went to the window, but the darkness reflected only her own anxious face hovering over the basin, and behind it the stove, and the table and chairs, and the kerosene lamp, a phantom room that extended into the night. She knew that Spec would be throwing the bottles into the water, and she thought she could detect each plunking sound, so hard was she straining to hear.

She was waiting by the door when Spec came in, and when he kissed her, she shivered from the cold of his clothes.

Trudy couldn't leave Spec alone, and she got word to Sam that she wouldn't be in to work for a while. Spec lay shaking on the floor by the stove, which Trudy kept going all the time, and she sat with him, whispering to him, holding his head in her lap when he wasn't

too restless to keep it there. She pulled the covers from the bed and
wrapped him in them, but still he shook and moaned "I'm cold, I'm so
cold," over and over, and then he threw off the covers and she found
he was bathed in sweat. She sponged his face, but he was shaking so
wildly she couldn't get his clothes off, and they dried hard and stiff and
sticking to his skin.

For five days, Trudy tried unsuccessfully to tempt Spec with food.
For five days and nights their home was the bed she had made for
them on the floor by the stove, but it seemed to her that he never
slept once, so great was his agitation. Later he told her how her calm
voice had drowned out the things he heard, and told her about the
terrifying visions that cursed his sleep and forced him from the bed.
But that was later, when he was able to articulate what it was he had
seen, when he could explain that he thought he alone understood
the mystery of life, that it had to do with a disgusting, loathsome
creature who began to fly apart and pieces of that creature became
other creatures, different creatures, vile as the first, and he knew this
first creature was himself. Most brutal of all was the sense that he
was caught in a time warp, or a timeless warp, in which these events
repeated themselves again and again and again, a horror movie he
had seen before and was seeing now and was destined to see for all
eternity.

Trudy tried not to fall asleep, but there were times when she
couldn't keep herself awake any longer. With Spec lying beside her as
she drifted off, her hand on his chest, the last thing she thought was
that his heart was racing so fast it seemed not to be beating so much
as flowing. Sometimes, after what felt like a few minutes, she would
awake to find him sitting bolt upright, his head shaking frantically, his

eyes open wide, his breathing unnaturally fast, and he would begin
yelling, "NO!" and thrusting his arm up to protect himself from what,
Trudy did not know.

She didn't realize until later that they had spent New Year's Eve this
way, welcoming in 1971 with Spec waking her with violent twitching,
which was quickly replaced by frantic brushing of his hands against his
legs, his chest, his face.

"Get 'em off me! Jesus Christ, get these things off me!" He leapt
up, tearing off the clothes that had again soaked through with sweat,
and began beating at himself. Trudy lit the lamp and brought it close
enough to see there was nothing on Spec's naked body, but still he
flailed at himself as if at an enemy.

It was Mitch Trimble, a friend of Trudy's who needed another
hand on his fishing boat, who came to Spec's rescue. Trimble had
married late in life and liked to say that, just two years before, all he'd
had was a brown bag with two, three pair of pants in it and now he had
a family and washing machine and everything. He hired Spec without
ever having met him.

Spring had come and Spec was ready to work, now that he was
released from the black moods that had enveloped him for much of
the winter. Besides, the shack was no longer available and it would
take two paychecks to pay the rent on even the modest place they had
found.

Mitch's boat was an old, wooden, 50-foot trawler named Mary Mae
("And don't go thinking Mary Mae's my wife!" said Mitch with a chortle),

whose deck was covered with nets and ropes and once-brightly-colored plastic floats. The first time Spec saw the tall, skinny ladder leading up, up, up to the platform, and the elaborate system of lines that was the rigging, he was overcome by a memory of a long-ago circus high wire act, with its intricate apparatus.

"You need a strong back and a weak mind to do this job," Mitch had warned, but it didn't take Spec long to fall in love with the sea and with fishing. It was an occupation tailor-made for someone just off drinking, miles away from the shore and the tavern and the temptation. Out on the water he had none of the sudden attacks of pure panic that sometimes came out of nowhere these days, when his pulse raced and his breathing quickened and he sweated through his clothes. Since he stopped drinking he found he often forgot things, simple things, that Trudy had asked him to do while she was at work, and at other times he apologized for not doing something he had actually done and then forgotten. He told Trudy that each day was like a completed jigsaw puzzle with a few lost pieces. The big picture was there, he told her, and most of the detail. Most, but not all.

Spec felt that the sea forgave him all this, and because remorse did not follow him onto the Mary Mae, he soon learned what he was supposed to do and how to do it. The work was physically demanding, but Spec found its straightforwardness refreshing. In time his hands learned to do the work, relieving him of the need to concentrate. His mind was free to roam over his life as it had been and as it was now. When he began to fish, he explained to Trudy, the jigsaw puzzle of his days became increasingly complete.

Spec had asked Trudy not to discuss his drinking with Mitch, who didn't know Spec's history, which meant that at sundown when they came in from fishing, if Mitch said come on, Spec, what say we go get ourselves a little nip, Spec said sorry, I've got stuff to do. There were times when he came close, but just picturing Trudy made the urge disappear.

Later, much later, when Spec had regained his sense of humor, he told Trudy that it must've been something like that for his horny friends back in high school, when their parents chaperoned the dances and made that urge, too, disappear.

"You know," he said, "I can still see ol' Gregory, Mr. Makeout, Mr. Go-All-the-Way, dancing with his girlfriend when his parents chaperoned a dance. Mr. and Mrs. Taber, they just smiled and bobbed their heads around like those bobble-head dolls people keep on their dashboards. Christ, he held her so far away his folks could've come over and stood between them."

"How about you?" asked Trudy. "Did your mother ever chaperone?"

Spec snorted. "She was more likely to work as a stripper than chaperone a dance. If she wasn't working, she stayed home. I could deep kiss a girl right there in the middle of the dance floor if I wanted to." He saw the question on Trudy's face and answered it before she asked. "No girlfriends. A hell of a lot of deep kissing, though."

He kissed her softly, a long, sweet kiss.

They were married on December 28, 1972, which they calculated to be the second anniversary of the day Spec walked out into the cold to throw away his habit. The ceremony, performed by a justice of the peace on the mainland, was witnessed by two penguin shaped, silver-haired women who stood knitting while they watched the proceedings, heads tilted to the side, smiles frozen, skeins of yarn tucked expertly under their arms. Until one laid down her knitting and played "Oh, Promise Me" on the organ as Spec kissed Trudy, the musical background consisted only of the steady click-clicking of knitting needles.

That morning, when Spec put on tan corduroys, buttoned a clean blue work shirt up to the neck and put on the striped tie Sam had loaned him, he wished he had a suit to wear alongside Trudy's pale blue silk dress. She wore the bright blue beaded earrings he had given her for Christmas, telling her they matched her eyes. Today he gave her a necklace, companion to the earrings, and said it was not only for this day, their wedding day, but for that lost Christmas when he was too drunk to know it was December twenty-fifth.

They stood before the justice of the peace, and Trudy's hands shook as she held the bouquet of plastic flowers provided by the witnesses. This was the first time Spec had seen her in a dress, and his efforts to glimpse her legs as she stood beside him made her cheeks flame with embarrassment and pleasure.

They had no honeymoon. The tavern was busy at this time of year, what with everybody depressed over the holiday season, so Trudy changed into work clothes, jeans and a bright red turtleneck sweater back at the house. She almost took off the earrings and put on red ones, but then thought better of it and smiled at herself in the mirror. She drove to the tavern as usual in the pickup, which she shared with Spec now that the sedan was no more. It was a lost day as far as fishing was concerned, since Trimble had gone out hours before with someone he'd hired to take Spec's place for the day, and Spec planned to spend the rest of the afternoon and evening working around the house.

He thought of this new dwelling as the mother of the old one, which they could just see from the living room window. They could afford the rent because the place was unfurnished, and because no fancy summer people wanted to be at this end of the Island.

Spec smiled, remembering the first time they'd seen the house. From the front it was long and low with a nearly flat roof, a scaled-down boxcar that had fallen out of the sky and happened to land right side up. The shingles, weathered gray, had been installed haphazardly. There was no landscaping; no trees, no bushes drew attention away from the mismatched windows, or from the signs that a front porch was obviously planned but never built. Instead, a single step led up to the front door, with its blistered red paint. This opened directly into the surprisingly oversized living room.

It was, he told Trudy happily, a "genuine, insulated residence," with electricity and indoor plumbing, though there was a stall shower and not the bathtub Trudy had hoped there would be. Hot water radiators heated the living room and kitchen, the bathroom, and the three bedrooms lined up along the hallway. Large, medium and small, Three Bears style, said Trudy, adding that it was really small, smaller, smallest. They ate their meals in the kitchen and did their laundry there, too, thanks to a small combination washer-dryer.

They had taken out a loan in order to buy some used furniture at a shop on the mainland. Trudy favored a cluttered look Spec privately found claustrophobic. It involved her covering the couch with so many little pillows that he had to move them out of the way in order to sit down, and the assortment of area rugs spread about the living room reminded him of a rug sale. To Spec's dismay, Trudy gravitated toward items that had been something else in a previous incarnation, and so they had a lamp made out of a copper kettle, a coffee table made from an old sled, and a chair made from a tree stump so heavy it had taken three men to carry it into the house. Spec reacted by refusing to admit these items had new identities, and he simply referred to the kettle, the sled and the stump whenever possible.

On this their wedding day, after Trudy left for work, Spec took off Sam's tie, realizing too late that he could have given it to her to return, and changed from his shirt and corduroys into a plaid flannel shirt and jeans. He had intended to chop wood while it was still light outside, but it had started to snow so he decided instead to do some painting and then make dinner, which they would eat at midnight when she came home. They rarely ate together, rarely even saw each other, since Mitch picked up Spec shortly after Trudy went to bed. And, Spec thought ruefully, they sure didn't have much sex these days. Life is nuts. When he'd been drinking, he mused, they'd had lots of time, but usually he was too drunk to get it up. "Natural birth control," Trudy called it. And now, when he was off the sauce and raring to go, she wasn't around. He turned on the television, a set that received one channel fairly clearly and two others with considerable interference, to keep him company while he worked. Someone was giving a weather report. Shit, said Spec to himself as he adjusted the picture, you can figure out the weather better by looking at the map behind the guy than you can by listening to him talk.

He opened the paint, poured some into the metal tray, and moved the roller through the pale gray several times before ridding it of the excess and beginning to work. As he spread paint on the bedroom walls, he gradually stopped listening to the TV and began to think about what he would make for dinner. There was chicken in the freezer compartment, he knew, and he remembered seeing a box of spaghetti and a jar of sauce in the cupboard. He didn't know whether there was any lettuce left over or not, but, now that they had a telephone, he could always call Trudy and ask her to run out and buy some. Suddenly he couldn't wait to see about the lettuce, so he put down the roller, went into the kitchen, and opened the refrigerator. There on the top shelf was a bottle of champagne and a note of congratulations from Mitch Trimble.

Trudy arrived home to find Spec asleep on the bed. Funny, she thought. He was hard asleep, but at last she was able to awaken him.

"Sleeping?" she said. "On our wedding night?" She was only half teasing.

"Come on, I have to show you something," said Spec groggily as he rose from the bed.

He led her into the kitchen and over to the sink where the bottle of champagne lay smashed, with only the gold foil-covered top and neck intact.

Trudy looked at Spec, confused.

"A present from Mitch Trimble," he said. "For us."

"No," said Trudy, smiling. "For me."

CHAPTER EIGHT

July 1971.

Frances held Miles on her lap, rocking him and wishing she had a proper rocking chair. She thought of the advertisements she admired in magazines, mother and baby in a rocking chair. There was always a rocking chair. That's what a little boy needs when he can't go to sleep, she thought, not just his mother sitting on a couch, moving back and forth.

Only Miles was awake; Thomas and Clara had gone to sleep some time before. Frances could hear Davis drawing air through his pipe, as he sat across the darkening room in his wingback chair. Even on a sticky summer night like this he sat by the cold woodstove, as if he needed the imagined warmth.

Miles showed no signs of tiredness, but kept up animated chatter with Frances. He spoke in the low, gravelly voice that she loved, a voice that disappeared in a whisper when he tried to raise it.

He talked now about the butterflies he and Thomas chased that day, about the beetles they picked up, about the spiders they watched. Frances cupped her hands around his chubby legs and stroked them while she listened, taking pleasure in the softness of his skin and in the jubilant smile on his wide, square face. Although he certainly favored Davis, Frances thought the person Miles most resembled was Jackie Kennedy. No matter that she was now Mrs. Onassis, to Frances she would always be Jackie Kennedy.

There was no denying it: Miles was awake. Frances rose and picked him up, a sturdily-built four-year-old and heavy for her to carry. Together they went into the kitchen for a pad and pencil, and then returned to the couch. Already Miles was exuberantly, hoarsely, singing.

"A-B-C-D-E-F-G!"

"Should we write something, Miles? A real word?"

He grabbed the pencil and began to write the letters of the alphabet. Gently Frances took the pencil from his hand.

"How about if we write your brother's name?" She printed "Thomas" in large, block letters. "Okay? Let's both try it."

Miles held the pencil and Frances placed her hand over his, guiding it, and together they traced the letters, over and over: Thomas, Thomas, Thomas.

"Now you," said Frances.

Miles carefully printed the name: T-H-O—and then—Frances wasn't sure whether he was impatient to finish or was simply unaware he had skipped two letters—he made a shaky 'S.'

"There," he said. "Thomas."

"You've got part of his name there. It's an abbreviation."

"But does it spell anything? Did I write anything?" he asked urgently.

"Well, I guess you wrote 'Thos,'" said Frances slowly, her tongue lingering between her teeth on the "th" sound.

"'Thos,'" repeated Miles, imitating Frances as he stuck out his tongue on "th," then exaggerating the "aah" as he did when his father used a tongue depressor to look down his throat, and finishing with a hissing "ssss."

"I'm going to call him Thos. Thos, Thos, Thos, Thos, Thos!"

Thos. Because Davis considered nicknames to be frivolous ("Les," for some reason, didn't count), he gave the children his names, family names, formal names, never consulted her. Miles. Thomas. Clara. Yes, she, too, would call him Thos, would whisper "Thos" in his ear, quiet as the breeze that came through the screenless windows on this summer evening.

Miles had gone to sleep, and Frances kissed his cheek and laid him on the couch, where she knew he would remain through the night. The dogs scratched at the door and she let them in. Peanut Butter was a big, old, yellow Labrador retriever, and Nighttime a bigger, older, black one. The children had renamed the dogs when Davis inherited them from a patient who moved away.

Frances could still hear Davis smoking his pipe, and she said into the darkness, "Are you coming up?"

"In a little while. You go on."

Frances went upstairs and sat on the edge of the bed. Slowly she pulled the elastic from her hair, shook off her shoes, and, still in her pale pink housedress, lay down, shrugged up the covers, and went to sleep.

When she woke the next morning, Frances knew Davis had never come upstairs, had slept again in his chair. She had not planned to change out of the wrinkled housedress, but the air was hot and still upstairs and she was sweating. She had little choice about what to wear, just an old, lavender, halter-top dress, which she'd regretted buying. She could still hear Gran's cross voice saying, "Well, I'm sure I don't know why you bought it in the first place," when Frances confided the mistake.

Combing her hair with her fingers and stretching the elastic to accommodate the wiry bundle at the nape of her neck, Frances paused at the top of the stairs as she did every morning, summoning the courage to continue down. The sight below was at once alien and all too familiar. There was more furniture than ever. The clinic Davis had been associated with finally disbanded, and his "share" was delivered by truck. Frances pleaded with Davis to have everything put into the barn, but he said no, that was impossible. He agreed to put his medical records and equipment there, but he said they could not encroach further on Johnny Johnson's garage space. "I'm getting a piece of his very successful business, and I'm not about to mess that up," he said with finality, and that was the end of that, and then he asked Hank to come and help them stack the furniture.

Hank suggested they create paths. "Least you'll have a fighting chance of getting around the place," he said, and so there were pathways that wound through the room. Davis pointed out that they seemed to have developed a workable burglar-proofing scheme, since it was impossible to get to the valuables. Hank made sure there were a couple of usable tables, as well as a few accessible places to sit.

Frances hated that the house smelled bad. Not fresh. Not clean. Bad. She had bought room deodorizers and stuck her finger through the ring and pulled up the heavily pine-scented wicks from their bottles, hoping they would perfume the stale air. But they had dried out without making any noticeable difference and remained where she had left them, candle-like fixtures adorning the room.

Now Frances hurried along the pathway to the kitchen. Her eyes the barest slits, she sucked in her breath to hold herself away from the filthy furniture. As she passed Davis sleeping in his chair, Frances saw that his stack of newspapers had tipped over, fanning the papers downward. He had taken off his shoes and socks; his shirt lay on the floor where he had thrown it when he became too warm during the night. Half a cup of cold coffee and an empty glass sat on the floor next to an overflowing ashtray. It was always a puzzle what she was supposed to do with the mess Davis created. When she cleaned up after him, he appeared to take it as a rebuke, even as he made frequent unflattering comparisons between Frances and his mother and her apparently legendary housekeeping.

Frances continued toward the kitchen, stopping outside the door to gaze at Miles, who slept unmoving on the couch by the kitchen door. Tiny drops of perspiration shone on his body, which was naked but for his diaper.

Once in the kitchen, she took the coffee pot from the sink, removed the basket, and deposited the grounds on top of the garbage that lay mounded in the step-on trashcan. The lid had broken off, but Frances could not break herself of the habit of stepping on the pedal. It had been a long time since they visited the town dump. Instead they waited until the large, foul-smelling cans that sat outside the front door were heavy with rotting garbage before dragging them to the edge of the woods to be emptied.

She added water to the coffee pot, letting it mix with yesterday's brew, and, without rinsing the basket, replaced it in the pot and measured out the coffee. She picked up the coffee pot, saw there was no room for it on the stove, and used her free hand to shove the pans from last night's dinner off to the side. While she waited for the coffee to perk, she stared out the window, watching the birch trees move effortlessly in the light summer wind.

Taking her coffee with her, Frances picked up a small parcel and carried it outside. She walked down toward the river, and then, seeing the shovel, stopped. Here she dug a shallow hole, laid the parcel in, and threw dirt on top of it.

"*Kotex*? Jesus Christ Almighty, you wear *Kotex* for your periods? That's positively antediluvian! What's the matter with Tampax? Getting a little late to be joining the twentieth century, isn't it?" And Davis, shaking his head, had walked out of the bathroom where he had found her one day, never knocked, just walked right in, as was his habit. But the thought of inserting something into herself made Frances ill, and so she quietly took her used pads and buried them, every month a series of little funerals.

As she entered the house again, she heard Thos coming down the stairs. She sighed. She'd been hoping to have a little more time to herself before the children woke up, but with that, Clara began to cry, which was sure to wake Miles, and everything started all over again.

It wasn't so bad in the warm weather, Frances thought, as she worked in her small flower garden later that morning. At least she wasn't cold all the time, indoors and out, no matter what she did.

The thing was, though, something was wrong, he'd rather be target-shooting in the woods than be with her and the children, or if he was with them, he had his camera hanging around his neck and kept snapping pictures of them. And then she'd taken that test in one of her magazines and there it was, plain as day: he didn't love her anymore, not the way he used to, anyway, when he paid attention all the time she was talking. She had tried putting her zinnias around the house in jelly jars, wherever she could find a level spot—"Brighten up the place," the article had said—but so far he hadn't seemed to notice. Well, she told herself, today, *today* would be better. The article had said to keep that in mind, too.

It was early but already hot as she pulled weeds, and her hands sweated in the cotton gardening gloves. Still, it was better than the feel of dirt. Frances hated the way it found its way under her fingernails and into the lines in her hands. She sat back and brushed a gloved hand against her shoulder, where a bee had landed. The bee flew off, but not before Frances had made a dark streak on her bare skin. She glanced at the mark, then tipped up her wide straw sunhat and took off her glasses. She blew on the lenses, and the dust shimmered for a moment in the air, reminding her of the face powder she used to wear. Then she put the glasses on again and turned to watch the children, scampering about with no clothes on. They didn't want to wear clothes and Davis instructed her to let them do as they pleased. But this "no clothing" business made her uncomfortable. People shouldn't go around naked, she thought, not even children. It wasn't natural.

At this moment Clara was chasing her brothers as the two aging dogs tried hard to keep up with her. She was two years old and very tiny, but she could run. Clara was about to get Thos—Frances loved the name, would always think of him as Thos—with the old, metal-edged shoulder-strap bag that Frances had given her to play with, but which had long since become a weapon in her hands. Whenever her brothers bothered her, she whipped the purse around and caught the culprit on the back, across the legs, over the head, wherever. It was not pleasant, and they had come to think twice before tangling with Clara.

Now she had slowed to a walk and was laughing. It always seemed to Frances that Clara danced rather than walked, and when they walked together, Frances felt that she, too, should be dancing, but that somehow she had forgotten the steps.

Thos, who was not much of an athlete, was down now, and Miles was laughing with Clara. It was playful laughter, not malicious. She wished Thos could laugh too, but he was always so serious and worried about everything, nothing at all like Miles. They could be mistaken for twins, both with wispy, black hair that blew in even the slightest breeze, and those dark, dark eyes. They looked like two versions of the same child, Miles solid and strong, Thos thin and fragile-looking. But Miles was busy all the time, running around and looking underneath everything to see it from another angle, while Thos was content to play quietly. She thought of how differently they played with the puzzles given to them by a patient. Miles forced the pieces and turned bright red, finally abandoning the effort, but Thos worked slowly, methodically, manipulating each piece until it slid into place, then picked up the next piece and did the same thing, until the simple puzzle was completed.

All the children, even Clara, who was fair, resembled Davis, and Frances felt the four of them were a unit that did not include her. Nothing came from her. Even the boys' black hair probably came from someone on his side. She thought of his older son, Leslie, Jr., and how much he also looked like his father. All four of his children had his straight hair, too. Davis hair would be afraid to curl, Frances reflected, at the same time grateful that her three had not inherited her thick, dark, uncontrollable mass, which she had despised since she was a child. As a young girl she had worn a kerchief to cover it, until her grandmother forbade it, saying she should be thankful for God's gift and appreciate it.

But Clara! Frances watched her flit around. She had eyes like her brothers', but otherwise she was as light as the boys were dark. Her hair was white-blonde, like Frances's grandmother (a trace of Taylor after all) in the photographs taken when she was young, before the blonde turned to gray and then to white. Frances felt the way she did whenever she thought of Gran. She no longer cared that they hadn't gotten on when Frances was growing up. She missed her, missed her so terribly that she hurt everywhere, her teeth, her scalp, every part of her body. She would not have been able to bear it had she known they would never see each other again.

Frances turned around at the sound of a car pulling into the driveway.

"Uncle Stuart! Uncle Stuart!" shrieked the children as they ran toward the red Volkswagen Beetle.

The man who emerged from the car appeared to be too large to fit into it, a mini-circus act. Stuart, who had played basketball in college, now had a desk job, a beer belly, and alimony payments from a marriage that had lasted less than a year.

"Hey, kids!"

They ran to him, Miles adding an intermittent skip he'd been working on. Stuart took notice right away.

"Well, I'll be a monkey's uncle!" he said admiringly.

"We're not monkeys!" Miles shouted, or tried to. He was laughing hard; he loved it when Uncle Stuart said that. Thos and Clara weren't quite sure what the joke was, but they joined in nevertheless.

With the dogs circling his legs, Stuart put Thos high on his shoulders, where the boy began pulling on his uncle's short, dark, ponytail. Then Stuart grabbed giggling Miles and Clara around their waists and lifted them off the ground. He pretended to ignore them while he greeted his sister.

"Hi, Francie, how's it going?"

Frances stood on tiptoe and kissed her brother on the cheek.

"Okay, I guess. How's Gran?"

"Fine, fine. Feisty as always." Of course, added Stuart to himself, she still cries a lot. She thinks about you all the time but she won't come down here because she can't stand the thought of seeing you with the great Dr. Leslie Davis. Then, as an afterthought, "She sends her love. And a vacuum cleaner that she bought for you."

"You didn't . . . ?"

"Are you kidding? What did we agree on? She was quizzing me pretty good after the last visit, so I had to say something. I didn't go into any details, just told her the place needed a—what did I say?—'a little sprucing up,' I think it was. Yup, 'a little sprucing up.' My exact words."

He raised his eyebrows and smiled a conspiratorial smile. Frances smiled back.

"I'm really glad you're here, Stuart."

Something in Frances's voice made him bend down as far as he could, adorned as he was by the three children, narrow his eyes and scrutinize her face.

"You sure you're okay?"

Before she had a chance to answer, Davis's "Hello, Stuart," came from the front step.

Stuart set Clara and Miles on the ground, reached up, and took Thos down from his shoulder. He wiped his hands on his jeans.

"Morning," said Stuart, walking over with his hand extended. He never knew what to call the doctor, and so he never called him anything. Nothing seemed right. Stuart had decided the man probably introduced himself by saying, "I'm Leslie Davis. My friends call me Dr. Davis."

Davis kept his right hand on the pipe that stuck out of his mouth, and Stuart rubbed his neck with the hand he'd extended, hoping it looked as if he'd meant to do that all along.

"Come in, Stuart, come in," he said, holding the door open.

Stuart looked back at Frances and the children, and he went inside. He followed the pathway to Davis's chair, of necessity leading the way through the airless room and not liking that. They sat down and Davis gazed at Stuart, puffing on his pipe and saying nothing. Stuart was sweating. He was hot, and he was nervous.

He glanced around, trying to locate the source of an overpowering odor that nearly made him gag. His eye caught a jar of flowers, then another, and he assumed there were others he couldn't see from where he was sitting. The flowers were dead, dried really, and the gelatinous, fetid water they sat in gave off the smell.

Davis had followed Stuart's gaze. "I must remind Frances to change the water for the flowers. Sometimes she forgets."

Stuart looked at him. How about changing it yourself, you bastard? he thought. It wouldn't kill you to give her a hand. Can't you see she's drowning, for Christ's sake? For a smart guy, you're a goddamn fool.

Much as he would have liked to, Stuart didn't say this aloud. He knew that Davis could easily keep them apart. Somehow Frances simply would not be available when he drove down to visit her and the children.

"I see your car's rusting a little, huh?" he said instead.

"Yes, but I don't drive much anyway. I've stopped renewing my driver's license. There's no reason to, really, for my infrequent trips into town. And of course I can walk to the office every day." He added, "An easy commute," and laughed quietly at his little joke.

You pretentious son of a bitch, said Stuart to himself.

Davis continued to smoke his pipe and look at Stuart, who felt increasingly ill at ease and finally rose.

"Think I'll go play with the kids for a while. Then I've got to get back to Philly. So."

Davis nodded absently and Stuart made his way along the pathway and out the front door. The children were running around, and Frances was standing where he'd left her when he went into the house with Davis. He put his arm around her and spoke loudly enough for the children to hear.

"Well, now, Francie, what say we take these kiddies down by the river? I brought some boats they might like to . . . ."

"Yippee!"

"Yay, Uncle Stuart!"

"Let's go, let's go, let's go!"

The children all spoke at once, jumping up against Stuart as if trying to attach themselves to him like bits of Velcro. No one saw Davis watching them through the window.

CHAPTER NINE

The weather had turned cold when Stuart visited Hardwick with the news that his company was sending him to England for a year. He hadn't intended to say anything to Frances until the end of his visit, because he didn't think he would be able to stand the look on her face, but the words tumbled out as soon as he saw her. She began to cry, as he had known she would, but he had not realized the sobbing would go on for so long.

"It's not forever, Francie! Come on, you know I'll write to you and the kids! It's just a year. Be over before we know it. Maybe you could come visit and we could go to Paris! You've always wanted to go to Paris!"

But Stuart knew she had stopped listening.

"When—when do you leave?" She could hardly get the words out.

"Next week. November tenth. Then I'll be home right around Christmas next year, mid-January at the latest."

"That's more than a year, Stu! You said a year! That's more than a year!" She began to sob again.

Stuart held her and stroked her back, whispering in her ear.

"Where are the kids?" he asked, when at last she had calmed down.

"Upstairs. The boys are sick."

As they walked along the balcony to the bedroom, Stuart glanced down at the two broken spindles. It wasn't the first time he'd noticed them, nor was it the first time he'd mentioned them to Frances.

"Those can't be very safe, Francie. Shouldn't he be fixing them or something?"

"He's pretty busy, but he'll get around to it, don't worry."

Miles and Thos were feverish, and Davis had fashioned a hospital ward out of their bedroom. Steam emanated from a humidifier, and on a chair was an array of over-the-counter medicines and a small enema bulb. The room was warmed by an electric heater that Hank had driven to Shoreline to buy. The old oil furnace wasn't up to the task of heating the upstairs properly.

The boys were asleep in bed, "bed" being an untidy heap of quilts on two foam mattresses that lay side-by-side on the floor. Usually they shared the mattresses with Clara, but now, with the boys sick, she slept in bed with Frances. With Davis, too, if he chose to sleep there.

Davis looked up when they came in, tipped his head slightly in greeting, and went back to the temperature-taking he was engaged in.

"He's hardly left their sides since they got sick," said Frances proudly.

Stuart nodded stiffly.

"Where's Clara?"

"Here!" said Clara, climbing out from under the chair where the medicines sat and knocking them over.

"Frances," said Davis at once.

"Yes, I'll get them," she said quickly, setting the bottles upright.

"Now, Clara," said Davis, "I told you to stay out of the room when your brothers are sick, or you might get sick, too, and you wouldn't want that, would you?"

Clara looked remorseful for a moment.

"A walk, a walk!" she shouted.

"Good idea," said Stuart, hustling her out of the room. "But first we'll have to get a coat and some boots on you. It's pretty cold out there."

Clara, who wore nothing but an undershirt, nodded vigorously. Pulling on Stuart's hand, she ushered him downstairs to the bathroom closet, into which coats had been thrown rather than hung, so that the door was forced open. She burrowed into the pile and emerged with a parka, a large fur hat, and a pair of boots, all of which she handed to Stuart. He helped her dress and they went outside, Clara's face scarcely visible beneath the hat, and the parka dragging on the ground like some unusual evening wrap. She promptly tripped, and her feet slipped out of the too-big boots.

"I don't think this is going to work!" said Stuart, smiling and shaking his head.

They went into the house again and Clara led the way back to the bathroom, this time to the great pile of clothes on the floor next to the tub. She selected a shirt and a pair of small blue jeans with an elastic waist, and Stuart, having taken off her fur hat and pulled the parka up and over her head, helped Clara into the shirt and the pants, which were much too long for her. He rolled up the cuffs until they looked as though sausages had been slipped inside.

"Now, I have a great idea, Clary! Find some more shirts and some socks in the pile, a whole bunch of socks, so we can keep your feet toasty warm. Then you're going to ride in a special place, and you won't even have to wear any shoes!"

Clara jumped up and down, clapping her hands. She found some odd socks, which were too big, but Stuart pulled them over her legs so they stayed in place. Then he layered the several shirts she brought to him, and he had a quick picture of what she would look like if she were not quite so thin.

"Okay! Let's go!"

Stuart, still wearing his parka, scooped up the little girl.

"Now watch this trick!"

He unzipped his jacket and tucked Clara inside so she faced forward, then zipped her in so that only her head and hands stuck out, a baby kangaroo in its pouch.

Clara turned and touched his face with her hand.

"Ooh, you hurt!" she said.

"Sorry, young lady, but I didn't shave this morning." Laughing, he adjusted her small body inside his jacket. "What do you say, should we go for our walk? You all set?"

Clara snuggled happily against him, and they went outside once again.

It was considerably colder and windier than Stuart had thought, and he walked as fast as he could along the narrow trail by the river. The path was frosted with a paper-thin layer of frozen mud, and the wintry-brown marsh grasses lining the path shivered in the wind. The river looked uninviting, forbidding.

Keeping one hand under Clara, Stuart breathed on the free one to warm it and then switched hands, regretting that he'd left his gloves in the car. He couldn't stop thinking about Frances and wished he could help her, but short of murdering Davis, he came up empty.

"How're you doing? Everything okay in there?"

Clara nodded her head several times in quick succession, but her attention was clearly on something else.

"Look, look!" She pointed to the road in front of them.

It was the biggest turtle Stuart had ever seen, more than a foot long. Clara was trying to get down for a closer look.

"Uh-uh, let's look at him from up here."

"A teeney-weeny dinosaur!" she yelled, struggling harder to get free.

Stuart stared at the turtle, a snapper, he was pretty sure.

"Well I'll be darned. You're right!"

Sure enough, the heavy creature with the saw-toothed tail bore more than a passing resemblance to a—what the hell was it?—brontosaurus?

"How do you know about dinosaurs?" he asked.

Stuart was aware that he was no authority on children, but he knew two-year-olds were not dinosaur experts.

"Books," she said, straining to get a better view of the turtle.

"'Books,'" echoed Stuart. "Amazing."

Stuart put his arms around the bundle in his jacket and knelt down near the turtle.

"Keep your hands inside," he warned, and he remembered Gran cautioning him with these same words as he sat in the back seat of the car, waving his arms out the window. "Young man," she would add. Then she'd tell him a horror story. Gran had had a horror story for every situation. She seemed always to know someone who knew someone that it happened to. "Don't make a face, Stuart. If the wind changes it will stay that way." Well, he'd tested that one, all right, made so many faces so often he was sure the wind must've changed several times over, but his face never changed with it.

They watched the turtle until it disappeared into the grasses on its way back to the river. Stuart stood up.

"Okay, home we go! Train leaving on Track Four!"

Clara turned to look at him, clearly mystified. Stuart smiled down at her and kissed the top of her head as he started back along the path. He didn't say anything because he didn't know where to begin.

Christmas was nothing but a chore, thought Frances, as she decorated the tree that Christmas Eve. The house smelled, not of pine boughs, but of the burned, ruined cookies she'd tried to make for the children, and for Dorothy.

Dorothy had said to her, "You know what I really want for Christmas? I want you to leave Les. Look at you! You're miserable, and things are only getting worse. You and the kids can stay with me until you figure out what to do next. You're an abused woman, Frances."

"I am not abused! He hasn't once laid a hand on me! Do you see any bruises? Do you?"

Dorothy had to admit that she didn't.

"And don't you understand?" Frances had raised her voice as much as she dared in Sally Bea's store. "He'd never, never let me go. Certainly not with the children, and I'd rather die than be without them. Besides, he—he needs us. Where would he be without us?"

And that was the end of the conversation.

Frances got halfway through trimming the tree and didn't have the energy to finish the task. She was in this by herself, since Davis had never had any use for the holiday. He had told her she could decorate all she wanted, the tree, the house, anything, but this year she didn't bother. What was a child's Christmas without Santa Claus?

"There's no point in lying to the children, Frances," he had said. And so they knew, from the time they looked at their first Christmas tree, that she had gone out and bought whatever gifts were under it. There was no mystery, and when they woke up during the night and saw her trimming the tree, as usually happened at least once, it didn't make any difference.

This morning was not so very different from any other. Miles was, as usual that winter, the first to awaken. He went downstairs, with his too-small undershirt riding up and his wet diaper hanging. ("He'll train himself when he's ready," Davis had pronounced. But he was four and a half now and Frances was privately beginning to wonder.) Miles in particular didn't mind the cold, not even on mornings like this when he could see his breath, before the furnace rumbled on and a fire burned in the woodstove.

Miles squatted down in front of the couch and peered underneath it, groping at the same time until his hands found the string he was looking for. He gave a yank, and with a clatter a dozen mousetraps, all tied together, came whipping out. He staked out a different territory each evening, and the previous night he had arranged the traps so they went under the couch and on under the long pile of furniture that led to the front door.

Miles took very seriously the responsibility of checking his traps. He still remembered seeing Mama crying when she found mice on the kitchen counter that first time. Hank told him about mousetraps and gave him some. He tied them together for the child, explaining that this was the way to catch a lot at one time.

"One, two, three, four." Miles counted carefully this Christmas morning, anxious to get all the numbers in the right order. "Five, six, seven! Oh, boy! I got seven!"

Dancing around delightedly, he removed the mice from the traps. All dead this time, he thought. That was the best, when they went in head first for the cheese. That was catching mice, not when he only got them by the tail, then had to take them outside to let them go. "See you tomorrow," he'd call to them as they ran off. But when they were like this, already dead, he could just stand in the doorway and throw them onto the ground.

"Well, well. And how's the littlest lobsterman this morning? Catch anything in your traps?"

Davis was descending the stairs and lighting his pipe. The dogs, who stirred when they saw Davis, lumbered up the steps to meet him, and he scratched them behind the ears.

"Yup. I got seven today!" said Miles, and wondered as he always did why his father called him "the littlest lobsterman."

"Merry Christmas!" called Frances.

A moment later, with Clara and Thos close behind, she appeared at the top of the stairs, wearing a plaid flannel shirt of Davis's buttoned over her nightgown. Thos's shirt, like Miles's, was too small, but Clara's hung down over her diaper. Frances knew better than to ask if they were warm enough. When she used to do that, on cold mornings like this, it was Davis who nodded yes.

Frances clapped her hands and rubbed them together. "Let's see what's under the tree!"

The tree stood off to the side of the woodstove, the only space in the room where it could be accommodated. They filed along the pathway, and, while Davis started the fire, the others gathered by the tree.

"This one says 'Miles,'" said Frances, handing him a package wrapped in the funnies from the Sunday paper. He sat down on the floor, the present in his lap, waiting.

"And this says 'Thomas.'"

Thos sat beside Miles.

"And this—"

"Says 'Clara,'" she interrupted, taking the package from Frances. It was large but not heavy, and she half-dragged, half-carried it over to her brothers and sat down.

A small package remained under the tree. As Frances leaned over to pick it up, her glasses slipped off, and Davis, turning away from the fire, which he now had blazing, stepped on them.

"It's all right," said Frances immediately. The glasses had snapped across the bridge of the nose, and she picked up the two halves. "Don't worry. I can fix these with some of that electrical tape, Les."

Davis smiled at her and shook the package she had given him, opened it, and said, "Pipe tobacco! Why, thank you, Frances."

He could not imagine why, after all this time, she didn't know the brand he smoked. Well, he could exchange it at the market. Or give it to Hank, who had taken up pipe smoking in a failed effort to give up cigarettes. Yes, that was a better idea. He'd give it to Hank.

"Nothing for you, Mama?" asked Miles.

"I seem to have forgotten that today was Christmas," said Davis, clearing his throat. "Maybe you'd like a nice, warm bathrobe," he said to Frances, glancing at her outfit.

"That would be nice," she said softly. "Now, what did you all get?" She tried unsuccessfully to sound excited, enthusiastic.

"What's wrong, Mama?" Thos looked worried.

Davis answered for her. "Mama's a little tired, Thomas."

Thos continued to look at her, but Clara and Miles, apparently satisfied, turned to their presents.

"You first," said Miles.

Slowly Clara unwrapped hers. "Goody, goody! Help, Miles!"

She was struggling with the box, but through the cellophane on top she could see a fire engine.

"Frances, may I speak to you for a moment?" Davis took Frances by the elbow and led her to the kitchen.

"A fire engine for a little girl? Surely you know that is not appropriate?"

Frances had suspected he would be displeased, but she'd hoped he would decide it was too late by the time the children opened their packages.

"Please, Les, what difference does it make? Clara was so excited when she saw a hook and ladder go through town. You can see how much she loves it. It's perfect for her."

Davis was shaking his head. "Not for this little girl. Maybe a tea set or a doll or something, but a truck? For a girl?"

Frances thought of the coloring book and crayons for Thos, whose first words had been colors. She didn't think Davis could object to that. Or to the checkers for Miles.

The boys had opened their presents by the time Davis and Frances returned. Davis cast a glance at Thos, already coloring a picture.

Clara was still trying to free the fire engine from its packaging.

"Mama made a mistake. She mixed up your packages," said Davis, plucking the box from her hands, and the checkers from Miles's.

Clara started to cry.

"Now, now. No tears. Remember the rule? No crying? We won't have any more of that." And he gave her the checkers.

Miles, who had been handed the fire truck, tried to put the lid on the box. One wheel broke through the cellophane.

"You can both color with me," said Thos quietly.

"Clara, you go over next to Thos," instructed Miles. "I can color upside down."

CHAPTER TEN

They'd begun celebrating all the children's birthdays at once. Miles and Thos shared a May birthday anyway, and Clara was born in June, which was close enough, Davis decided. "Pointless celebrations," he had said. "We'll just get it all over with," which had turned out to be fine with Frances. For the first couple of years she was disappointed to have all the excitement at one time, but now she was glad. A single day, a single cake, a single party.

The birthday was on no particular date each year and therefore brought none of the frenzied anticipation that Davis found so irritating. Instead, one May night he would say, "How about tomorrow for the birthday?" and she would say fine, yes, fine.

Today's the day, thought Frances as she awoke this morning, surprised to find Davis asleep beside her. She wanted nothing more than to put her head under the sheet and sleep for hours, days even, but she forced herself out of bed, picked up the faded gray jumper from the floor where she'd thrown it the night before, and pulled it on over Davis's undershirt, which she had worn to bed. Before going downstairs she re-read Stuart's latest postcard, an upbeat message as usual, written in a scrawl that even Frances sometimes had trouble deciphering. She tucked it into her pocket. She was impressed that, with the many cards he had sent, he had managed not to duplicate any. She knew there were no two alike because she had kept every one and often spread them out on the floor to admire the London landmarks, the royal family, and Queen Elizabeth, with and without Prince Philip. It had gotten so that, simply by looking at a given picture, she knew just what message was on the other side. But Frances had not written to Stuart. He couldn't possibly want mail from this place, and there was no news to report, anyway. Then, too, she knew that Davis would find a way to keep her cards from reaching Stuart. He would always find a way.

The children were perched on the counter eating breakfast when Frances walked into the kitchen. They were drinking from a bottle of grape juice and eating from little boxes of cereal into which they had poured milk, as Frances had shown them one morning when she couldn't face another day of rinsing out yesterday's bowls, with their tiny bits of cereal cemented to the inside. This morning they had splashed milk onto the counter and the floor, but Frances didn't seem to notice.

The children stopped talking and smiled at Frances, but she paid no attention to them. They looked at one another. Miles put his finger to his lips and opened his eyes wide at the other two, furrowing his brow with the effort. "Sh-h-h," he mouthed, without making a sound. They watched as Frances took a glass from the pile in the sink, poured in a swallowful of juice, drank, and put the glass back where she had found it. She left the kitchen, and they heard the front door click.

"Good morning, children," said Davis, coming into the room a few minutes later. As usual, he wore khakis and a graying T-shirt. He smoothed his thin hair with the palm of one hand and with the other flipped on the Pittsburgh Pirates cap he wore every day. Hank had taken the cap off his own head and presented it to Davis when the doctor admired it.

"Good morning, sir," the children chorused.

"Where's Mama?" he asked.

They shrugged and went back to eating their cereal. Davis leaned over and tightened the laces on his boots.

Frances knew she would be at the store too early to see Dorothy, but she wanted to get the shopping over with. By the time she got back, carrying a small grocery bag, the children were outside playing with the dogs, trying with limited success to ride them. They hung on as the dogs lumbered around the yard and trampled Frances's plot, which this year grew nothing but weeds. Davis sat in an oversized wooden armchair, smoking his pipe and watching the activity. The chair, once polished, was bleached and peeling from a life outdoors for which it was never intended.

"You're going to have to take the car and go get ice cream," said Frances, on her way inside. "It would've melted by the time I walked home."

You should have let me teach you to drive, thought Davis, but he knew better than to talk to Frances when she got like this.

A few minutes later she heard the car cough several times and finally start up. The children were asking to go with Davis, but she could hear him say no, stay with Mama. She began to unpack the bag, setting aside the "Happy Birthday" paper plates and napkins and taking out the frozen cake lying on the bottom. Rotating the aluminum foil pan, she bent the edges back so she could remove the cardboard top and the paper liner. This worked best when the cake was frozen solid, Frances had discovered, but the walk home in the warm weather had softened the icing, and most of it stuck to the liner when she peeled it off. With her finger, she put the icing back on the cake, then tried to spread it smooth. The white frosting came apart and pulled across the top of the chocolate cake, picking up chunks as it went, and by the time she finished, it appeared to contain chocolate chips.

Frances unwrapped the cake decorating kit, hard sugar letters that spelled Happy Birthday. She took the yellow letters off the paper backing as carefully as she could, one at a time, unable to prevent bits of paper from sticking. Then she poked the letters deep into the icing to keep them in place. "Happy" worked out all right, but she misjudged "Birthday" and had to take the letters off and start over, in order to fit the entire word on one line.

Now for the candles, said Frances to herself. Using her teeth to rip the cellophane around the box, she opened the package. They sure aren't going to show up too well, she thought, but I didn't have much choice, white was all Sally Bea had, and I was lucky to get them, her last box. She stuck the candles in at random, using the entire box.

Frances retrieved three red rubber balls from the bottom of the bag. She looked at them as she held them out, waist high, two in one hand, one in the other, as if ready to juggle them but unsure how to go about it. She was thinking that this was it, her last idea for presents for the children that would make them happy without making him angry.

When Davis came back with the ice cream, he found Frances seated on the couch outside the kitchen, still holding the balls, still seemingly in the act of figuring out how to juggle them.

"Frances? I've brought the ice cream."

She didn't answer.

"Frances?"

Her head tilted slightly to one side and she looked frozen, staring at something in the middle distance that he could not see. Her glasses, mended across the bridge with black tape, were askew. Davis adjusted them, then knelt down and covered her hands with his.

"Come, Frances. It's time to celebrate the children's birthday. You'd like that, wouldn't you? We can all have our ice cream and cake, and we'll sing Happy Birthday together."

Frances moved her head slowly to where his voice was coming from, but her gaze never met his. He patted her hands and stood up.

"All right, you sit here for a while. You're tired, I know. When you feel like joining us, we'll be outside."

He went into the kitchen to get the cake. Jesus Christ, he thought when he saw her handiwork. How could you screw up a frozen cake? Holding the bag of ice cream with one hand, he slipped the other under the foil pan, balancing it like a small tray, and walked past the couch to the front door. Frances had not moved.

"Someone come open the door for me, please! It's a special day today!"

Clara, closest to the house at that moment, reached up to open the door and held it for her father.

"Yummy!"

"Oh, boy! Birthday day!"

"That means cake and ice cream and everything!"

Davis set the cake on his chair and distributed the Dixie cups from the bag.

"Can I do the spoons?" asked Miles.

"*May* I do the spoons. Yes, Miles, you may."

Davis handed him the strip of paper-covered wooden spoons. Miles pulled them apart and started to unwrap each one.

"I want to do my own!" said Thos.

"Me, too!" echoed Clara.

"Miles, give Thomas and Clara their spoons so they can take the paper off themselves."

"Yes, sir," said Miles, handing them their spoons. "Can—may I do yours?"

"Yes, you may."

There was one spoon left over when he had finished distributing them.

"Isn't Mama coming to our party?"

"Mama's feeling a little tired this morning. Maybe she'll come outside later."

They heard laughter from inside the house.

"Is Mama watching television?" asked Thos.

"I'll go and see. I'll be back in a minute."

He found Frances still on the couch, laughing at something deep inside her mind. Then she was quiet again. Davis reached down and gently pried the red balls from her hands.

"Mama must have turned on the television set for a minute," said Davis as he came through the door, "but now she's turned it off again. Let's have our party. Presents first!"

The balls were greeted with shouts of delight, but louder still was the reaction when Hank walked into the yard, and the children raced to him, anxious to show off their presents.

"Look what he gave us!" said Thos, while Clara reached up and patted Hank's back as she always did, reassuring herself that this was his skin, and the tattoos just seemed to be a T-shirt.

"Well, I'll be! Looks like it's somebody's birthday today!"

"Mine! It's mine!" chorused the children.

"That so?" he said to them. "Let's see what we can do about that!"

He reached slowly into the pocket of his jeans and took out a large penknife.

"What say we go get Hank some wood, something he can hold on to?" As they ran off ahead of him, he said to Davis with a chuckle, "Naked as jaybirds, eh, Doc?"

They emerged from the woods a few minutes later, the children solemnly bearing at arms' length the red maple shoots Hank had cut for them. While he went to work making whistles, tapping and slipping the bark, Davis passed out the Dixie cups and loosened the lids for the children. He watched them finish the job of removing the top and licking it before starting on the ice cream. Miles and Clara vigorously mixed the vanilla and chocolate together and turned it into soup before eating, but Thos took a tiny bite of vanilla, then chocolate, then vanilla again.

"If Mama is too tired to come to our party, maybe Hank can have her ice cream," said Miles, sucking his spoon.

Hank looked up, concerned. "The missus feeling poorly today?"

"Don't talk with your mouth full, Miles. Yes, Hank, she is a bit tired," said Davis, holding out a Dixie cup.

"Thanks, but I can't say I'm much for ice cream."

While the children ate, Davis rearranged the candles on the cake. He put three in one corner for Clara, four in another for Thos, and five along the bottom for Miles. The rest he dropped on the ground. Then, using his pipe lighter, he lit the candles ceremoniously, cautioning the children not to blow them out yet. When he began to sing, everyone joined in, although Miles's voice disappeared as he sang:

"Happy birthday, dear Miles-Thomas-Clara, happy birthday to you!"

"Happy birthday, dear Miles-Thomas-Clara, happy birthday to you." Frances's voice came like a warbling echo from the doorway.

"Mama, Mama! Look at the balls he gave us!"

"And Hank's making us presents!"

"You're just in time for cake, Mama!"

Miles, who was still holding the extra spoon, went over to his mother, put his arms around her waist, and leaned his head against her stomach. They stayed there for a moment as the others watched silently, while the candles burned themselves out. Then Miles walked to the cake where it rested on the chair, put some on the spoon and took it to Frances. She looked at it strangely, as if unsure what it was, and then smiled faintly at him.

"Thanks," she whispered.

While she stood licking the spoon, Davis and the children crowded around Hank, watching him carve three crude whistles. He worked quickly, making short strokes. Every once in a while the children ran and dug their spoons into the cake, always making certain one of them took a small piece to their mother, who continued to stand apart. Then it was time for blowing the whistles, which made a satisfyingly piercing sound, and the children were so enthusiastic that Davis and Hank could hardly carry on their conversation.

It wasn't until the following day that Davis found the unopened birthday plates and napkins on the kitchen counter. He never realized the children had not blown out their candles.

"Sister," said Sally Bea one day that summer, "our little girl needs some pretty clothes."

Dorothy, who was just leaving, laughed and waved good-bye to Frances.

"No clothes! I don't like clothes!" said Clara in a jump-rope singsong as she bounced up and down, and Frances smiled helplessly at Sally Bea. Clara was wearing just her brother's T-shirt.

"But she's only three," said Frances

"Never too young to wear clothes, I always say. Why, you could make them yourself! Nothing to it."

The next time Frances was in the store, Sally Bea had found out about a sewing machine that was available.

"Owned by a widower, a man whose wife upped and died, and he can't wait to empty the place of her things. You got yourself a good price, too. He says he'll even bring it out to the house."

"I've got to ask my husband," said Frances, who had long since stopped hesitating over the word.

Davis astonished her by declaring it a fine idea.

"She missed her calling," he said of Sally Bea. "She should have been a matchmaker."

It was a treadle sewing machine, on its own stand, and Frances had it put in the kitchen with the stool that came with it. Navigating around the kitchen was now nearly impossible, but Davis kept that thought to himself.

In time the counters were covered with fabric and thread and bits of tissue paper patterns that concealed the food-encrusted pans and dishes that lay beneath. All that summer and into the fall she sewed, making a pile of little dresses that lay on the floor by the sewing machine, dresses Clara refused even to try on.

One rainy October afternoon Davis returned from his daily walk in the woods—always with the .22 caliber pistol he used on small animals—and found the children racing along the pathways and shouting to each other. They wore the matching red sweatshirts, much too big for them, that Uncle Stuart had sent from London last Christmas. The dogs were jumping up against the furniture and barking at the children.

Davis took off his yellow slicker and dropped it on the floor, beneath the hook that Frances had installed. The mud on his boots made dark, wet marks as he followed the pathway to the ivory box. He put away the gun, locked the box, and slipped the key under *Gray's Anatomy*.

"Where is Mama?" Davis had to raise his voice above the din.

The children stopped where they were. The dogs, too, were still.

"She's sewing," said Miles, gesturing toward the kitchen.

They could hear peals of laughter, and Davis went in to find Frances pedaling fast, very fast, too fast, on the treadle, shoving the material through rapidly and laughing loudly, a girlish laugh turned coarse. Her thick hair hung forward, uncombed, hiding her face.

"Can you tell me the joke?" asked Davis.

Frances was sewing frantically, laughing even harder. And then everything stopped. She was silent. Her feet continued to move on the treadle, but slower now, and slower, until the needle, in its constant up-and-down motion, moved so slowly that Davis could follow it with his eyes. Then she was still. Her feet remained on the treadle and her hands on the fabric she was working on, and she reminded Davis of the life-like wax figures he had seen in a London museum.

The children crowded around the doorway, and the dogs pushed in beside them.

"What's the matter, Mama?" asked Clara.

Frances didn't move.

"Mama is—Mama is sick today," Davis explained.

"But you're a doctor," said Thos. "Can't you fix her and make her better?"

"Yeah," added Miles. "Isn't that what doctors do?"

Davis thought he detected a hint of sarcasm, but decided no, five years old was too young for sarcasm.

"She'll get well all by herself," said Davis, "if we leave her alone."

"Take her to a different doctor! Maybe she needs a different doctor!" Miles was shouting.

"Miles, please keep your voice down." Davis spoke quietly. "Because I *am* a doctor, I know what's best for Mama."

He turned and left the kitchen, following the pathway to the woodstove. He gave the fire a poke, sat down in his chair, and lit his pipe. Then he leaned back and pulled the visor of the Pirates hat over his eyes.

The children gathered around Frances. Clara put her nose against her mother's and stared into the unseeing eyes.

"Mama? Mama? Where are you, Mama?" She started to cry.

"Talk!" yelled Thos into her ear.

Still Frances did not move.

"Come on, let's go play upstairs," said Miles. "Maybe she wants to rest." Then, on the off chance that she could hear, he added, "We'll be back later, Mama," and kissed her cheek.

"Wait, I think she might be cold," said Clara.

She ran to the front door, picked up Davis's slicker, and ran back again, the slicker dragging on the floor. Miles helped her position it over Frances's bare shoulders, over the lavender dress with the halter top.

The children followed the pathway past the woodstove to the stairs. Davis did not speak to them as they walked by.

"Is he sleeping?" whispered Clara.

"No," said Thos softly. "You can see his pipe puffing."

CHAPTER ELEVEN

Frances rather liked "going away," as she began to think of it. She was disoriented when she came back, but not upset, not scared, just not quite sure where she was, exactly, or where she had been. The time away seemed no longer than a sigh, time unattended, but the clock told her it had been hours, sometimes many hours. She returned feeling lightheaded and weightless, certain that, were it not for her clothing to anchor her, she would float away. She felt peaceful, rested, as if she'd had a deep, dreamless sleep in some distant and nameless place. Her nights by contrast were filled with disturbing dreams, and she had to push them aside to make way for morning. She dreamed Gran was with her, smiling and talking, but there was no sound, as if the volume on a television set had been turned off. She dreamed she went to the store to buy pineapples—why pineapples? she wondered the next morning—and when she got back, Davis and the children didn't recognize her. And she dreamed again and again of this house, sometimes looking as it did when she first saw it, other times with the piles higher than ever and off balance, spilling into the already narrow pathways and blocking them completely.

Frances had not always come back with a feeling of serenity. The first time it happened, she was frantic, unable to find the gold watch

Davis had given her for her birthday. She knew she'd left it on the kitchen window sill, could picture it perfectly, with the tiny crystal gleaming in the sunlight, and the thin gold band tapering gracefully to the clasp. She emptied the sink, drained the gray water, thinking it must have fallen in. She searched everywhere she could think of, finally bringing herself to confess to Davis that it had disappeared, and he said I don't know what in the world you are talking about, there was never any watch.

For a few days after being away, the texture of her world was softened; sounds were muffled, and Frances felt as though she were peering through a haze. She had spun a cocoon for herself, she thought, like the caterpillars she had seen at the science fair in elementary school. As soon as she came back, the children welcomed her into their lives again, but Davis wouldn't speak to her or look at her for the next twenty-four hours. "Tell Mama I'm going for my walk," he would say in her presence to one of the children, as he loaded the .22 and avoided their eyes, or "Ask Mama when she will be going to the laundromat," although he knew very well that such trips had become nonexistent.

Then Davis, without alluding to her time away, would speak to her directly, and she felt she had been forgiven.

She told Dorothy about going away, what it was like, and Dorothy urged Frances to tell Davis that she wanted, needed, professional help. Dorothy even offered to accompany her when she broached the subject. But Frances was terrified at the prospect.

"If he ever thought I had a friend," she cried out, "he'd never let me walk to town again! We wouldn't be able to have our talks, and I couldn't live without them! I haven't even told Stuart about you! Promise me, PROMISE ME, you'll never say anything to anyone!"

And Dorothy, through her tears, promised.

But it was a promise that she couldn't, in good conscience, keep. She skipped their meeting at Sally Bea's one day in order to find Davis home alone. Indeed, he answered her knock so promptly she suspected he'd been watching her car pull up.

"Hello, Dr. Davis," she began, already feeling perspiration form in her armpits. "My name is Dorothy Turner, and . . ."

"Yes, I know who you are," said Davis quietly.

Of course he would know. He would have his sources, all those grateful patients, thought Dorothy, aware that the perspiration was now soaking the underarms of her denim work shirt. For a moment she was fascinated by this, and wondered what process made it happen. But Davis's dark, staring eyes brought her back.

"I'd like to talk to you about Frances."

"Please," said Davis, and Dorothy imagined that he stepped back from the door and asked her to come in, form an alliance with him against the madness that was assaulting Frances.

"Please," he repeated, "don't come here any more." And he closed the door.

She'd been away again, and when she came back this time, Frances was forced to listen to a sound she assumed she alone could hear. But it was familiar somehow, and finally she understood it was an autumn rain, heavy, steady, pounding, and the roaring she heard behind it was inside her head.

Frances saw that Davis had abandoned his chair by the woodstove and was standing at the window that overlooked the river. He stood immobile as always, the only sign of life the puffs of smoke that emanated from his pipe. Frances went over and stood beside him, but he did not acknowledge her presence. Clutching Stuart's most recent postcard in her hand, rumpling the thin cardboard, she stared out at the driving rain that hung between the house and the river, bridging the scant seventeen feet separating them. It was impossible to see the river's contours, but Frances could make out debris rushing by, logs and branches traveling at a terrific rate, many times faster than she'd ever seen before. And then she realized the roaring in her ears was the river.

Miles came over and took her hand.

"I think he's worried," he said, glancing at his father. In order to make himself heard he had to strain his voice, raising it as if trying out for his first stage role. "He says the water's rising pretty fast."

By the afternoon of the fourth day of rain, the river, which had already left its banks, made its way under the back door and into the house.

"We'd better go upstairs," said Davis to Frances and the children, who were watching the water creep toward them and ease into the living room. Then to Frances, "Will you be all right? We need you here, with us. This is an emergency."

The children turned to look at her.

"Yes," she said, "I know."

He called the dogs. Clara started to cry and Thos followed. Miles's lip quivered, but he wouldn't give in.

"Now, now, will tears stop the river? Of course not. And remember the rule. No crying. *We don't cry.* Thomas? Clara? Come along. I'll get my black bag and something from the kitchen for us to eat and meet you all upstairs."

"Bring lemons, too, Les," said Frances, "and the big drawing pad and some pencils."

Davis had no idea what she had in mind, but he located the pad and pencils. From the drawer of the almost-empty refrigerator he took the two lemons that Hank had brought one day after Frances mentioned that she never remembered to buy lemons for her tea.

As Davis continued to gather provisions, he thought about what he was headed for upstairs. Christ, he said to himself, Miles is the only one who has figured out that you don't just leave human waste wherever you happen to be at the time.

He shook his head, sighing deeply, and picked up the bag of dried dog food. There was little to choose from in the way of food for himself, Frances and the children. It was a point of pride that he left the shopping, no job for a doctor, to her. He discovered they'd used the last of the canned soup and baked beans, their usual fare. He gathered together a package of stale cookies, some apples, a jar of peanut butter, and a loaf of white bread, the soft kind he detested. He filled a jug with water. It was all they would have for two days.

The river continued to rise for twenty-four hours. They watched from the balcony as it seized possession of the main room, coursing toward the front door, and, as they looked on, the piles came apart and collapsed into the water with a sound so muted it all seemed to be happening far, far away, and the pathways were gone. It occurred to Frances that this might be just another of her dreams.

While Davis kept a constant watch on the water, as if his vigilance would prevent it from rising higher, the children ran wild, racing between the two upstairs rooms and jumping on the bed in their parents' room. They blackened the mattress with the soles of their bare feet, then charged back to their room with the dogs chasing after them, and slid on the blankets they had pulled off the foam mattresses.

"Frances, can't you keep them quiet?" said Davis finally, as he wrote in his notebook, and so she curled up with them on the double bed, and they drew pictures together.

Several minutes passed. Then Clara looked over at Frances's paper and cried, "That's me! That's me!"

Frances, glancing from time to time at Clara, was indeed sketching her face. Using the side of the pencil lead as she shaded the child's cheek, she smiled without looking up.

"You are really good at drawing!" said Miles, admiringly. "How come we didn't know that?"

"Oh, I used to draw a lot when I was a little girl, but . . . ." She let the sentence go.

"Did you draw with your mama?" asked Thos.

"I didn't know my mama." Frances continued her sketching. "But *her* mama took care of Uncle Stuart and me. My Gran."

"Did you draw with your Gran?" Miles was insistent.

Frances sighed and laid down her pencil. Looking from Miles to Thos to Clara, she said, "Gran was too busy. I used to draw by myself, in my bedroom. I played there a lot. I liked to have pretend tea parties, and the guests were pictures I drew and put on chairs. Then I made believe they were talking and everything."

"What else did you play?" asked Thos.

"Well, I loved to play library. They don't have one here in Hardwick, but it's a building where they have lots and lots of books, and you get to borrow them. You don't have to buy them. You can take the books home and read them and then take them back.

"Once I got a special stamp for my birthday with an ink pad—you could change the date and everything. I took all my books and put little papers in the back, just like they did at the real library, and I stamped the paper with the date the books were due. I drew pictures of all the people who came in to borrow those books."

She smiled in memory. "Now let's see your pictures."

Clara's doodles were beginning to take some shape, Frances noticed, and she was staying on the paper, no longer ignoring its edge and continuing her creation directly on whatever surface she was working on.

"You are doing such a good job, Clara! What a hard worker! It's not so easy to stay on the paper, is it?"

Thos's rendering of the rising river and the debris it had collected was executed with great care.

"The river looks so different now, doesn't it, Thos?"

But Miles's was the drawing that fascinated her. His tongue working the corners of his mouth, Miles was using a sort of X-ray technique to show the house with the family inside. He had drawn the outline fairly accurately, Frances thought, and was busy revealing the interior. A horizontal line, positioned more or less in the middle of the house, divided the upstairs, which he was still drawing, from the downstairs, which he had completed. Frances recognized the piles and pathways in the main room, here depicted as dark, tight swirls, like thick smoke, broken by a bit of white space. Using lighter strokes, Miles had shaded the entire area all the way up to the horizontal line.

"The water," he said to Frances, glancing at her.

The upstairs particularly intrigued her—his drawing of her and the three children, and the bed on which they were sitting at this moment.

A very large Frances, distinguished by her wiry hair, sat next to the children, whom Miles had drawn just alike, the three of them, all in a row, all the same size, no separation between them. Everyone held a pencil, and he had meticulously drawn fingers around each pencil. The bed took up the entire upstairs.

"Where is he?" asked Frances gently.

Miles stopped drawing, cocked his head to the side, and looked at his picture. He thought for a minute.

"I didn't have any more room, I guess," he said, and went back to work.

When they tired of drawing, she told stories, one after another, until she fell asleep and they were at it again. The sound of screaming woke her up.

Thos, reaching under the broken spindles of the balcony to throw wadded paper down into the river flowing through the main room, had ripped his arm open. Frozen with terror, he was unable to pull the bleeding arm back up, and the blood ran down, down, through the air, into the muddy water below. By the time Frances got to him, Davis was already at his side.

"Let me see it, Thomas. Come along, now. Bring it up."

"NO! NO! I CAN'T!" shrieked Thos.

"I'll help you, then," said Davis.

Crouching next to Thos, he reached beneath the shattered spindles and eased the wounded arm back up, applying pressure to stop the bleeding. He could see the bone.

"Frances, bring me my bag. We'll take a few stitches here and Thomas will be fine. When the weather improves, we'll see that he gets an inoculation. There's no rush on that."

He worked swiftly, suturing the wound, while Thos screamed a high-pitched scream that sounded to Davis like something out of a horror movie, quieting finally when the needle was put away, and even then he could not take a breath without shuddering.

"Now," said Davis, "there's no more bone showing, no more reason to cry. I'm going to swab this with alcohol, and it will hurt, but you're not going to cry. Do you hear me? You are not going to cry."

"Yes, sir," said Thos, nearly inaudibly.

Frances, Miles and Clara, standing close together, had been watching Thos's face, and their own faces mirrored his reactions.

"Don't cry, please don't cry, Thos," urged Miles.

But Thos couldn't hold back. He shrieked again and again until his voice was hoarse, and Frances, who could not bear to listen to the sound, sank to the floor, lowering her head to her knees and pressing her hands to her ears. She had always hated to hear their crying, but this—this was different. It was nothing at all like the crying when Davis had first put alcohol on their cuts and scrapes, before they had learned, long ago, his harsh lesson that crying was forbidden. They learned the lesson well, and instead of tears, she would see faces that strained with the effort of keeping them back, but in time it was only their eyes that registered the suffering, and then they, too, went flat.

Now, as Davis dressed the wound, Thos cried not only because of the pain but because of his failure and because of the look of anger, disapproval, disappointment on his father's face. Davis, without saying a word, grasped Thos's head so the boy could not turn away. He gazed hard until Thos stopped crying.

"Look, Thos!" said Miles, walking over to the broken spindles, the splintered ends of which were darkened with Thos's blood. He knelt down and slipped his arm underneath, and then, his eyes locked with Davis's, yanked his arm back and ripped it open. Frances fainted.

Again the blood ran down into the water below, but Miles needed no help from his father to get free. He walked over to Davis, supporting his injured right arm with his left hand.

"Sew it," he ordered, his voice scarcely shaking.

Davis examined the arm. Not as deep as Thomas's, he said to himself, but in need of suturing nevertheless.

"Now for the alcohol," said Davis when he had finished.

Miles stared at Davis as the alcohol was rubbed over the wound. His lip didn't even tremble.

"Come on," he said to Thos and Clara, after his arm had been bandaged. "Let's go play."

He was speaking to them, but he was looking at Davis.

The second day Frances asked Davis for the lemons and his penknife and she cut them in two. Sitting on the balcony with the children gathered around her, she tore some sheets from the pad and handed them each a piece of paper and a lemon half.

"Okay, now squirt some of that juice onto the paper and let's see what will happen."

"Nothing! I get nothing!" grumbled Miles after several seconds.

"Yeah, nothing."

"Me too."

"Do a little more drawing," suggested Frances.

"More drawing? I can't see any at all!"

Miles was clearly annoyed, but he kept at it, rubbing the lemon over the paper. Thos did the same, but Clara developed her own method, skipping the lemon across the paper.

"Come on with me now," said Frances, and the children followed her into the bedroom she shared with Davis. "This is something I haven't done since I was a little girl!"

She switched on the bedside lamp, forgetting that the power had gone out. She had to plead with Davis for the flashlight he kept in his black bag, as he was afraid they would exhaust the batteries.

"See what you see," she said, when she had positioned the light behind one of their papers.

As the hidden shapes emerged, the children giggled and tried to make sense out of them, as they had done so many times with Frances, lying on their backs in the yard and studying the passing clouds.

Forty-three hours it was, Davis said, but Frances hadn't thought about the time, merely of trying to keep the children occupied, teaching them number sequences using their ages as a counting device, and there was the background of noise and turmoil and everyone complaining of hunger, and the dogs' disgusting messes, but it was the plastic wastebasket they used as a makeshift toilet that Frances would never forget, nor would she forget trying to catch Clara and Thos before they dirtied themselves, nor the fact that she had no water for cleaning them up, all that rainwater gone to waste, and in her worst dreams at night, she imagined the smell was still there.

They ventured downstairs when the water finally slid back and left the house alone. With great difficulty they climbed over the fallen piles and saw the brown silt that was everywhere. It combined with the ashes that had spilled from the woodstove, and spread over the floor. It coated the bathtub and toilet and turned them into giant chocolate toys.

The muddy water left a mark along the walls, which Davis measured: two feet, three inches, just eight and a half inches shy of Clara's height. They're all quite small for their ages, mused Davis as he released the lock on the tape measure and watched it whip back into itself. I wonder how Leslie would have fit in here. Was he small for his age? I doubt it. These genes must be Frances's.

No one spoke as they picked their way through the house, or when they went outside into the brilliant, mocking sunshine and saw the damage there, saw the snakes, black and brown and green and long, that hung from the trees in which they had taken refuge, away from the land that was covered with leaves, logs, branches and dead fish. And silt. A thick layer of brown silt. The children's eyes were wide as they gazed upon the familiar landscape turned alien.

Finally Davis broke the silence.

"Do you notice there's no odor? That's because this river is so pure we could drink out of it if we wanted to."

But Frances wasn't interested in the purity of the Hardwick River, preoccupied as she was by the thought of the back-breaking work ahead of them.

"Is this ever going to happen again, do you think?" she asked Davis.

"If you live by the river, you know the water will get you eventually," he replied.

The barn, on higher ground, had escaped all but the rain that had leaked in, so Davis and Hank, along with Johnny Johnson, turned their full attention to the house, spending many hours carrying the furniture outside to dry, scraping off the worst of the dirt, then shoveling the silt from the floors before stacking the peeling tables, the mildewed chairs and sofas, inside again. They spread the clothes on the bushes and hung them on branches, and Hank said he'd see to it they got to the laundromat after they were dry. Frances overheard him ask if he could help inside, but Davis said no, there was no need for that. Then the men began to hose down the land around the house, and she was on her own for the rest of the indoor cleanup.

She worked with a wire brush, removing most of the coating from the bathroom and kitchen. When she tried to wash the rest, it turned to mud that made great swirls like huge finger paintings. At night her knees were sore from kneeling, and fine dots of sprayed dirt freckled her arms, her dress, her face, her hair. She swept the floors as well as she could before mopping them, but again it was like washing with mud, and the children frequently interrupted her to use the pathways for a narrow skating rink. She did her best to clean the coffee table and brush off the leather chairs and the couch, but she knew they would never be clean again, the chairs would be two-toned and the couch would be forever stained and crusty.

Frances looked at the dried brown mud that graced the newly stacked furniture and realized that each table leg and drawer front and lamp base and chair back had come in contact with the river. She examined the dirt so deeply embedded in her nails that she knew they would have to grow out before they would be clean, and she stopped working. It had been three days of laboring and listening to the broken rhythms of Davis's target practice. Davis never said anything about the fact that she had given up, and for that she was thankful, but neither did he in any way acknowledge what she had accomplished.

While Frances cleaned the house, Davis, his work done, practiced shooting paper targets, his newest hobby. It gave him great pleasure, but now his face was red not only with concentration, but with anger at Frances. What was the woman thinking? he asked himself. Couldn't she see that the place would never be clean? What the hell was the difference if there was some dried mud around? Trying to wash it off only made things worse. She could have saved herself a lot of trouble if she'd let it dry and then swept it up.

As always, Davis took a deep breath and held it to steady himself as he pulled the trigger. This time, however, he closed his eyes for a moment before firing the shot. In that flash of time, Davis cleared his mind of Frances, of the house, of everything. Then he was ready for the pastime he loved above all others.

He enjoyed target practice more than ever, now that Hank had introduced him to wadcutter cartridges. Davis kept his first gun, the modified .38 revolver, loaded with these flat-nosed bullets that contained less gunpowder and were therefore less powerful than a regular cartridge. They were designed to make a nice, clean cut in the paper, a perfectly round hole, rather than rip through it the way a conventional bullet did. Using a wadcutter, he could see precisely where he hit the target and what his score was. Every day he nailed the target to a tree and shot from 25 yards, a distance he'd painstakingly measured. Sometimes he fired single action, sometimes double action, but always, now, he hit the black. No more 5's and 6's in the outer, white circles.

He was hitting a few 7's, mostly 8's and 9's, and, with increasing frequency, the coveted bull's-eye, the 10. Davis had targets tacked around his office, each labeled with the date and time. He enjoyed looking at them when he went to the barn, as he did more and more often now, to watch Johnny Johnson work on cars, or simply to sit among his belongings and think about the years at the hospital.

"What time will you be wanting supper?" Frances would ask when he left, as if they sat down to a formal meal each night.

"Oh, six o'clock will be just fine," Davis would reply, humoring her, or seven o'clock, or eight, knowing it didn't matter anyway. On the rare occasions when she fixed something that did not come directly out of a can, it would be ruined because he was not back on time, and Frances would be in tears.

"You know," he said one day, "you might come along over to the office to fetch me, or send one of the children," which she did, but he resented the interruption, saying, "I'll be there shortly," and it was an hour or more before he came in.

Tired of carrying heavy cans from the market, Frances often simply boiled water to make instant mashed potatoes or soup. When she had ruined the second pot, forgetting she had put water on to boil, Davis asked Hank to pick up a whistling teakettle for them. The following day he came in from target practice and was greeted by the demanding sound of the kettle. Frances was standing and shaking in the corner of the kitchen, her hands over her ears.

Davis turned off the stove and looked at her. She smiled and went back to fixing dinner.

At least he's spending more time with the children, thought Frances, as she watched them together. The information that Davis gleaned from his books on astronomy, geology, botany, zoology, he had begun to share. It started with their obvious interest in a baby pig, a runt, given to Davis by one of his patients.

"Charlotte!" said Frances excitedly, when they were searching for a name.

"Why 'Charlotte'?" asked Davis.

"Charlotte! You know, Charlotte!" said Frances again. "It was a story about a pig. I had it when I was a little girl."

"All right, then, 'Charlotte' it is," said Davis with unaccustomed heartiness.

Frances felt she could take at least some small measure of credit for having come up with what was clearly just the right name. It wasn't until a few nights later that she woke up, heart pounding, sick with the realization that the book she had been thinking of was *Charlotte's Web*, that Charlotte was a spider and Wil-something—oh, God, Wilbur!—was the pig. I can't tell Les, she thought. Please, Lord, don't let him find out, she prayed silently, and added this particular prayer to the ever-lengthening one she prayed each night.

The interest in Charlotte led Davis to explore the outdoors with the children. He sprinkled birdseed so they could identify various kinds of birds. When the weather was poor, he brought nature into the house to better explain its mysteries. Together they dissected rabbits, squirrels and other small animals Davis had killed when he was out plinking.

"Home schooling," he said. "There's nothing better."

Frances thought that Miles, who was five years old, should be in kindergarten with other children. But she couldn't conceive of her days without him, and so she didn't say anything.

At night Frances left it all behind and dreamed of Gran's house in Philadelphia, of the perfectly straight rugs on the floor, the spotless, polished, wood surfaces, the carpeted quiet of Gran's bedroom, the peace that pervaded everything. Sometimes even in her sleep Frances knew she was dreaming, and she awoke to find her face wet with tears.

CHAPTER TWELVE

"Well, this is a first for me," said Davis, looking at the court summons he had just been served. "Apparently our man-eating dogs have nipped somebody once too often. Looks like I'll be going to court."

"Court?" said Frances worriedly. "You have to go to court? Will they take away Peanut Butter and Nighttime?" She sounded to Davis like one of the children.

"We know they've been biting people, and they undoubtedly bit Mr. . . ." he looked at the summons, "Brigham. Yes, I'll have to go to court, but I promise you, no one will take away the dogs."

Davis was as good as his word. With Frances and the children in tow he went to court in Crispin, the county seat, armed with a dozen dog photographs he had taken. He did not choose to be represented by legal counsel.

"May I question the witness, Your Honor?" asked Davis, after Mr. Brigham had presented his case.

"By all means, Doctor," replied the judge, at which point Frances and the children, seated in the front row, squeezed each other's hands. Sally Bea had "begged, borrowed and stole," as she liked to say, and seen to it that the children were appropriately dressed for the occasion.

Producing the photographs he had brought along, Davis showed them to the witness. "Are you absolutely certain these were the dogs that bit you?"

"Yes, I am, absolutely sure," said Mr. Brigham.

"There can be no mistake? There is no doubt in your mind that the dogs in the photographs you see before you now are the very same dogs that bit you as you walked by my house? That is your testimony?"

"No mistake, I'm sure," said Mr. Brigham, sitting up straighter in his seat and looking pleased with himself.

"Well, Your Honor, I have a confession to make. The dogs in these photographs are not my dogs. They belong to a neighbor of mine, and I took the liberty of snapping a few pictures for identification purposes." He reached into his pocket. "These, however, *are* my dogs."

He handed this new set of pictures to the judge.

"Well, Mr. Brigham," said the judge, as he looked through the pictures. "Have you anything to add to this?"

Mr. Brigham shook his head and looked confused.

"Case dismissed," said the judge. "Next."

"Brigham didn't know what hit him," said Davis as they walked to the car. "I'm almost hoping he goes after those other dogs. He'll find they don't have a tooth in their heads." Laughing at his cleverness, he said, "I think this calls for ice cream cones all around!"

As Davis licked his cone, he recalled with pleasure how Brigham had mopped his forehead, couldn't look Davis in the eye, squirmed in discomfort. Davis had destroyed his victim, and he had loved doing it.

Frances had no idea how it had happened this time. She suspected he'd taken her while she was asleep, because she could scarcely remember when they'd last made love. Or, as he liked to put it, "had sex." Still, "once is all it takes," Miss Miller had warned in her menacing voice in a long-ago Health class. Her baggy cardigan sweater hung open and her stiff white shirt was buttoned up to her chin, and everyone had laughed, but now Frances supposed she'd had a point after all. It was just a matter of figuring out the right time to tell Les.

But it turned out there was no right time. Mealtime would have been the obvious opportunity, but it had been a long while since they'd sat down to eat together. She and Davis and the children simply helped themselves to whatever was there whenever they were hungry, taking soup or instant mashed potatoes right from the pot, or pork and beans from the can in which they'd been heated. And so the days passed with Frances looking frantically for a moment when she could break the news, but it never arrived, and finally she came out with it one November afternoon while the children were playing upstairs, when Davis walked into the house after his varmint-shooting.

"I'm pregnant again, Les."

Her eyes were wide and she was breathing rapidly. She twisted her hands together and looked expectantly at Davis, who gave the low whistle he'd adopted from Hank.

"Good God," he murmured.

He started to ask if she was certain, but she had produced three children and should certainly know the signs and symptoms by now.

He said instead, "I'm sure you agree the ship here is pretty full already, don't you, Frances?"

She nodded hesitantly, still twisting her hands.

"You know we don't have a lot of money coming in?"

She nodded again.

"Well. You also know what the solution is, I presume?"

She swallowed hard and nodded a third time.

"Then it's settled. Let's get working on it tomorrow."

The discussion over, Davis put his gun away, tucked the key under *Gray's Anatomy*, took off his hunting vest, and went into the kitchen to fix himself something to eat, leaving Frances standing at the door, where she had greeted him with her news.

The next morning when Frances awoke, the house was quiet and just beginning to brighten with morning light. She reached over and picked up yesterday's postcard from Stuart, the one that said he would not be coming home soon after all. It was November, one year since he left. They were keeping him a little longer, but not much longer, really, he wrote, just until May or June. July at the latest. He would let her know as soon as he had more information.

She slipped out of bed. Barefoot, she crept into the children's room, stepping over them as they slept, all three of them, on the two foam mattresses pushed together on the floor. Impulsively she leaned over and kissed each one lightly on the forehead. Then from the closet she took the plastic bag that held her wedding dress.

Back again in the bedroom she removed it from the bag, which had grown so stiff she could hardly slide the zipper. She held up the dress and stood before the dust-covered mirror. The dust created a soft, filtered effect, and for a long time she stared at herself, pictured herself, then slowly hung the dress back on its padded hanger and zipped it into the bag.

Frances carried the dress bag downstairs and outside, where she laid it gently on the ground. She tipped over one of the overflowing garbage cans that sat by the door and dumped out as much as she could manage. With difficulty she righted the can, stuffed the dress into it and replaced whatever garbage she could fit on top, leaving the rest where it lay on the ground, indistinguishable from the rusting tins, the moldy food, the wet papers, that were there already. She wiped her hands on her nightgown and went back inside, closing the door so carefully she could hardly hear it shut.

From under the kitchen sink Frances took a dust cloth, black with grime she did not see, and went into the main room to give a quick, light dusting to the surfaces, as if to put the house in order. Flicking the cloth as she went along the pathway, she slipped past Davis, heavily asleep in his chair. She straightened the newspapers piled on the couch, glancing over to make certain Davis wasn't moving in his sleep, but then, noticing how the newsprint had blackened the upholstery, she spread the papers again to cover the cushions. When she reached the shelf where *Gray's Anatomy* lay, she slid her hand underneath, found the key to the carved ivory box, and unlocked it, pausing before selecting the larger of the two guns. She wanted to do this right.

Somehow it was the smell of the gunpowder, rather than the gunshot, that would linger in the children's memories. Davis found Frances lying on the bathroom floor, conscious and talking to Miles, who had seen everything from the doorway. The warped door wouldn't close, and it had never locked. Today she had wanted more than anything to lock herself away forever.

"I'm sorry. I'm so sorry," she was saying over and over.

Davis laughed harshly. "Jesus Christ! If you're going to kill yourself, at least use a gun that was made for killing! Don't you know by now this is the one I use for shooting targets? There's hardly any powder in those goddamned bullets!"

Indeed Frances appeared to be uninjured, a scarcely noticeable powder burn surrounding the small spot of blood already drying on her nightgown, over her heart.

"Miles," said Davis shaking his head, "run and get Hank. Tell him he might as well go someplace and telephone for an ambulance."

Miles flew out the door and headed for Hank's cabin, thinking that Mama was wearing the same nightgown she'd been wearing last Christmas when Davis promised to buy her a warm bathrobe. If you gave her the robe like you said you would, he screamed at Davis in his mind, this wouldn't have happened.

While Miles was gone, Davis fixed himself some coffee. The sound of the gunshot had awakened Thos and Clara, and now they stood outside the bathroom, holding hands and quietly watching their mother. Frances, who did not realize they were there, lay thinking how unexpectedly heavy the gun was, how unwieldy it had been to hold it backwards, using her thumbs to push rather than pull the trigger, how the trigger had been surprisingly easy to push, and the gun had fired almost before she was ready.

When Miles returned with Hank, Davis ushered him unceremoniously into the bathroom.

"Tell him what happened, Frances," said Davis. It was important there be no misunderstanding about this.

"I shot myself," she said. "I don't want to live anymore."

Miles, who had gone over to stand between Thos and Clara, put an arm around each of them.

"Did you hear that, Hank? Say it again, Frances, so Hank will be sure to hear."

"I shot myself. I don't want to live anymore."

Miles pulled Thos, who had started shaking, closer to him.

"Well, then. Hank, did you call an ambulance?"

"Yessir, yessir I did. I did do that. Used the Bartons' phone. Called the police, too." Hank was trembling and fiercely wiping his eyes.

"The police? Yes, I can see that would be a good idea. Thank you, Hank. Thank you very much."

The ambulance arrived shortly afterwards, and the children, now huddled together at the top of the stairs, watched their mother being carried away on a stretcher. Her eyes were closed and they did not call out to her, afraid they might disturb her.

"We'll be taking her to Shoreline," said the driver, as he climbed into the ambulance.

"Fine, fine. I'll be along soon," said Davis, thinking it would be a good idea for him to be at the house when the police came.

"Hank," said Davis as they waited, "I wonder if you would be good enough to give me a lift over to the hospital. I'm not sure my car will make it that far. I was surprised we didn't break down on the way back from court in Crispin."

"Oh, don't you worry about it, Doc. Be happy to take you. Kiddies be all right here by themselves?"

Davis glanced around and caught sight of them at the top of the stairs.

"You'll be all right, won't you children?" Without waiting for an answer, he added, "We won't be gone long."

There was a knock at the door.

"Come in, officers," said Davis, holding the door and then showing them into the bathroom. "We've had a little accident here. Hank, tell these gentlemen exactly what Frances told you."

When the questioning was over, one of the officers knelt beside the gun that still lay on the bathroom floor where Davis, anxious not to add his own fresh fingerprints, had left it. The officer covered it with a cloth, picked it up carefully, and slipped it into a plastic bag.

"Routine," he said, ill at ease under Davis's gaze.

"Oh, of course, of course," said Davis. "I would like to mention that you should expect to find my prints on the gun, because I use it to shoot targets every day."

He paused, and then added, as if as an afterthought, "I'm sure you can understand that I'd like to make a note of the serial number before you take it away. After all, it *is* my gun. I want to be certain I get it back."

Frances died on the way to the hospital. The wadcutter, neither powerful nor deadly, had lodged in her heart and killed her. It was November 16, 1972. She was twenty-seven years old.

Sally Bea picked out the dress she was buried in, the flowered one Frances had worn years before, when Davis took her out to dinner to celebrate her birthday. And once again she saw to it that the children had something appropriate to wear.

"Lordy, lordy," she said to her brother Eldon repeatedly. "Seems like yesterday I got those kiddies dressed and ready to go to dog court with poor, dear, little Frances."

The funeral was small, just Davis and the children, Hank, Eldon, Sally Bea, Stuart, Johnny Johnson, and Dorothy, who had called Gran with the news. Stuart, who had flown back from London for the funeral, had urged Gran to come say good-bye to Frances, but she said no, she would do it in her own way, far from the man who, she insisted, had killed her granddaughter.

The funeral parlor reminded Stuart of a dentist's waiting room, with its synthetic wood paneling, light green leatherette sofa, unmatched, uncomfortable, armless chairs, and cheap prints in their supermarket frames, but instead of the antiseptic smell of a dentist's office, a mock floral fragrance hung heavily, cloyingly, in the air. Taped electronic organ music played, crackling and sputtering and intrusive. Each time Stuart turned it off, the funeral director, after what he apparently considered a polite interval, turned it back on.

When it was clear that no family member was going to speak, he welcomed them in a deep, lugubrious voice and said a few generic words about the tragic loss of a wife and mother and how much they would all miss her.

"Children grow up and make their own lives," he said. "The greatest loss is suffered by the devoted husband," and he looked sympathetically at Davis. He concluded by saying, "Always remember that she misses you, too," and then it was over and they were out in the parking lot and Stuart was yelling at Davis.

"How can you treat her memory like this? How can you subject her spirit to elevator music, to crappy white-bread creepy awful stuff? My God, her life was good until you came along and fucked it up!"

Davis, gazing placidly at Stuart, did not respond, a tolerant parent indulging the tantrum of an unruly child.

It wasn't until later that Stuart realized he hadn't met the tall, gray-haired woman. He'd meant to introduce himself. And Dorothy, for her part, had wanted to meet Stuart, had intended to talk to him after the funeral, but the moment clearly wasn't right, and she slipped away unnoticed.

Frances was buried in the Hardwick Cemetery, a short walk from their house. The children located the site by pacing off thirty-three steps from the big oak tree, and so they were able to visit her whenever they wanted, even though no stone marked her grave.

The death was never discussed in the house; Davis didn't mention it and the children didn't ask, as if doing so would break the spell that might, just might, allow Frances to come back to them. They didn't cry, either. They'd been trained. You may cry if bone is showing, and there wasn't any bone showing now. There was only an emptiness so powerful, so crushing, so vivid, that each of the children felt it must be visible.

The pattern of their days was unchanged, making it almost possible to pretend that their mother wasn't far away, but in the night the odor of gunpowder penetrated their sleep.

CHAPTER THIRTEEN

Stuart's first order of business was to get the kids away from Davis. Any fool could see the man was an unfit parent. He and Gran had been talking about this for a long time, and they were prepared to take Miles, Thos and Clara to live with them in Philadelphia. It wouldn't be easy, they knew, but they'd get through it somehow. Stuart had done the requisite nosing around, and now he wrote a letter, a detailed letter, to the Bureau of Children's Services, the state agency whose mission it was to protect children.

He provided his name and address, and affirmed that he was the uncle of the children in question. And then he described it all: the naked children ages three, four and five, the lack of proper meals, the condition of the house and the plumbing, the foul odors, the garbage inside and out. Davis wouldn't stand a chance. Stuart refrained from making personal accusations. Let the facts speak for themselves.

He couldn't give an address for the Davis house, since nobody had such a thing in Hardwick; residents picked up their mail at the post office. But a stop at any store in town would get the agents the necessary directions when they went to check things out. He knew the agency wouldn't call ahead to say they were coming, not that Davis had a phone anyway, and Stuart relished the idea that the old man would be caught off guard.

Jesus, it would be worth everything to see the look on his face when these guys show up, thought Stuart. If Davis didn't know what I look like, I swear to God I'd pose as someone from the agency. Son-of-a-bitch should be on trial for murder, not just have his kids taken away. At least we'll get them out of there, give them some kind of decent place to grow up.

He had neglected to take into account, however, the fact that Davis was always one step ahead.

The day after the funeral, Davis asked Hank to gather all the men who had worked on the construction project, as well as any interested townspeople, to come to an important meeting the following evening. He was pleased and astonished at the number crowded into the barn, around the cars that Johnny Johnson was in the process of working on. He suspected that Sally Bea had done her level best to convince them not to come.

While the children played in his office, Davis told the assembled group what was on his mind.

"Thank you all for coming tonight. I know you work hard and are tired at the end of a long day, and to come out like this when it's colder than a witch's—well, it's damn cold, isn't it?"

Appreciative laughter filled the room.

"Anyway, I'm very, very grateful."

"We're grateful to you, Doc! You're our hero!" shouted a man.

"We'd do anything for you!" called out another, and there was a roar of cheering and clapping.

Davis's eyes filled with tears and for a moment he could not speak, something that didn't happen very often. Finally he was able to continue.

"I think most of you have seen my house. It's a little, you know, disorganized."

More laughter.

"But now I have a problem, which is why I asked you to come tonight. I'm hoping you can help me out."

"Tell us what you want, and you've got it!"

More clapping.

"Well, to get right to the point, I'm pretty sure the authorities are going to try to take my children away. You know how it is. You don't fit somebody else's idea of a parent, and next thing you know, you're not fit to be one. My idea is to fool the authorities."

The room was still. Davis wasn't sure whether they were intrigued or appalled, but he pressed on.

And so it was that the Bartons, who lived in a cozy house not far away, and whose telephone Hank had used to call the ambulance and the police, were chosen to be the leading characters in Davis's little play. They were ideal, Mary Barton agreed, since their children had "flown the nest." Members of the community donated toys for the children, as well as clothes for them and for Davis. They helped Mary Barton put everything away in drawers and closets, and then they waited.

Sure enough, one week later a strange car pulled up at the gas station and asked directions to the Davis place. The attendant did as he'd been told, and gave extremely poor directions that were sure to confuse the driver and the woman with him. He then ran inside and called Tom Barton, who drove his pickup over to Davis's house. Davis and the children climbed in and were at the Bartons' in no time, where they washed their hands and faces and changed into the clothes Mary Barton had laid out on their beds. Mary tied back Clara's matted blonde hair and used a big pink bow, hoping it would be a distraction. The boys' hair, she decided, would pass muster. It looked as if Davis literally put a bowl over their heads from time to time and gave them a trim.

"Wow!" breathed Miles to Thos. "Look at our room!"

It was bright and sunny, with stuffed animals on the beds. Clara's was a perfect little girl's room, with pink curtains that matched the pink bedspread. The Bartons' room now "belonged" to Davis.

"Okay, Doc, I guess you're on your own," said Tom Barton to Davis. "We'll go get ourselves a cup of coffee. Good luck, buddy."

A car drove up a short time later, and Davis went out onto the porch. The children stayed upstairs, following orders. A man and a woman, who looked to be in their late thirties, early forties, got out of the car. His suit was ill-fitting, and her dress was a style long out of fashion.

"Can I help you?" asked Davis with as much innocence as he could manage.

"Yes," said the man, as he glanced down at a paper he held in his hand, "We're looking for a Dr. Leslie Davis. Would you know where we can find him?"

"Actually, you've found him. And you are . . . ?"

He listened to the irritation that glittered in his tone. The irritation rapidly turned to curiosity as he watched the reaction on the man's face and wondered how he would proceed.

"Oh. Yes. I'm Edward Potts and this is Helen Carson. We're from BCS."

"BCS?" said Davis. "And what might 'BCS' be?"

"Sorry. The Bureau of Children's Services. We're a state agency charged with protecting child welfare."

"I see. What business have you here?"

Davis was starting to enjoy himself as he watched Edward Potts and Helen Carson squirm uncomfortably. He thought of Mr. Brigham and the dogs.

"We—we've had a complaint. Is it all right if we look around?"

He had dropped his voice, and, although Davis had heard perfectly, he asked the man to repeat what he'd said.

Then, "Come in, come in. Please, look around all you like. The children are upstairs in their rooms."

"They're not in school?"

"No, no. I home school them."

"I see," said Edward Potts, nodding.

Davis held the door for the pair and followed them inside. This was ideal. He looked polite, but it served a larger function in that he could conveniently let them find their own damn way around the house. Personally, he had no idea where anything was.

Edward Potts and Helen Carson stayed no more than fifteen minutes. Davis walked behind them, eavesdropping on their murmuring. They peered at Davis's medical school diploma that was hanging prominently in the living room. They looked in the spotless oven, in the refrigerator filled with fruits, vegetables, and fresh meats, in the cupboards stocked with cereals and crackers and cookies. They checked the flow of the water, flushed the toilets, ran their fingers over doorways and found no dust. The house was immaculate.

Davis followed them upstairs. The children were playing quietly on the floor in the boys' room. They looked up when they saw their father with the two strangers, but they kept silent as they'd been instructed to do. They pretended not to pay attention as the closet door was opened, as dresser drawers were pulled out and the contents inspected.

Edward Potts and Helen Carson couldn't apologize enough.

"Obviously there's been some dreadful mistake," the woman said. "Someone is a good candidate for the loony bin!"

She laughed weakly. And they left.

"Okay, children, get your clothes on!" called Davis up the stairs. "Just about time to go!"

"Gee, I wish we could stay here. This is really nice," said Miles, slowly pulling off his shirt."

"Yeah," said Thos.

"My room is pretty!" crowed Clara.

Then they put on the London sweatshirts from Uncle Stuart and went home with their father in Tom Barton's truck.

Stuart read the BCS letter three times and then asked Gran to read it aloud. They could not believe the words on the page:

Thank you for your concern, which we very much appreciate. Indeed, it is only because of interested third parties such as yourself that we are able to protect our children. In this case, however, there has been a clear misunderstanding on your part. We do not wish to refer to your communication as a "crank letter," but the fact remains that we were sent on a "wild goose chase." It was an embarrassment for our agents, who felt they were accusing a medical man of negligence where his children are concerned. We have absolutely no doubt that Dr. Leslie Davis is providing a safe and nurturing environment for his three children, who, by all evidence, are thriving. It is obvious that they are well cared for, and that their well-being is paramount to Dr. Davis. The house you described, and conditions therein, bear no resemblance to the abode visited by our representatives, who observed that the children had well-appointed bedrooms filled with appropriate toys and books, as well as proper clothing. The kitchen was stocked with fresh vegetables and fruit, and with healthful snacks. In sum, we at the agency are more than satisfied that Dr. Leslie Davis is a fit, concerned, nurturing, and fully qualified parent.

The door slammed in their faces, and they could hear the click of the lock.

"Shit!" screamed Stuart. "Shit! Shit! Shit!" Then he caught the look on Gran's face and stopped himself. "The bastard! He used somebody's house! Oh, my God, those poor kids!"

He'd had one chance, and he'd blown it. He was overcome with despair, and with hopelessness.

CHAPTER FOURTEEN

Almost a year and a half had passed since Frances died, and Stuart was making one of his occasional, unannounced visits to Hardwick to see the children. This summer morning, however, he did not present himself right away, but parked down the road and walked the rest of the way through the trees, in order to observe unnoticed.

From his vantage point Stuart could see Charlotte in her pen, rooting around for the slop she was eating off the ground.

Jesus, he said to himself, that's the biggest goddamned pig I've ever seen.

Indeed, Charlotte had grown to such a size that she looked inflated and not precisely real, an animation come to life, with her white skin decorated with black designs that appeared to have been drawn on with a crayon.

Stuart also had an unexpectedly excellent view of Davis sitting in the hot sun with another man, whom he recognized from Frances's funeral. He and Davis looked to be of the same vintage,

Hard to tell, though, thought Stuart, they all look like hell down here, with their scraggly beards and thin, messy hair, and their missing teeth and long, dirty fingernails.

The men had taken off their shirts, revealing sunken chests that, Stuart supposed, were bordering on hairless, although it was impossible to see from where he crouched in the bushes. He did see, however, that the shirt lying across Davis's lap was the same one he was wearing whenever Stuart saw him, and assumed the pants were, too. The children had told him how, when Davis felt the infrequent need to change his clothes, he went into the bathroom and checked the pile for the "cleanest" ones by sniffing them, piece by piece, until he was satisfied.

Miles and Thos, naked as usual, were playing what looked to be an elaborate game they had set up in the dirt driveway. Stuart thought he could hear Clara whimpering, a sound that seemed to be coming from fairly high up, and he realized she had climbed a tree and couldn't get down.

"Aw, come on, she's just a little tyke," the other man was saying to Davis.

"You climbed up there, Clara, which means you possess the ability to climb back down," Davis said, ignoring the man's remark.

Jesus H. Christ, said Stuart to himself, she's a little kid! What in hell does he expect?

Davis's companion was clearly having trouble keeping his mind on the conversation, casting frequent glances at the tree Clara had climbed. Miles and Thos disappeared from his view, and then he heard them cheering her on.

"Come on, C! You can do it!" This was Miles.

"Let's go, C!" shouted Thos.

When she had managed to get herself down, Davis greeted her with, "Do you see? Didn't I say you could do it by yourself?"

Clara, as naked as the boys but for her mother's large sunhat that she was putting back on her head, paid no attention to him and ran inside.

"Women," scoffed Davis with a degree of disgust that disturbed Stuart.

Miles and Thos went back to their game, the men continued to talk quietly, Clara came outside to join the boys, and Stuart assumed the fireworks were over. He turned away, preparing to come out of hiding, but then he heard Miles announce,

"I'm going to have to do this all over again! It looks like shit!"

Davis interrupted himself to say, "That will be five cents deducted from your allowance, Miles," and resumed his conversation.

"But you say it all the time! Who deducts it from *your* allowance?"

"Ten cents for talking back. That will be a grand total of fifteen cents so far this week."

"*This week?*" said Miles incredulously. "But today is Saturday! Allowance week *starts* on Saturday!"

"Twenty-five cents," said Davis, who wove his comments to Miles artfully into the tone of the conversation he was having with his companion.

"But we only *get* twenty—"

Miles stopped so abruptly that Stuart assumed Thos and Clara had stepped in.

The men's dialogue caught Stuart's attention. The companion was suggesting that Davis might like to get someone in to help with the children and the housework, adding that he knew a lot of people in town who would be happy to have the work, and that he could bring them around and let Davis talk to them, see who he liked best.

"I know who these people are," replied Davis, "and I can tell you that I have no intention of putting my children in daily contact with someone who doesn't have the faintest idea how to put together an intelligible sentence. The children and I are managing fine by ourselves."

Stuart had the distinct impression Davis was about to finish with a sarcastic "thank you," but thought better of it.

"Isn't there some law or other that says you have to go to school when you're six or something?" inquired the man after a pause, changing the subject. If he felt he'd been insulted, he didn't show it, thought Stuart.

"How old are they now, anyway?"

There was another pause. For a minute Stuart thought Davis was going to ask to have the question repeated, sounding like a contestant on a quiz show stalling for time. But it was Davis himself who repeated it.

"How old are they? Well, now, let's see. Miles is seven. Thomas is six. And Clara is—Clara is five. They're small for their ages, but that's what they are, seven, six, and five. Small is a handicap, I'm afraid. My family tended to be tall, so I assume the short gene came courtesy of their mother.

"And I don't care about any damned law. Schools are for trash. You associate with trash, you turn into trash. I can teach them everything they need to know, right here, and what I can't teach them isn't worth knowing. And do you know why they're so healthy? Why they don't get sick? Even though they haven't had a single vaccination? Because they don't go to school, that's why. School is nothing more than a cesspool of germs. The boys were sick once, *once,* and Clara, never."

After this exchange the men grew quiet, and, figuring this was it for the time being, Stuart returned to his car. A few minutes later he drove up to the house, careful to stay clear of the game set up in the driveway. He was greeted with great fanfare, as the children shouted his name and rushed to meet him.

"Hello, Stuart," said Davis. "I was wondering when you were going to come out of the trees and let us see you."

He got up and went inside, and it dawned on Stuart that Davis's discourse had been for his benefit. He saw that the good doctor had a revolver strapped to his hip.

Stuart stood by the steps as the children held hands and danced around him. He was embarrassed, the other man mystified, and then Stuart's curiosity got the best of him.

"What's with the gun?"

"Aw, anyone comes around, he tells them to get off his land, and he means it, too," came the reply. "He can be nasty with a gun." The man was chuckling. He waited a moment and said, "Eldon. Eldon Speen," and stuck out his hand stiffly. "Me and my sister, Sally Bea, we own the market here in town."

"Stuart Taylor. Sorry," he added, and laughed, glancing helplessly at the children, whose antics made it impossible for him to shake hands.

Eldon put his hand back in his lap. "Uncle Stuart. Yeah. Saw you at the, at the—service. For the missus."

He examined his fingernails for a long moment. They seemed to remind him of something, and he gestured with his head toward the house.

"Don't mind the Doctor. He just gets a little, well, ornery sometimes. He doesn't mean anything by it."

The children were clambering all over Stuart, who excused himself and followed them to their game.

They had created a series of squares, large enough to walk around in, by stacking bricks to a height of, Stuart guessed, about twelve inches. The squares were connected by narrow walkways, four bricks across, laid flat.

"We're playing Society!" squealed Clara.

"'Society'?" repeated Stuart.

"Oh, yeah, they play it about every day," called Eldon from his chair.

"Come here," said Thos patiently, taking Stuart's hand, "we'll show you."

With some difficulty, Stuart followed him along the brick path, their clasped hands raised in a kind of minuet, with Miles and Clara close behind.

"See," Thos continued, "it all started when he was telling us about how societies began a long, long time ago. About institutions and everything."

He. Stuart had noticed some time back that the children were not comfortable calling their father anything. The situation was an awkward one, in the same way that it is for a new son- or daughter-in-law. To each other, the children referred to Davis simply as "he." When direct address could not be avoided, it was always "sir."

"Who got the idea to build a society?" asked Stuart.

Thos peered around Stuart to look at Miles and Clara, who nodded as he said, "We kind of all got the idea together. Then our friend Hank gave us these bricks. So," he went on, as they made their way through the system, "here are the houses, and here's the school, and the courthouse, and the penitentiary. And over here is the restaurant, and the general store, and here, right where we're standing, is the hospital!"

Stuart was impressed by how detailed it all was. Using model glue and scraps of wood, bits of cloth, sticks, pebbles, apparently whatever they could find, they had made everything they needed. The children pointed out the hospital beds, the emergency room, the operating room, the X-ray machine.

"He used to be a doctor," explained Clara. "He told us a whole lot of stuff."

"Yeah, like he told us that this guy Roentgen discovered X-rays," said Miles.

"Roentgen," said Thos. "He was a German—physicist." He stumbled over the word.

"And Madame Curie. She was this *lady* physicist from France, and she figured out something about measuring radioactivity, I forget what. They named the curie after her, I remember that," said Clara.

"'Curie'?" repeated Stuart.

"That's how you measure—"

"How you measure—"

"Radioactivity!"

The children were all talking at once.

"Ah," murmured Stuart, "so that's how you measure radioactivity."

The restaurant featured tables and chairs, a counter with stools along it, and a short-order stove behind the counter. There were pots and pans, dishes, a coffee pot, even hamburgers cooking on the grill. Stuart picked up one of the people sitting at a table. It was made from a bendable plastic straw.

"Look," said Thos, taking the straw-person from Stuart. "He can move his hand! See? He can wave and everything!" Thos demonstrated.

"They can't actually sit, is the thing," said Miles. "But we prop them up and lay them down."

"And they don't disintegrate in the rain," added Clara. "The ones we made out of paper didn't last at all. We got so excited when we saw these straws at the market, and Eldon said we can come in whenever we feel like it and take as many as we want!"

Stuart looked over at Eldon, who was nodding "yes" as he sat in his chair by the door.

At the courthouse, Miles said, "Sometimes we have trials here."

He showed Stuart the courtroom, the jury box, the judge's bench, even the tiny gavel they had fashioned out of aluminum foil.

"We had this one guy who murdered somebody. We had a trial and we found him guilty, and C and I wanted to hang him from a tree, lynch him, like they used to do in the old days," he said, "but Thos wouldn't let us."

"Yeah, Thos thought that was mean," Clara chimed in. "So we just kept the man in prison for a while. Detained him."

"Then we had another guy," said Thos, "and we didn't feel like having a trial 'cause we were busy doing something else, so we stuck him in the penitentiary instead. But he told us you can't do that. It's called 'habeas corpus.' You have to have a trial, or else you have to free the guy, so we let him go."

Inside the school was a classroom containing a blackboard and several rows of desks; a cafeteria; a gymnasium; and an auditorium. A playing field lay behind the building. Stuart heard about the homework assignments and the quizzes, the sporting events and the plays, the food fights and the after-school detentions. He couldn't resist.

"How do you know so much about school if you've never been there?"

They answered together. "All the TV kids go to school!"

"He made us have school here a couple of times," said Clara.

"It didn't work out too well, though," added Miles. "He said it was time for us to learn something, so he took a stick and he wrote some numbers in the dirt and he said some stuff we didn't understand, and then he handed us sticks and told us to do it. We didn't even know what we were supposed to do! It was kind of stupid.

"But there's a neat word game we play," he went on. "It doesn't have a name, at least I don't think it does, and it's just so we learn big words. He really likes big words. He gets out the dictionary and he reads us a bunch of words and their definitions, and he reads them pretty fast. Then he goes back and reads the definitions again, one by one, and we have to say what word it is."

"Does it help you read?" asked Stuart.

"Oh, we can't read," said Thos, the tour guide explaining the peculiarities of the inhabitants. "Once he did try to teach us, though. He showed us one of those medical journals he gets in the mail and he started telling us how to read, but we couldn't do it."

"So what happened?" asked Stuart.

"Nothing," replied Miles. "He never gets really mad or anything. I mean, he doesn't yell at us. 'Course he won't talk to us for a while."

"Sometimes I wish I could go to school with the kids on TV, 'cause the teachers look really nice," said Clara. She thought for a minute.

"If we're outside when the school bus drives by here, all the kids get on one side of the bus and look at us and I get a really scared feeling. Then he says if we do something bad, we're going to have to ride on that bus with those mean kids." She pulled Stuart's sleeve. "Let's go see the houses. Yesterday there was a community picnic!"

The houses showed the same attention to detail evidenced throughout. Each house had a living room, dining room, kitchen, bathroom and two bedrooms. There were tables and chairs, lamps and sofas, beds and nightstands.

"You know about this from television, too?" asked Stuart.

The children nodded vigorously. Stuart looked at each of them.

"What do you suppose it would be like to live in a house like you see on TV?" He almost said, "a real house," but didn't.

The children looked at each other. They'd all thought the same thing, that once, for a little while, they had lived in a real house. But their father had warned them that it was to be a secret, and they were never, never to tell anybody about it.

The children giggled. "Most of the real houses are just on TV! It's pretend!" they all explained at once.

Nobody actually lives like that, was what they meant, Stuart said to himself. He tapped his tongue rapidly against the roof of his mouth. Then, "How about you guys go play while I talk to Eldon?"

They ran off and Stuart walked over and sat heavily in Davis's chair.

"Uncle Stuart," said Eldon. "Their mom's brother."

"Half-brother, actually. Older, by a couple of years." Stuart felt he should volunteer something more. "Our grandmother raised us."

Eldon's eyebrows shot up.

"No mama, huh? Looks like you've got something in common with the kids."

Stuart was appalled that he'd never made the connection.

"Your grandpa was the breadwinner, eh?"

"No, he died a long time before we were born. She did it all by herself. Tutored kids, took in laundry, did some bookkeeping and secretarial work for small businesses in town, anything to keep her home with us. She was awful strict, but she got us through. Me and Francie."

"'Francie,' you called her? Your sister was a heck of a lady. She used to come into the market a lot, walked into town with the kids. Always polite, and real nice. Pretty, too."

"Yeah, she was," said Stuart quietly. He had to change the subject. It hurt to talk about her. "So, what about this game?"

"'Society'? Aw, just something the kids figured out to occupy their time. Keeps them out of trouble."

But what about habeas corpus and Roentgen and Madame Curie? Stuart wanted to ask. Why 'Society'? Why everything?

After a long time, resigned to being unable to sort through his thoughts, he began again. "So. How did you and Davis meet?"

"The Doctor? Well, like I said, Sally Bea and me, we own the Hardwick Market, and the kids, they're always hanging around. They're nice kids, good kids, and I give them stuff. Candy bars, popcorn, ice cream, sodas, and all like that. How we come to get friendly, is, back a few months ago when the kids were over to the store, I asked them if their dad was home. Miles, he said sure, he's always home, where would he go? So I said come on, I'll give you a ride. It's not far, like you probably know, maybe a mile or so, but that was a big treat for the kiddies 'cause they don't spend much time in cars, I can tell you that. Anyway, they jump into my old Buick and we ride them home. Now I'd heard from a whole lot of people in town that the Doctor is a real nice man, nice to all his patients. Doesn't even charge them. It's different when you don't pay. You kind of put up with things. Conditions. No waiting room, and like that. Anyway, I had some kind of boil on my head I wanted him to look at. So the kids, they hop out of the car, yank off those elastic-waist shorts they wear when they come into town, and they run off to play. I knock on the door and the Doctor, well, he couldn't have been nicer. Lanced the boil for me and everything. I tried to make conversation. How have you been making out since the missus had herself that accident? But it was like he didn't hear me. Never said a word, and of course I never did bring it up again. Not to this day."

He was quiet for a short while.

"You didn't have to be real smart to see they weren't making out well at all, not at all. Things were, you know, kind of helter-skelter around the place, so the next day I came back with a couple of bags of food. The Doctor wouldn't let me pay for lancing the boil, and I wanted to do something for all of them. Besides, owning the market like I do, food doesn't cost me all that much. Here, I said, I thought maybe you could use a little something to eat. He takes the bags and nods thanks, and he starts to close the door but then he opens it and asks me in. Guess he was pretty lonely. Told me later, matter of fact, time was when he had some big-shot doctors coming down from the hospital to visit him, groups of them used to come together, the top brass, you know, but seems like they just finally stopped coming."

Top brass? Stuart thought skeptically. Well, whoever they were, he probably called them disciples. Davis's Disciples. He would've liked the sound of it.

"We talked a while," Eldon continued, "and then, Jesus, I had to take a piss in the worst way, so I say is there a bathroom or an outhouse here or something? So he shows me the bathroom. Well, the toilet wasn't working but that didn't stop them from using it, no sir. Smelled something fierce, all backed up like it was. It's got some kind of real slow leak, so there's times it empties enough so you can use it, but most times it's spilling all over the floor and you have to use the Great Outdoors. Truth is, I was wondering why somebody or other from the health department never showed up. Then the Doctor, he sees me kind of looking around and he says don't you worry, I know the right people. I got my contacts, he says. Seems like he does too.

"Anyway, that's how I happened to see the pile of laundry in the bathroom. All their clothes in there, *all* their clothes. So when I left, I said why don't you let me take that laundry. Said the wife will be glad to do it up. Those clothes were filthy, the dirtiest clothes I ever saw in my whole entire life. Stained with dog shit and God knows what all. Lucille wasn't any too happy to see it, especially from those kids that . . . well, I guess she figured she'd never been able to have kids herself and I never said a thing about it, but she knew I wanted kids practically more than I wanted a wife. Then too, she's home all day with nothing to do but watch her soaps, so when she had everything washed and ironed and folded in boxes I took it over to the house. Couple of weeks later it was right back on the floor there in the bathroom. I never did tell Lucille."

There was a lull in the conversation.

"Sounds like there's not much money coming in," said Stuart. "I mean, you're bringing food and everything."

"You said a mouthful. No sir, not much money is right."

"So—how does he pay his bills? Taxes? I guess that would be the big one."

Eldon ran his tongue around his teeth, as if assuring himself they were firmly in place.

"He told me when he and the missus first came down here, times were different. He had plenty of money from his doctor days. He got himself a lawyer and set up something so that's all taken care of. Taxes get paid when the time comes, no problem. 'Course he doesn't have a mortgage or anything. Paid for the house all at once."

Eldon smiled proudly, then went on.

"You know, I think he figured money problems were coming his way, and he wanted to make sure he had a roof over his head."

Stuart nodded and waited. Eldon didn't say anything, and Stuart tried to think of another question.

"Have you always lived in Hardwick?" he asked.

"You bet! Born and raised. Truth is I've never been more than about thirty, forty miles from here in my life. Hardwick's a real quiet place. Has been during my lifetime, anyway. But it wasn't always like that. They found iron ore around here about a hundred years ago, and there were furnaces and forges and everything. A genuine industrial center. Next thing you know, there's better ore someplace else, and everything pretty much collapsed and most everybody moved away. Me, I'm destined to die right here. Doesn't bother me. Unless I die soon. *That* would bother me." He chuckled to himself.

"So you see Davis, um, the Doctor, a lot?"

"Every day or close to it. I bring the newspaper, maybe some money if he gave me some little check to cash the day before. Bring it along with a batch of groceries. How are they going to eat if I don't? Suppose one of his patients shows up with a basket of potatoes instead of something they can eat without fixing it? Those potatoes will sit there 'til they stink up the place. I know, 'cause I've seen it happen more than once. I don't worry about a balanced diet. Just want to fill them up is all. They like cookies and sugary cereals and all like that, maybe some peanut butter. The Doctor, he lets them rip everything open and go at it as soon as I walk in the door, food sprays all over the place, he doesn't say anything."

"Wouldn't you think he'd be more concerned about what the kids eat? I mean, he's a doctor, after all."

Eldon laughed.

"You know the Doctor!" He glanced at Stuart. "I guess you don't, do you? See, he's doing some kind of experiment with the kids, trying to approximate their 'living in the wild.'" Eldon said the words slowly and deliberately. "I guess that's where the naked stuff comes in, too. He says nobody in the wild sits down to a nice, home-cooked dinner every night. They take what they can get and make do with that."

He shook his head, then shrugged his shoulders and put his palms up, smiling slightly.

"I have to admit, seems like a pretty good childhood to me. Those kids can do whatever they please, so long as they ask the Doctor's permission first. He's very strict on that."

"Does he ever say no?" asked Stuart.

Eldon thought for a minute. "Well now, I can't recall a single time when he said no to those kids. He just likes knowing where they are."

More silence, and he went on. "Come holiday time, I get Lucille to cook them a big turkey with all the trimmings. Ham at Easter, like we have over to the house. She's not real crazy about it 'cause she doesn't approve of the Doctor and his ways, but she's a good egg."

He paused.

"He's a mighty brilliant man, you know. Mighty brilliant. Trouble is, now he's got no money coming in, just his share of the garage business, and he's got the kids. Somebody has to take care of them. So we kind of do it together, know what I mean?"

Stuart nodded, though not in agreement. Amazing, he thought, how some people work the system, any system, even one they've created.

"Does he have any friends?"

"Hmmm. A lot of people come to him as patients, so he knows them, but not like you'd call them friends. Nope, I'm about it."

Eldon sat for a bit, working his tongue against his teeth. He made loud sucking noises.

"I'm thinking about getting me some false teeth," he said, leaning toward Stuart and speaking in a confiding tone. "You kind of lose your vanity after a while. Figure who the hell cares, right? But I'm out in front of the public all day. Not like the Doctor." He nodded toward the door. "Me, I have to keep up appearances."

"He's let himself go, that's for damn sure. Looks like hell, if you ask me." Stuart realized too late that he was talking about Eldon, too, but the man didn't seem to notice.

"Yeah," said Eldon, "the Doctor doesn't take much pride these days. But he's got himself a girlfriend, he does. Always has had some lady-friend or other, far as I can tell. Real pretty ones, too. Must be some women get turned on by the mess in there!" He laughed coarsely.

"Holy shit! How does he meet these women?"

Stuart could hardly get the words out. He doubted there was a pimp around here, but it was the only explanation he could come up with on short notice.

"Patients, mostly. And then I guess the word just spread. He must give off some kind of smell like animals do, you know? Attract the opposite sex? I've never seen anything like it. He's a devil, he is!" He chuckled, shaking his head. "This one, every week, like clockwork, she drives over in a real nice car. Shows up right around noontime. The Doctor tells the kids, now you leave us alone, don't you be coming upstairs, and up they go, the two of them, and a little later down they come. Doesn't take them long, that's for sure. She hops in her car, hair mussed, clothes looking like she didn't have time to take them off, but a sort of satisfied smile on her face. Cat that swallowed the canary. Never says a word to me or the kids. The Doctor, he comes back and sits down again, right where you're sitting now, calm as you please, and starts in talking to me like he never even left. Right in the middle of a sentence, seems like."

Eldon grew quiet again, and Stuart, anxious not to lose this opportunity to talk about Davis, said, "Tell me, what in hell does he do all day?"

It was a while before Eldon answered.

"Now that's a mighty good question. One thing he does do a whole lot is read. He never gets tired reading those medical books he's got, or the 'journals,' he calls them, that come in the mail. They gave him some kind of 'honorary lifetime subscription,' he says. Yeah, that would be his number one activity. Reading. Then he writes in his notebooks. He keeps a lot of notebooks, all about the kids, and their progress, and whatnot. Of course he shoots his targets and his varmints. Cleans and oils that shotgun of his, too. And then naturally there's the office. He spends a lot of time over there. Talking with Johnny Johnson, mostly."

The sky had been steadily darkening, and now it began to rain.

"Come on inside," said Eldon. Then, as he saw Stuart glance in the direction of the children, he added, "Don't worry. They'll be all right. We let them stay out in all kinds of weather. The Doctor says they're 'drip dry.'"

It was the first time he had been in the house since before Frances died, and Stuart found himself nearly retching. Christ, he thought, it smells like a fucking kennel crossed with a garbage dump. It's time to say adios to the dogs, that's for damn sure, dragging around and shitting all over the place and nobody in a hurry to clean it up.

He turned to Eldon at the sound of thudding and rustling. "Snakes," said Eldon with a chortle. "Neighbor kids know the Doctor is a sucker for living things, so they come around with snakes they catch and then they threaten to kill the little buggers if he doesn't buy them, and he does. Ten cents apiece. It's blackmail, I tell him, and he says well, it's for a good cause. Sometimes the snakes get loose in the house before he can get them outside, but they're harmless. He takes them 'cause he can't stand to see anything die that doesn't have to. Can't stand it, is all. Loves all God's creatures. That's how come those poor old dogs are still hanging around when anybody else would've had them put to sleep by now. Even loves the varmints he shoots at. Says he has nothing against them, but he's higher on the food chain. Naturally he doesn't eat them or anything." He laughed to himself.

While Eldon was talking, Stuart had followed the thudding sound and was watching snakes slither up the outside of the stair rail, fall off, and disappear under the papers on the floor, under the piles of furniture, under anything they could find. It crossed his mind that they had plenty of choices.

"Showing Stuart around, are you, Eldon?"

The doctor's voice momentarily drowned out the sound of the television set, and pipe smoked added to the already hot, airless atmosphere. The lord of the manor, thought Stuart bitterly.

"Yessir, I am."

As Stuart left, he heard Davis snort derisively.

"What do you say we go down to the dock and have the muffins I brought before it's time for me to go?" asked Stuart when he got outside and found the rain had stopped. The feeling of nausea was beginning to subside.

At Miles's insistence they sat on the dock in order of height, although Thos and Clara made it plain it was only for a few minutes because they wanted to sit next to Uncle Stuart, too. And Thos pointed out that he and Miles were practically the same height. Indeed they were, thought Stuart, but Miles was strong and muscular, while Thos was frail. They were simply growing into bigger versions of their young selves. Clara, too, was still tiny, although she was becoming a little beauty.

Stuart took a muffin from the bag and handed it to Miles, who gave it to Thos, who passed it to Clara. By the time hers slipped out of her hands and fell into the water, Thos was holding his own muffin.

"Here," he said, breaking it in two, "you can have half of mine."

It was one of the few pieces of the day he could relate to Gran. "There wasn't a split second missed in the cosmos before this kid shared," he told her. "He didn't even have time to think about it. It was unbelievable."

On the way back to the house, they heard gunshots. Before Stuart could say anything, Miles said, "He's shooting the rats that hang around the garbage. It's okay. He does it a lot. He doesn't want to scare them away before he can shoot, so he leans out the upstairs window and they don't even know he's there! Pretty smart, don't you think?" Without waiting for an answer, and responding to something in Stuart's face, he added anxiously, "He doesn't bust up the garbage cans or anything. He uses his plinking pistol. Really. Don't worry. This one's specially made for killing varmints."

They walked on in silence until Miles said, "After Uncle Stuart leaves, let's play 'Anne Frank.'"

"What's 'Anne Frank'?" Stuart was almost afraid to ask.

"She was a little girl that was hiding and then somebody came and took her away because she was Jewish," said Clara.

"Okay, that's right," said Stuart cautiously. "How do you play a game of 'Anne Frank'?"

"Well," said Thos, "C is Anne Frank and she hides and Miles and I are the Gestapo and we find her and we carry her away!"

He jumped from one foot to the other.

"And then what?"

"That's all. We just take her away."

"What happens to Anne Frank?"

"Nothing," interjected Miles. "Oh. They killed her, really," he added, and shrugged.

CHAPTER FIFTEEN

Letter-writing time again, thought Stuart, as he tried to figure out what to say to Davis. The effect he was striving for was, he told himself, polite but not ass-kissing, because the old guy would spot that a mile away and he, Stuart, would be dead meat.

His proposal was this: It might be worthwhile for the children to spend a weekend now and then with Stuart and Gran at their house in Philadelphia. He didn't feel the need to mention that they shared the house because Stuart had never been able to see his way clear to move out. That, aside from his time in London, he'd pretty much spent his whole life there. Stuart would, he told Davis, be happy to pick up the children and bring them back. He suggested a date several weeks hence, and, wishing that Davis would emerge from the Stone Age and get himself a telephone, included a stamped, self-addressed envelope so Davis could respond if he wished. If he heard nothing, Stuart wrote, he would assume the arrangements met with Davis's approval.

Each day he checked the mail but there was no reply, and so, on the appointed Saturday morning, Stuart arrived in Hardwick. The children were waiting for him and had climbed into the car before Stuart had a chance to turn off the motor.

"Hey, guys, how about saying good-bye to your father?" he said.

Grudgingly they got out, and, standing at some distance from Davis, they chorused, "Good-bye, sir."

"I guess they don't need me now that they have you," said Davis as they scrambled back into the car. "That's gratitude for you, isn't it?"

Stuart kept his mouth shut. He knew a genuine question when he heard one, and this wasn't one.

"Um, you'd better put on some clothes," he said to the children, trying hard to picture the look on Gran's face when he arrived with the three great-grandchildren she had never met, their hair filthy, their fingernails dirty, and stark naked to boot. Gran, proper Gran, hair tucked into a perfect bun, dressed in the black dresses she'd worn every day since Frances died. She was, Stuart knew, in perpetual mourning for Frances and for the opportunities she, Gran, had missed as both a mother and a grandmother. The black dresses plunged straight down from the shelf of her ample bosom and over her box-like figure. She had never worn lipstick or powder, and her only jewelry was her thin gold wedding band and a watch that had belonged to the husband who was dead before his thirty-third birthday. No, Stuart couldn't imagine Gran greeting the naked children, not without risking a heart attack. Clothing them might not guarantee her good health, but it would help.

For the second time the children got out of the car, and when they scrambled back in, barefoot and topless and wearing grimy, elastic-waist shorts, Stuart simply asked if they'd be warm enough.

"It's fall, you know. It gets pretty cold, especially at night."

"We'll be okay, Uncle Stuart," said Miles.

"Can we bring our bikes?" asked Clara.

"Bikes? You have bikes?"

"Hank made them for us out of spare parts. They're really neat!" cried Thos.

"Two problems," said Stuart. "First off, this car, as you can see, can barely hold the four of us, much less three bikes. Second, you're going to see that Philadelphia is a city, a big city," he paused, "like you see on television." The children were nodding seriously. "And because there are lots of cars, it's not a safe place to ride bikes. But we'll do other things, and then your bikes will be waiting for you when you come back tomorrow. Okay?"

"Okay!" they shouted together, and they were off.

Stuart hadn't realized Gran was such a good actress. If he hadn't known better, he never would have suspected she was the slightest bit taken aback by the children's appearances. The fierceness that sometimes vied with kindness in her face was gone today, and she hugged them and kissed them and told them how much they looked like their mother. They stood still with their arms at their sides and smiled, unaware that some people, finding themselves in that situation, hug back.

"Now," said Gran when they were inside. "The first order of business is baths! Do you take baths at your house?"

The children shook their heads.

"Not in winter," said Clara, "because the river gets too cold for the soap to lather up. But in summer we sometimes wash when we go swimming, if that's what you mean."

"No, I mean in a bathtub with plenty of nice, warm water and bubble bath and boats and rubber toys to play with!"

With that she took Miles by the hand and led him upstairs.

"Stuart," she instructed, in the no-nonsense tone he knew so well, "while I have Miles soaking, you give Clara and Thomas the chicken sandwiches I've fixed, and some of that chocolate cake and a big glass of milk, I think."

For the next several hours, the children rotated so that each had two long baths. "It's like doing the laundry, except these are human beings," Stuart murmured to her as they met on the stairs.

The dirt had grown into their skin in some places, and these Gran gently rubbed with baby oil and cotton. She shampooed their hair, but it was badly matted and she decided to give them haircuts.

"I cut your Uncle Stuart's hair once a month," she said, as she worked on Miles, "so you can consider me a professional."

When it was Thos's turn for a haircut, he took to heart Gran's admonition to stay still so he wouldn't get hurt, but Miles and Clara were too excited for that, and they were so intrigued and opened their eyes so wide that Gran had to cover them with her hand when she brushed the hair from their faces.

The haircutting completed, she said, "All right, Miles, Thomas, Clara. You come with me."

"Um, excuse me," said Clara, "but could you call me 'C'? I like that a lot better. He's the only one who calls me Clara, and I hate it! I know it's my real, real, *real* name, but it sounds like a girl."

"Why I think it's a perfectly lovely name, but if you prefer to be called C, then I will gladly call you C."

"And I'm Thos. Not Thomas. Thos." He looked at her eagerly.

"All right," said Gran heartily, "we have Miles and Thos and C! Good enough! Now, come see what I have for all of you!"

Spread out on Gran's bed was a dress for Clara, shirts and pants for the boys, and three bright red nylon jackets. Three pairs of sneakers with balls of red socks tucked inside them sat on the floor.

They headed first for the sneakers.

"Hey, look at these! We've never had our own shoes before! Shoes, we have shoes!" they exclaimed, talking on top of each other, and they sat on the floor and pulled them on. Stuart, about to tell them the tradition is to wear socks with the sneakers, was silenced by a look from Gran.

She'd had no idea what sizes to buy and had simply told the saleswoman that the children were six, seven and eight years old, and so the shoes were far too big. But Miles, Thos and Clara wiggled their feet forward and dragged them along delightedly as they walked, until Gran explained they could have smaller ones that would fit their feet.

"Today?" asked Thos. "Will we get them this very day?"

"This very day," said Gran.

The boys' clothes, too, were much too big. They, however, thought they looked wonderful, and admired themselves in the full-length mirror hanging inside the closet door.

As far as the dress was concerned, the size was irrelevant since Clara refused to try it on, and ran off screaming, "NO! NEVER! I HATE DRESSES! I HATE BEING A GIRL!"

Miles and Thos went running after her. "C!" called Miles, "It's okay! You don't have to wear the stupid dress!"

Gran and Stuart looked at each other. Then Gran quietly folded the dress and slipped it into the Strawbridge and Clothier bag. She'd always prided herself on knowing when she'd lost, but this—she hadn't even realized there was a contest. At any rate, she comforted herself, I didn't cut the tags off. And I do have the receipt.

Things settled down quickly, and while Gran showed the children around the house, Stuart drove to Strawbridge's and exchanged Clara's dress for pants and a shirt like the boys'. Gran wanted to have him return theirs for smaller ones, but they refused to take them off. He took with him tracings of the children's feet so he could exchange the sneakers for the proper sizes.

The house fascinated the children. "It's so big," they said over and over, but Gran, knowing the house was actually quite small, probably smaller than the one they lived in, did not mention their situation in Hardwick. They ran their fingers over the smooth, gleaming surfaces of the furniture, dragged their bare feet on the waxed wood floors, and jumped from one area rug to another. Later, the children admitted to each other that they were confused. This house looked like the houses they saw on television, but Gran didn't even own a set, so how did she know? And their father, who knew very well what TV houses looked like, lived in a place that looked nothing at all like them. They couldn't figure it out. What were houses supposed to look like, anyway?

Best of all was the baby grand piano. They loved it when Gran told them that their mother had sat on this very bench and touched these very keys, and they sat together and pounded away.

They asked countless questions about her—What did she like to eat? What was her favorite color? Did she have a bike?—but they never said "Mama." None of them, not Miles, not Thos, not Clara, could say the word aloud.

"What are these?" asked Clara, pointing to a collection of greeting cards neatly arranged on the piano.

"Well, dear, when there is a special occasion, like a birthday, or an anniversary, or a holiday, people send you cards like these. I like to decorate with the ones I've received over the years. In the winter I put out all my Christmas cards. In the spring I put out my Mother's Day and Easter cards. In the summer there are the birthday cards, because my birthday is in August. Now, you see the Thanksgiving cards and Halloween cards that your mother and Uncle Stuart and friends of mine sent me a long time ago. I've never thrown any of them away."

She picked up one and read it to the children. It was signed "Francie," which had been crossed out and "Frances" written in its place. "Everybody called your mother 'Francie' except me. I called her 'Frances.'"

"And our father. He called her 'Frances,'" said Miles suddenly, a memory surfacing.

"Yes, your father. He called her 'Frances,' too."

The children had many more questions as they sat with Gran and Stuart in Frances's room, poring over the photograph albums Gran had taken out to show them.

"Was she my age in this picture?"

"How come she's wearing that fancy dress?"

"Who are all these other people?"

"Is Uncle Stuart older or younger than our mother?"

"Look! Look! She's playing the piano that's downstairs!"

Stuart kept a close eye on Gran for signs that she might break down, but she kept up the same strong front he'd admired earlier in the day, and it wasn't until he heard her muffled sobbing in bed that night that he understood how painful this was for her.

Stuart and Gran had planned to take the children to the park on the day they arrived, but they were so enthralled with their clothes, their shoes, the house, that it was decided they'd all stay in. The kitchen became the center of activity, and they helped Gran make soup and roast chicken, bake rolls and cookies and a pumpkin pie. Stuart showed them how to set the table, but when dinnertime came the children used their fingers to eat. Stuart, remembering the lectures on table manners that Gran had given him, was impressed that she didn't say a word, but he knew she was biding her time and would teach them a thing or two when the moment was right.

After dinner Gran went to put on a sweater, saying there was a chill in the air.

"Let's put on our jackets," said Clara to her brothers. "Gran's cold."

Then they filed into the living room and Stuart said, "Why don't you give a show for Gran and me? I'll bet you guys know all kinds of tricks!"

They didn't have to be asked twice. While Stuart and Gran watched from the couch, Miles did somersaults, laughing and tangling himself in the too-big jacket, and Thos rolled over and over on the floor, and Clara danced around, crowing delightedly. "It's like a three-ring circus!" chuckled Gran, and indeed they performed all at once, with no notion of the concept of taking turns.

In the car on the way back the following day, the children chattered about the house.

"It's gigantic!" marveled Miles. "No piles or anything!"

"Everything smells yummy-yum-yum," said Clara, licking her lips at the memory of good things cooking in the oven.

"Our beds were so comfy I didn't want to go to sleep," added Thos.

Stuart came so close to saying something he would regret that he took one hand off the wheel and held his lips together with his fingers.

When they were a short distance from the house, Miles started to undress.

"You'd better keep these for us, Uncle Stuart."

Thos and Clara, too, took off their clothes, and, like Miles, folded them clumsily and left them on the seat of the car when they got home. Davis, who was waiting at the door, turned away as soon as he saw the children.

"It's the haircuts," whispered Thos. "He's angry about the haircuts."

Hoping to appease their father, they ran to put on the paper painter's caps that Hank had given them, but it was no use, and two days passed before he spoke to them again.

It was the last time the three children went together to Philadelphia. When Stuart would arrive in Hardwick, Davis would announce that one was going, or another, or maybe two, but never all three at the same time. Once, he refused to let any of them go, so Stuart visited with them in Hardwick and went home to tell Gran, who cried all weekend.

On their trips to Philadelphia, they were greeted by the smells of turkey roasting and bread and cookies baking. Piles of storybooks from the library sat on the kitchen counter, ready for Gran to read while they nestled together on the deep, soft living room sofa, and she licked her plump finger genteelly to better turn the pages.

There was always a treat planned to follow the ritual soaking in the tub. Gran searched *The Philadelphia Inquirer* for special events that would be going on when the children came, and they went to libraries and museums, plays and magic shows.

Gran never gave them haircuts again, but shampooed and combed their hair as best she could, and then, very carefully, she cut the mats out, smiling and putting her finger to her lips when she brought over the scissors, and they smiled back, her co-conspirators.

It was, of course, most difficult for the child who stayed behind.

"He gets up in the morning and I watch him start the fire in the woodstove," Miles reported to Gran and Stuart. "Then he sits there and stares at the stove, smoking his pipe. He doesn't talk, and I never know what to say. It feels so weird. Then he kind of watches me play. When he looks at his sports stuff on TV, I go over and sit with him, but I don't understand it at all. Not one bit."

Between visits Gran took great pleasure in buying clothes and making parcels to send off to Hardwick, but when Stuart went to fetch the children one rainy Saturday he saw the clothes lying on the ground, muddy and soaked, and he had to tell her not to bother sending them anymore.

CHAPTER SIXTEEN

S pec was having a recurring dream. Three nights in a row he'd dreamed that his father was standing in front of a pet store, looking through the window at a tan Cocker Spaniel puppy. The dog was jumping delightedly against the glass and seemed to be barking, but Spec couldn't hear the bark in his dream. After a minute, Davis turned and walked on.

"What do you think it means?" asked Trudy, when Spec told her about it.

"If I knew, I'd tell you, Trudy," he said exasperatedly.

"Well, let's think. You're dreaming about your father—and a dog. Why a dog?"

She saw the irritation on Spec's face and decided this was not the time for Dreams 101. She continued.

"This dog is trying to get your father's attention, trying to please him, wouldn't you say? Sort of 'Buy me! Buy me! Buy me! Love me! Get me out of here and take me home with you!'"

"Yeah," said Spec slowly. "I think I see what you're getting at."

"Good. Tell me."

"I'm the dog, and I'm trying to get my father to notice me? But he isn't listening?"

Trudy smiled. "This isn't a quiz, Spec. There's no right or wrong answer. If it sounds right to you, then it is."

He grinned. "I sure wish my courses in school had been like that." The grin disappeared. "So what do I do? Frankly I'm getting pretty sick of dream re-runs."

"Maybe we should go see your father."

"What good would that do?"

"Well, it might stop the dreams."

"You mean it would prove once and for all that there's no pleasing the old man, and I should give it a rest?"

"Something like that. And you could introduce me. That might be interesting. If nothing else, we'll have a nice ride in this gorgeous summer weather."

<hr>

The day was indeed beautiful, but Spec wasn't thinking about the weather. His mind was on the house in Hardwick and his attempts to prepare Trudy for it, although there was really no way to do that.

"You won't believe it, Trudy, really, you won't. Seven years later and I can still picture it. So much crap everywhere you can hardly walk around," said Spec, as they drove south on the Interstate.

This was not the first time he'd tried to describe it, but he wanted it to be fresh in her mind. She'd embarrass herself, and him, if she looked shocked when she saw the place.

Trudy patted his arm.

"It's okay, don't worry. I'm a big girl, Spec. I can handle it."

"No, you don't understand," he said, raising his voice. "It's not like anything you've ever seen. Me neither, for that matter. The guy is crazy!"

"So? Fathers can be crazy. It's no reflection on you."

"I hate this, Trudy, I really do. I just hate it."

"Then why are we going? Let's turn around and go home. Whatever you want. Your call."

Spec pulled the pickup onto the shoulder and turned off the motor. He put his forehead on the steering wheel.

"Jesus Christ, I don't know what to do."

"All right. Talk to me. Tell me what's going on in that pretty little head of yours."

Spec gave a loud, exaggerated groan and paused for a long moment.

"I guess I liked what you said—you know, that you could meet the old man," he finally blurted out. "Or maybe I thought I'd like to show you off, have him see that I did pretty well, catching you."

Trudy rubbed the back of his neck. He sat up and she laid her head on his shoulder.

"Gee, thanks for the compliment," she said playfully.

"And the kids. I want to see them."

Trudy picked up her head and looked at Spec. He stared straight ahead.

"I have a hard time with kids, Spec. You know that. I think we should stop producing them and let the world age and die a natural death."

"An interesting if unrealistic idea. Anyway, these kids are here already, so even if everyone on the planet said, 'All hail, Trudy Payton!

Nevermore will a child be born on this earth!'—well, these particular kids would still be here. And frankly, I'd like to see them."

Spec ran his fingertips over her silver necklace.

Trudy took his face in her hands and kissed his forehead.

"What are we waiting for?" she asked. "We have a long drive ahead of us. Let's get going."

All these years later, Spec remembered how to get to the house. He half-expected to see the dog with three legs, the welcoming committee. This time he didn't miss the driveway, even though it was barely visible through the thicket.

He knocked on the door, waited several minutes, and knocked again. There was no sound from inside the house.

"Down by the river, I guess," said Spec as he opened the door, relieved he could show Trudy around without his father there to watch them. She didn't say anything, but stayed close behind Spec, pulling her thin gray cardigan tight around herself.

"Much worse than it was the last time. One of the circles of Hell, that's for sure," he said.

The filth, the vile smell reminded him of stories in the tabloids. The first stop along the pathway was the bathroom, and Spec pushed open the warped, creaking door so they could go in. He tried unsuccessfully to flush the toilet.

"Apparently they use this whole room as a hamper," said Trudy, her words muffled by the hand she held over her nose and mouth. She was trying to ward off the terrible stink that, she was afraid, would make her vomit, right here, in this hellhole. She kept herself at a distance from the pile of laundry that spilled down from its impressive height in one corner. She walked on tiptoes in order to minimize physical contact with the house.

The stench in the kitchen, too, was overpowering. Curious, Spec opened the refrigerator door.

"This thing isn't even cold. No wonder everything's spoiled. Hasn't been cleaned in a damn long time, either." Trudy walked over to peer warily inside, at the opened, crusty cans, the rotting food soft and dark, the shelves and walls spattered with blackened stains. A feeling of great sadness swept over her. She thought of her mother, whose greatest pride was her kitchen, particularly the refrigerator, and who was fond of saying you could tell everything about the way a family lived by looking in their refrigerator. Indeed, she had something of a reputation for peeking into her friends' refrigerators when she thought no one was watching. Her mother would pass out if she saw this one, thought Trudy.

Grease coated the kitchen's marble counters. In the sink, dishes lay in a shallow bath of murky water. The cabinet doors were rough and discolored, and the curtains were gray and sticky. Wondering if cooking was a possibility, Spec turned on the stove. He discovered that one of the four burners still worked, but barely.

As they continued along the pathway, they were greeted by a new and putrid odor, and nearly tripped over an aquarium that sat on the floor. Decaying fish floated on opaque water. No ordinary burial for these fish, thought Spec, since they couldn't be flushed down the toilet.

On the way upstairs, Trudy noted the Oriental rugs hanging from the balcony, then turned to look at the chaos below. When they reached the bedrooms, they saw there were no sheets on the beds, no pillowcases on the pillows, just a tangle of blankets that smelled strongly of mildew.

"These kids aren't babies, are they?" asked Trudy suddenly.

"No, the youngest is, uh, seven years old. How come?"

Spec's gaze followed her pointing finger to a pile of old, soiled diapers stiff with age, a macabre sculpture.

"Christ almighty," said Spec, "this goes back so far you can't even see where the rot begins. And it certainly doesn't end."

Hearing voices in the distance, they went downstairs and made their way to the front door. The children, just coming into the house, hung back at the sight of visitors, but Davis pushed past them and approached the pair.

Spec inhaled deeply.

"Hello, sir," he said. "I'd like you to meet my wife, Trudy."

Davis turned to Trudy, looked her up and down for so long that she began to blush, and then greeted her by saying, "Are you afraid of snakes?"

"No, not exactly," she replied uncomfortably.

"That's good, because we have a whole hell of a lot of them here!" Davis laughed at his joke.

By now the children, curious, had gathered around. Spec, realizing that Davis was not about to bail anybody out with introductions, turned and faced them.

"You were too little to remember when we met the last time, but I'm your brother and this is my wife." For a moment, he couldn't think what should come next.

While they looked on in confusion, Spec said to his father, "Where's Frances?"

The children froze, their eyes on Davis. He had not mentioned her since the early morning that seemed at once yesterday and long ago.

"Dead," was all he said.

The children glanced at each other and looked away. It was the end of their pretending. Even when they rode their bikes to her grave, and found the site by pacing it off from the tree, they told themselves she would come back to them one day.

"Well, as long as you're here, you might as well come in," Davis was saying. Spec noted that, though his words expressed a certain amount of reluctance, his father spoke with surprising enthusiasm.

Behind his back Trudy looked imploringly at Spec, but he avoided her eyes and followed his father to the chairs by the woodstove, and she came after, with the children trooping behind. Davis himself cleared off the chair opposite his and made a gallant, sweeping gesture that was almost a bow.

"Won't you sit down, Trudy?"

Seeing that she had no choice, Trudy sat, glad she was wearing pants and boots, and tucked her feet under her. She gathered her long hair, pulled it over one shoulder, and began to stroke it nervously. Spec glanced around and, finding nothing to sit on, stood stiffly beside Trudy, as if posing for a formal photograph. Davis leaned forward and turned on the television set, adjusting the sound so it was too low to listen to but sufficiently loud to be distracting, then sat in his chair. The children sat down on the floor in a single, seemingly choreographed motion. Davis made idle conversation with Spec and Trudy about where they were living and what they were doing. He glanced frequently at the television.

All at once Trudy jumped up, pointing to a bag that sat on top of the television set.

"What's that?" she shrieked.

The bag had started to move. Davis chortled.

"You women are all alike," he said with more than a hint of nastiness. "No sense of humor at all."

"They're snakes!" said Clara. "When the TV gets warm, they wake up. He puts them there 'cause he likes to scare—"

She caught Davis's look and stopped.

"You three run and play. We grownups want to talk," said Davis.

The children disappeared outside. Spec could hardly wait until they left.

"Frances *died*? How?"

"Oh, she had a little accident. With a gun. Not a good mix, guns and people. Not when they don't know what they're doing."

"What happened?"

"I'm not quite sure, to be honest. She said she wanted to kill herself, but she used a gun that can't really do that. It's made for shooting targets, not game, let alone people. It killed her, though. If that's what she wanted, that's what she got. Left me with quite a full plate, as you can see."

Spec was enraged by the unfairness of Davis's suggestion that all of this was somehow Frances's fault. His anger emboldened him.

"Why didn't you give her a hand with the kids and the housework?" His voice was shaking.

"Was I trained as a scientist or a servant?" replied Davis evenly, in the irritating manner he had of answering one question with another.

"She was drowning! How could you let her drown?" He was inexplicably desperate to defend a woman he had met once, and briefly at that.

"What, precisely, would you have expected me to do?" Again, quiet and controlled.

Spec was unable to let go yet unable to argue effectively. When he and Trudy got into the pickup to leave a short while later, he was soaked with sweat, and he saw, to his embarrassment, that he had wet himself.

Trudy drove home. Neither she nor Spec said anything for the first half hour of the trip, and then, in order to fill the void, she turned on the radio. Spec immediately reached over and turned it off.

They continued without speaking for another hour. Then Trudy cleared her throat.

"My mother used to take me to antique stores to look at rugs like the ones hanging over that railing," she said, as if Spec had just asked how she and her mother passed the time.

"She'd pretend she had the money to buy them, got us both all dressed up to go shopping, and then, when the salesman had taken a long time explaining each rug's history, she'd step back, put her hand to her chin, shake her head very slowly, and say no, the color's wrong, or no, she guessed she didn't really want a Tabriz."

Trudy glanced at Spec, but he was quiet and didn't look at her. She opened her palms against the steering wheel and stretched her hands. They drove in silence all the way back to Kings Island.

CHAPTER SEVENTEEN

"Is it all right if we go to the market?" asked Miles after Spec and Trudy left, knowing the answer would be yes, which it was, and so they rode their bikes to see Eldon. They had to talk to him.

Eldon knew better than to suggest they ask Davis about Spec and his relationship to them. He walked around to the front of the counter, crouched down, and pulled the children to him.

"Well now, a mighty long time ago your dad had a different wife, some other woman, not your mama. And they had a little boy, and that little boy grew up to be the man you met today. So that makes him kind of your brother, at least halfway, being that you got the same dad. The same dad, but different mamas." He paused. "Understand now?"

They nodded slowly, seriously, still digesting the information as they walked out of the store. They didn't hear Eldon call after them his offer of ice cream sandwiches.

"Why didn't he tell us we had a brother?" asked Thos on the way home.

"What would he say? 'Oh, by the way, I forgot to tell you. You're not the first family I ever had, you know,'" said Miles.

"He could've," said Clara softly, "but he didn't."

The children put away thoughts of Spec. Such thoughts were too intrusive for these summer days, when they stayed in the river much of the time. They jumped off the dock, they had swimming races, and they had contests to see who could dive deepest and who could stay under longest. They sat on the edge of the dock and watched themselves in the tea-colored waters of the river that formed a funhouse mirror. It reflected and distorted their images, while it hid whatever lay beneath its surface. They sat on each other's laps and looked in the water, laughing at the way their naked bodies seemed to form one person.

They played Society and flew the box kites Hank made for them. They climbed up on the kitchen counter, pushed the dishes aside, and jumped out the window, then ran back inside to jump again. When they were hungry, they stuck a finger in the jar of peanut butter and sucked off the salty goodness without a break in their game.

Often they rode their bikes to Gravity Hill, the bump in Hardwick's otherwise flat landscape. Eldon had introduced it to them. He'd also introduced the idea of optical illusions. Get in the car, he ordered one afternoon, and they drove out of town and down a long dirt road to what appeared to be the bottom of a gentle hill. Now watch this, he said, bringing the car to a stop. He shifted into neutral and indicated that his foot was on neither the brake nor the accelerator. Slowly, magically, the car was drawn forward, up the hill to the top, where it coasted to a stop, as if an invisible foot had applied the brakes. The children found they could do the same on their bikes, first settling themselves at the bottom, and then, legs out to the sides for balance, they rolled up, up, up Gravity Hill.

When Eldon came by with groceries one day, he brought along a plastic ball and bat, and the children convinced Davis to pitch for them.

"That was fun!" Clara said later to her brothers, and Miles agreed.

But Thos said, "You think it's fun 'cause both of you can hit the ball really hard. I can't do that, and he thinks it's funny when I'm up at bat. He lobs two at me and I miss them, and when I think okay, now I'm ready, he throws it really fast and strikes me out."

They were afraid he would start to cry. That was the worst. When he cried.

Clara got the idea from another television show, one in which the children gave their father a surprise party for his birthday.

"But we don't know when his birthday is," protested Thos.

"So, we'll make up a birthday," said Miles, warming to the idea.

When Eldon heard the plan he volunteered to have Lucille bake a cake, and Hank said he'd bring along Dixie cups "and those little wooden spoons where you can eat from both ends."

Sally Bea had to stay and "mind the store," she said, but she contributed wrapping paper and hats and noisemakers, and on the appointed day, a typical fall day, damp and chilly, they set up the party while Davis was busy with his target practice. They would have to celebrate outdoors, no matter the weather.

Hank and Eldon arrived. While they waited for their father, the children played a game of Giant Steps. Miles was "It" and permitted

Thos and Clara to take giant steps, or baby steps, or twirling umbrella steps toward the goal, as long as they remembered to say "May I?" Then they made up steps—slithering "snake" and arm-flailing "swimming."

"Hank, what do you do every day? Do you have a job, like Eldon does?" asked Thos, when they'd tired of their game.

Eldon chuckled and looked at Hank.

"I've got lots of jobs, all kind of jobs," he replied. "Anybody needs something fixed, they tell old Hank, and he takes care of whatever it is that needs fixing. Say, maybe you three would come help me sometime. What do you say?"

Before they had a chance to answer, Davis rounded the corner of the house, they all shouted "Surprise!" and it took him a minute to realize this was a birthday party, and it was for him. He looked around with pleasure at the brightly wrapped presents, at the ice cream and cake, at the smiling faces of Eldon, Hank and the children. They couldn't know this was the first birthday party he'd ever had in his life.

Ice cream and cake were served first, followed by "Happy Birthday," to which the children scarcely knew the words; a confusing chorus of "Happy Birthday, dear Doc-Doctor-sir" overlapped and blended near the end of the song. The last line was interrupted by Hank's terrible coughing, one of his spells during which he couldn't catch his breath. He turned crimson and coughed so hard that no sound came out, and the children thought his lungs would come exploding out of his mouth.

"I've told you many times, Hank, those cigarettes will kill you." Davis's words were stern but his voice was gentle.

Hank, who tried to talk but couldn't, managed a smile. Still coughing, he wiped the tears that streamed from his eyes.

Davis found himself looking forward to opening the presents. He'd heard about stacks like this, but long ago he had given up hoping there would ever be such a pile for him. Well, well, well, you never know, he said to himself, pleased, as he reached for the first present. But when he opened it, he saw that the children had wrapped one of his pipes. The second present was his latest medical journal. He couldn't hide his disappointment, and he laid it down, half opened, and went inside to watch television, leaving the rest of the packages untouched.

The children did indeed take Hank up on his offer and tagged along as he made his repairs. All that fall the three watched him re-hang doors, replace rotted steps and railings, fix roofs and floorboards and windows and chair backs. He painstakingly explained what he was doing and let them help as much as he could. They saw him use a hammer and chisel to loosen stones so he could repair a wall. He was a plumber and an electrician as well, and they thought he could do anything.

What convinced them of this was his skill with cigarettes. When Hank came by for them in his pickup, he was already smoking. He continued to smoke throughout the day, taking each cigarette out of his mouth only when it had burned all the way down. Then, in a series of carefully orchestrated maneuvers, he removed it with one last inhale and lit the new cigarette with the barely-smoldering butt, which he then flicked away. At first the children couldn't stop looking at the cigarette that spent all but the last moments of its life in Hank's mouth, as the ash grew longer and longer until it fell off. Except for the way Hank squinted against the smoke, it was, they thought, as if he had forgotten that the cigarette was even there.

When the harsh winter descended, the children were forced to give up for the time being their frequent trips with Hank, and they stayed indoors a good deal of the time. Although by most standards the house was cold, it seemed to Davis and the children to be a warm, cozy haven compared to the bitter winds and the snow. He, however, was never without a fleece-lined hunting jacket over his flannel shirt. Only occasionally did the children pay homage to the weather by finding something to wear in the laundry pile, which had continued to grow. Periodically, Davis arranged for Sally Bea to order new things for the children from the Sears catalogue, but he never disposed of the outgrown clothing that had by now gone through all three of them.

Most often they played the indoor games they had invented, another whole set of games, and Davis was impressed by their ingenuity and by their seemingly inexhaustible supply of ideas, which he remarked on in his notebook. Since the children were born he had filled exactly one each year. When they were published, as he had no doubt they would be, he'd be known as the new, improved Dr. Spock. The famous pediatrician had believed in a permissive approach to child rearing, but he, Davis, was taking that to a new level.

He often thought how unfortunate it was that he hadn't collected data on his oldest son's development. The split-generation aspect would have provided added appeal to a publisher. And now that Leslie was married to that woman with the snake phobia, well, he would have had a lot more material. He wondered what their marriage was like, how the sex was. He had a lot of questions, and Leslie would be able to answer them, but of course he wouldn't. Not now. The boy had run like a scared rabbit and would clearly not be coming back. No backbone at all.

Early one icy morning, as the children were climbing a particularly stable part of the furniture pile and trying not to trip on the Phillies T-shirts from Uncle Stuart, there was a knock at the door. Davis, used to this sort of interruption, opened it to find an elderly man accompanied by a young girl, who wore a bored expression.

"Doc Davis?" he said, before Davis had the door fully opened. "Hate to bother you, but see, I got a stomach ache I need to talk to you about." The words tumbled out in a rush. "Sorry about bringing Winnie here, but her mama's run off, so now it's me and Clarice taking care of her, and seems I'm on duty today. Couldn't leave her alone. You can't leave a seven-year-old alone, am I right?"

He laughed nervously, as if aware that he was having difficulty ending his own monologue.

"That's perfectly all right. Please come in," said Davis, ever the professional.

Miles and Thos, who had disappeared into the kitchen and were eating cereal by the handful, came out and peered down the pathway long enough to determine that this did not interest them, and returned to the kitchen. Clara, perched with one leg on the edge of the staircase and the other on the pile, called out, "Hey, Winnie! I'm seven, too! Come on up and play! Follow the pathway around to the stairs. I'll meet you there!"

Hearing her name, Winnie turned toward the sound of Clara's voice until she saw the girl, who looked to her like a Christmas tree ornament that had been lowered from the ceiling.

"How did you get up there?" asked Winnie.

"Come on and I'll show you! You can do it too!"

Winnie edged closer to her grandfather and twirled her finger around the ponytail that she wore on the side of her head. She looked down at her feet, at the pennies in her loafers, and then, apparently having made a decision, she glanced at her grandfather for a nod and started off in Clara's direction.

"Keep on going. Okay, right, you're almost here," said Clara, whose vantage point allowed her to monitor Winnie's cautious progress. They met halfway up the stairs.

The girls eyed each other awkwardly. Davis, watching them, realized how very much smaller Clara was than Winnie, even smaller for her age than he had thought, and he made a mental note of the fact. She looked, it seemed to him, like some grimy, life-size doll.

At first the girls were silent, each taking the measure of the other. Winnie saw a tiny girl whose eyes were bright and whose hair and skin were dirtier than anything she'd ever seen. The streaks that ran down her legs and along her feet made Winnie think of the lines that appeared on her grandfather's truck after a rain. Clara wore a T-shirt that was much too big, making the short sleeves appear long. Her thin arms looked dusty, and black lines, visible underneath the long nails, bordered her fingertips. Except for its fairness, Clara's hair reminded Winnie of the wig she had worn on Halloween, which had come from the store so tangled and matted that she couldn't comb it, and then her grandmother had told her that was the way it was supposed to be, you weren't meant to comb it. But Winnie couldn't get over how pretty Clara was. Her grandmother was always saying dress nice, now, so you'll look real pretty, and here was Clara, not dressed nice at all, but prettier than anybody she'd ever met.

Clara thought Winnie looked exactly like the kids they saw on TV, and was pretty sure that underneath the duffle coat and scarf there would be a plaid skirt and a sweater with a collar peeping out. As she looked at Winnie's perfect ponytail with the big curl at the bottom, she touched her own hair, but she quickly took her hand away and said,

"What do you want to play?"

"What games do you have?" asked Winnie.

"Well, we could make faces in the mirror. Or we could play the climbing game. That's where you climb up the side of the stairs and then down that pile of furniture. Like I was doing when you came in."

Winnie shook her head. "Not that kind of game. I mean, you know, Mr. Potato Head? Parcheesi?"

Clara raised her eyebrows and shrugged.

"I have an idea," she said. "Let's go up."

As they ran up the stairs, Winnie observed, "We're both staying with our grandfathers!"

"That's not my grandfather," said Clara, stopping and turning to look at Winnie, who had stopped on the stair below. "That's my father. And I'm not 'staying' here, I live here."

"You *live* here? You mean this is your house? Wow!" She gave a low whistle that was more air than sound.

When they had reached the children's bedroom, with the two foam mattresses pushed together on the floor and the blankets mounded on top of them, Winnie was dumbfounded.

"This is your bed? This is where you sleep? Here? On this?"

"Me and my brothers. I have two brothers," answered Clara. "Well, I really have three brothers, but only two of them are kids. We sleep here unless we don't want to. We can sleep anywhere we want.

Sometimes I sleep by the woodstove in our father's chair. Unless he's sleeping there. He does that a lot. Then maybe I sleep in his bed. Or if he sleeps in his bed, sometimes I sleep on the floor next to him. Different stuff. That couch downstairs is pretty good. There's a littler couch down there too, it has flowers all over it, but there's so much junk on it and I hate to have to move it off. I sleep in lots of places. Miles too. Thos—Miles and Thos are my brothers—Thos sleeps in here, especially in the winter. He likes to be bundled up at night, he says, and you can't really get bundled up when you sleep in a chair. Me and Miles, we don't need any covers. We don't get cold at night like Thos does. He—our father—says the only cold we feel is sangfroid." She laughed. "We used to have two dogs, Peanut Butter and Nighttime, but they got really old and they died. Two days apart. He says that happens a lot in nature, 'cause creatures get used to living together and they want to stay together for always. He says you can learn a lot from nature."

This reminded Clara of something, and she screwed up her face trying to remember what it was.

"Oh, and he used to have a hawk that was like a gun! You were watching killing in slow motion, he told us!"

Clara had been rummaging in the dresser while she talked, and now she brought out the colored pens and pad of paper Gran had sent her. "She shows talent," Gran had told Stuart. "Talent like that needs to be cultivated."

"That's it?" Winnie was incredulous. "Paper and pens? That's how you play? No Barbie? No Ken? No car and stuff for them? No clothes?"

Clara was shaking her head.

"No, just this," she said.

"Oh, well, guess it's only for a little while," muttered Winnie, sitting down and dumping the pens onto the floor.

Soon, however, she crowed, "I love your house! You can throw garbage anywhere!" and she crumpled her paper and gleefully threw it across the floor.

"You can not!" retorted Clara, standing up and putting her hands on her hips. She walked over and picked it up from where it lay next to the remains of a piece of bread covered with mold. She crushed the paper in her hands and formed it into a ball, then played with it as she looked around. Abruptly she stuck it under the pile of bedding and sat down again to work on her drawing.

"Let's take these down to be judged," said Winnie after a while, looking from her clown to Clara's unicorn and back to her clown. "Maybe they'll give the winner a dollar!"

Winnie's grandfather wondered how they would get out of this one gracefully. Goodness sakes, he thought, Clara's could be in a storybook! But he was spared the decision.

"Now, Clara," said Davis, "you know perfectly well there's no such thing as a unicorn. And Winnie has drawn—what is this, Winnie?"

"A clown! See? This is his big nose?"

"Yes, of course, I see that now. Well! Winnie has drawn a real clown, so that makes her the winner. Here's your dollar, Winnie."

Clara had already gone upstairs and closed the door.

Miles, meanwhile, had been watching Winnie, and decided this might be more interesting than it had first appeared.

"Congratulations, Winnie!" he bellowed extravagantly, walking over to her.

Davis interrupted this display of incipient manhood, as he later referred to it in his notebook entry, by grabbing Miles's arm and saying, "They're on their way out."

Miles tried to step forward, but Davis restrained him. Then as soon as the door had closed behind Winnie and her grandfather, he released his grip, leaving finger marks on the boy's forearm.

He turned to Miles.

"*Winnie?*" he said, with disbelief. "You're interested in *Winnie?* Come, now. I'm sure you can do better than that."

CHAPTER EIGHTEEN

Spring came, and with it the news that Johnny Johnson was leaving. He hated to go, he told Davis, but the garage business was down and he couldn't hang on any longer. He'd been lucky enough, he explained, to find a good job with a place in Florida, a nice guy who'd even advanced him a couple of months' pay. Davis knew he would miss their talks, as well as this particular excuse to spend time at the office. But Johnny Johnson's wife was expecting again, and Davis knew this was their sixth in as many years and said no more.

He came to say good-bye one morning when Davis was outside talking with Hank about Charlotte the pig, back from her "winter vacation at Johnny Johnson's," as Davis put it.

The children went off to feed Charlotte, and a moment later the men were interrupted by the sound of screaming. The sow had ripped through her wire pen in order to get to the food the children had spilled on the way to feed her. No one had realized that, over the winter, their pig had grown too strong for the enclosure.

At this moment Thos was hanging onto the bucket of slop, trying to outrun Charlotte, trying to figure out where to go, too frightened to toss aside the pail, the contents of which sloshed as he ran and held him back. Miles and Clara were shouting at him to throw down the slop, but he didn't hear them. The pig charging after him had grown mean and surly, not like a pet, he was thinking, not like Charlotte, and it seemed to him they'd made a terrible mistake to give a name, any name, to an animal like this. Then his thoughts became tangled and he didn't know what he was running from, knew only that he had to escape, had to move faster than he was doing right now, because this was his nightmare come true and whatever it was that was chasing him was gaining on him and was going to get him. It was hard running through the high weeds in the field, and his foot caught and he tripped and nearly fell before catching his balance again, and he figured he would surely be attacked now, but no, he continued to run and scarcely felt the thin, thorny branches tear at his bare skin, and then he was out on the road again where the going was easier, and still he ran and still he gripped the handle of the bucket.

By this time Johnny Johnson had circled around and was preparing to tackle Charlotte, divert her, give Thos a chance to get away, when all of a sudden a gunshot ripped the air and reminded the children of a day long ago.

"Here's a going-away present for you, Johnny Johnson. All the bacon you can eat for the rest of your natural life," said Davis, the faintest quaver in his voice. He walked quickly back to the house, cradling his shotgun.

The three children and Johnny Johnson gathered around Charlotte's body, and Hank, wheezing, joined them. They stood without speaking for a long time, with only the sound of Hank's difficult breathing to break the silence.

"You guys make real sure you take good care of your dad," said Johnny Johnson in a husky voice. "He's one in a million."

He patted each child on the head before going to see about hauling away the pig.

Hank and the children stared at the bleeding mound of flesh lying in the road. Thos was shaking. Miles and Clara knew the tears would come later, and Thos would have to be led away from the house so Davis couldn't hear his crying.

Hank came by the following day and found the children sitting on the front steps. He cocked his head to one side.

"Hey! Why the long faces?"

"We were just talking about Charlotte," said Clara.

"Thos is still kind of upset," added Miles.

Thos nodded.

"Can't have that!" exclaimed Hank. "Hmm," he said, drawing it out. "How about we tell one of our stories?"

The children were all for it. They jumped up and grabbed for his hands.

"Sorry, but I've only got two hands for three kids," said Hank, laughing. "Let's see about that."

Miles was already holding his right hand. He spread wide the fingers of his left so that Thos and Clara could both hold on, and the four of them walked over and sat down by their story-telling tree. Hank settled himself against it.

The children viewed Hank, who had spent his entire life in the Pine Barrens, who had never set foot outside New Jersey, as an authority on the Jersey Devil, that legendary creature who roams the Pines and terrorizes local communities.

"Dead of night, it was, over by Lumberton," began Hank. "Not too far from here, you know."

He looked from Miles to Thos to Clara. They huddled up to him as if a cold wind had started to blow through the spring afternoon.

"Man and his wife, they'd just about got themselves to sleep, when all of a sudden . . ." he looked menacingly at the children, "they heard a frightening, horrible sound, kind of a screech and a shriek and a scream and a howl, all mixed up together. 'Oh, my God in heaven!' the woman said." Hank spoke in as high a pitch as he could manage. "'What in the world can that be?'"

He looked at the children, who shouted on cue, "The Jersey Devil!"

He eyed them suspiciously and said, trying not entirely successfully to hide a smile, "Now wait a minute. Did you hear this before?"

"No! No! We promise! Go on, go on!"

"Wel-l-l-l," he said slowly. "Okay. So this woman tells her husband he better go look out the window and see what can he see. Well sir, he goes over to the window, and there he sees something he never, ever forgets 'til the end of his days, which were more than likely shortened by the sight, but that's another story altogether. He only catches a glimpse, 'cause it's flying nearly out of sight by this time, but what he sees, what he thinks he sees, what he's pretty sure he sees, is, he sees this giant bird of prey, except it's not a bird, more like a kangaroo, except it's not a kangaroo, more like—well, yeah, a kangaroo with bat wings and kind of a serpent tail, and its head!

"Its head is sort of like a dog, except it has this big chicken beak for a mouth . . . but you don't want to hear about that."

"Oh, we do! Please!"

Hank needed no more urging. "Nothing on God's green earth could keep that beak from tearing limb from limb, and then some, anything it had a mind to. So the man sees this—this thing, at least he thinks he sees it anyways, and real quick he hides under the bed. His wife, she's got the covers up over top of her by this time, and the two of them make quite a sight, I can tell you that."

The children laughed, but nervously.

"'What's going on?'" Hank had pitched his voice higher again. "The man starts telling her what he saw, what I've been describing here, and she starts laughing at him! 'Been drinking again, have you?' she says. Doesn't sound real nice, neither. Yelling is what she's doing. 'What did I tell you about drinking?' Nothing he can say will change her mind, no sir. Won't believe him, no way, no how, no matter what he tells her. 'Fine,' he says, and gets back in bed, kind of hoping she's right, 'cause after all, he did have himself a nip that evening.

"Next morning she takes one look at her husband and sees his hair's gone completely white. Overnight. Just like that. She doesn't say anything, goes on downstairs and outside to feed the chickens, like she does every morning, and back inside she comes, white as a sheet. Same color as her husband's hair, now that I think about it. 'What's the matter?' he says, 'cause he's coming down for breakfast. Didn't look in the mirror as yet, and he doesn't know about his hair. 'Chickens,' she says. 'Somebody killed the chickens last night.' But was it some*body*? Or was it some*thing*? Let me ask you that! They never did find out how those tracks got there. But I can tell you one thing. No pair of shoes anywhere leaves tracks like that."

"But we know what it was, don't we?" asked Thos.

"Could be," answered Hank. "Then again, we can never be sure, 'cause we didn't see it with our own eyes, now, did we?"

He covered his eyes with his hands, then opened his fingers and peeked through. When he took his hands away he was smiling broadly. The children smiled back.

Hank got up stiffly. "Have to be getting back now. Be seeing you real soon."

He walked down the road, facing forward but waving his hand behind him at the children, and he could hear them laughing as they imagined he was watching them with the eyes he swore he had in the back of his head.

No one knew that, from the years of Gran's reading to the children, from looking at the comics that came in Davis's newspaper, from seeing television advertisements, Miles had taught himself to read. Or that he had, in turn, taught Thos and Clara. Clara, in particular, was extremely proud of all of them.

"Well, it's about time we knew how to read," Miles grumbled one day. Davis was out in the woods with his pistol, and the children were able to talk freely.

"What do you mean?" Clara sounded worried.

"He means," Thos said, "that most kids learn how to read when they're much younger than we are."

"Well, how old *are* we, anyway?" she demanded. They had celebrated their birthdays only twice since Frances died, and she had lost track.

Miles was ready. "Okay. If this is 1978, and you were born—when were you born, C? Do you know?"

"1969. I always remember that."

"1969. That means you're nine. Then we go right in a row, so if you're nine, that means Thos is ten and I'm eleven. Nine, ten, eleven."

"And when can other kids read?"

Clara hated the idea that they were losing some sort of race.

"I don't know," said Miles.

"Neither do I," said Thos, "but sometimes little kids on TV can read. I figure if kids on TV shows can read, it must not be all that unusual."

"Well, so what? We can read, anyway," said Clara. "When should we tell him?"

They intended to tell their father soon, thinking it would be a fine surprise, but somehow they put it off, and then they decided it might not be such a good idea to tell him after all. Maybe he wouldn't like the fact that they had been able to do for themselves what he had been unable to do for them, and they figured it was safer not to risk it.

Whenever Davis was out in the woods, they combed the house for things they could read. There were mostly medical texts and journals, some of which they could make out but most of which were in technical language they did not understand. They tried to read the notebook in which he wrote about their development, but they couldn't decipher his handwriting.

One day, in their search for something to read, they came upon a folder containing a series of letters between Davis and the Hardwick Cemetery Association; included were copies of letters between Gran and Uncle Stuart and the Association. Thus did the children discover that, when it became clear that Davis would not be providing a tombstone for Frances, her family volunteered to pay to have one made. Having gotten Davis's permission, they sent a check to the Association to cover the cost of the tombstone, but after some months it was returned because Davis had changed his mind. Now, close to six years since Frances's death, Gran and Uncle Stuart were trying to bypass Davis, so far unsuccessfully. The last letter was very recent.

They made sure to put the folder back where they had found it.

"C and I were just with Gran and Uncle Stuart, and they didn't talk about this at all," said Thos.

"No," said Miles, frowning, "no, they wouldn't tell us." After a minute he said, "Let's go to our tree."

The children had discovered an abandoned estate just outside of Hardwick. Only the foundations of the immense house remained, and next to those they found their tree, a weeping beech tree, Hank told them. Its height was unimpressive, but it had spread out in such a way that it was considerably wider than it was high, a tree upon which a spell had been cast. To the children it appeared to be something out of the forest in *The Wizard of Oz*, a television favorite of theirs. Its branches had grown up, but then apparently changed their minds and began to grow down again, past the trunk that was off to one side, so that the drooping branches, thick with leaves, formed a tent. There were large, flat rocks underneath, and the children used them as tables, as chairs, as beds.

"Maybe we could make her a tombstone," said Thos, getting off his bike. "She should have one, shouldn't she?"

"Oh, yes," said Clara, nodding slowly, thoughtfully.

Indeed, on their visits to the cemetery, the children found it increasingly difficult to be certain they were pacing off correctly the distance from the oak tree to their mother's grave. Because they'd grown taller, they were afraid they were taking bigger steps.

Miles pointed to one of the smaller rocks. "This looks something like the other tombstones over at the cemetery."

They inspected it thoroughly. Low and box-shaped, it seemed to have broken off a nearby rock and therefore wasn't half-buried in the ground like the others, which meant that, when it was finished, Hank would be able to help them get it to the cemetery.

When their father arrived home, they were in the driveway, playing Society.

Later they would disagree on when the fire started, whether it was that night or the next. Miles, who had been sleeping on the couch, woke up and went outside to urinate. He could see flames through the trees.

When Davis and the children reached Hank's cabin, they could hear Hank calling as if from a great distance.

"I want you three to run for help. I'll take care of Hank," directed Davis. "And bring a blanket," he added, disappearing around the back of the cabin.

And so, once again the telephone at the Bartons' house was pressed into service. Tom Barton, still in his nightshirt, drove the children back to the cabin and told Davis, "Ambulance is on the way."

By the time they returned, the neat, spare, one-room cabin that had contained nothing but a bed, a chest of drawers, and a wooden chair, plus a woodstove and a kerosene lamp, had burned nearly to the ground. Davis had managed to pull Hank out through the door, which was next to his bed, and he lay on the ground, barely conscious. The upper part of his body was so badly burned that Davis asked the children if they were sure they wanted to see him.

It turned out that Thos and Clara couldn't look at Hank. Blackened pieces of skin drooped from his face, his eyes were barely visible, the hair had burned off his head, and already his skin was becoming hard, pale-colored leather.

"Why isn't he bleeding?" asked Miles through tears that, for once, Davis didn't question.

"Because the burns cauterized, sealed off, his blood vessels," explained Davis.

Miles went and sat next to Hank.

"What happened, Hank?" he whispered.

"He was smoking in bed," Davis answered for him. "He's too weak to talk right now."

Davis knew the man was in shock and wasn't sure he'd last until the ambulance arrived and he could be put on a breathing machine. It wouldn't be long before severe swelling would impede his circulation, and he'd lose his arms.

Hank spent eight months in the burn unit at Philadelphia Founders Hospital; Davis saw to it that Eldon called every day to check on his progress. Through Eldon, Davis knew that Hank had to undergo extensive skin grafting, as well as orthopedic surgery on the bones that had been exposed by the fire. The amputations Davis had feared had been avoided.

One day he announced to the children, "Hank is being released today. He will come to stay here with us."

"Maybe he'll look like he always did," said Clara when the children were alone.

"Yeah, maybe," said Miles doubtfully.

But he didn't, of course. They would never have recognized him. His eyes were tiny and lidless and without eyebrows; his lips were gone; his mouth was a hole in his face; and his head was completely hairless. The taut, shiny scar tissue that was his face never moved, which left Hank expressionless. Even the tattoos that had imitated the shape of a T-shirt had burned off, and in their place was a thickened, unnatural-looking skin.

Hank stayed upstairs on the foam mattresses. Davis tended to his bedpan and brought him the soft foods that Eldon had Lucille fix every day. It was difficult for him to eat, and the food fell from his mouth, but Davis stayed with him, feeding him patiently, because he could not use his hands. Miles alone among the children ventured up to see their friend, and found himself carrying on both sides of the conversation, repeating what he thought might be the words Hank was trying so hard to say.

He died a few weeks later.

"His life ended in the fire," Davis told the children. "We just helped him until he could catch up with himself."

That was all he had to say on the subject. There was no funeral. The children, having learned when Frances died that death is not an appropriate subject of discussion, did not remark upon it even among themselves. Nor did they talk about the desperate, terrifying sense that something had dropped away, something that had made them happy. But Hank, with his cigarettes and his tattoos, continued to visit them in their dreams.

While their father was occupied taking care of Hank, the children had had time to work on "the project," as they came to call it. It was arduous labor, and they took turns using the hammer and chisel they'd found among some tools that had been left at the office.

Carefully, painstakingly, they carved the name they'd seen in their father's folder of correspondence: FRANCES TAYLOR. Then, to be safe, they added DAVIS. They weren't sure if the date in the correspondence referred to the day she died or the day she was buried, and, having no idea when she was born, they voted not to put any dates at all and wrote simply "OUR MAMA."

When the stone was finished, they often went to look at it, not quite ready to face the problem of how to get it to the cemetery now that Hank couldn't help them. But they needn't have worried.

One bright afternoon Davis appeared under the weeping beech tree, where the children were gathered around the stone. They parted automatically, uncomprehendingly, making way for him, and watched while he picked up their stone with a force they didn't know he had, then wordlessly dropped it on the much larger rock that sat close by. A piece broke off the tombstone. He lifted it again and dropped it again, and again, and again, until he had shattered everything.

CHAPTER NINETEEN

Leslie Davis, M.D., was well aware that he had a heart condition. He couldn't make it up the stairs without stopping to catch his breath, and the pain was sometimes so fierce it filled his mind and wouldn't allow him to do anything but clench his fists and wait until it passed. He should be on medication, he knew, but what was the point? He didn't much care if this was it, his allotted life-span, sixty-five years, because the truth was, his life was coming apart. The deals he'd made, the Eden he'd created, the child-rearing experiment—everything was in jeopardy. And all on account of a snake bite.

On a rainy morning in late March, two men came to the door, one limping badly and leaning heavily against the other.

"I don't think we've met," said Davis genially, escorting them in.

"No, we're in town on a construction job. Billy here got bit by a snake. All the guys say you're the man to see."

Because they'd heard about the house as well as the doctor, the men did not appear to notice anything out of the ordinary as Davis led them to the couch outside the kitchen. The bite was swelling rapidly.

"Don't worry," said Davis reassuringly, as he proceeded with the washing and dressing.

Billy's friend stood at the end of the couch without speaking, shifting from one foot to the other, alternately watching Davis and glancing away.

"There are probably a dozen different kinds of snakes living around here, not a single one of them poisonous," Davis was saying. "Stay off your feet and make sure you keep that leg up to prevent more swelling." He demonstrated. "Sometime in the next day or so, take a ride over to the hospital in Shoreline. They'll give you a tetanus shot, to be on the safe side. They may prescribe antibiotics, too." Davis could hardly remember writing prescriptions at this point. "If they do, see that you take the pills until they're gone. Even if you're feeling fine, it's important that you finish the prescription."

The standard speech. And he sent them on their way.

The next day Billy was dead. Which is how Davis learned that there is one deadly snake, the timber rattlesnake, that inhabits the Pines. Unfortunately for Billy, this one was active earlier in the year than is common.

Word spread rapidly. Eldon, self-appointed defender, did his best to allay fears, said it could happen to anyone, and called it an honest mistake. But Davis told him a doctor doesn't make "honest mistakes." Davis, who hadn't considered himself a doctor in years, realized he had indeed been a doctor in Hardwick, and a good one. Until now. His ignorance had cost Billy his life, and he was no longer worthy of seeing patients.

In the weeks following, death was always on his mind. Before going to sleep, he often found himself thinking of his hawk, of the deaths it caused, and of the speed and efficiency with which it destroyed its victims. When he finally drifted off, it seemed as if he himself soared up and away. He knew with certainty that one night he would soar for the last time.

Davis had taken to saying good-bye to the children before going upstairs to bed. He wanted to die in bed, he told them. He explained that if he did not awaken, he would be in Valhalla, the heaven that was waiting for him. There he would see his hawk, and Peanut Butter and Nighttime, even Charlotte, who would be kind and gentle like she used to be.

When Davis began the practice of ending his day with good-bye, the children were terrified he would die in the night, but by now the cloud of fear had dissipated. Thos continued his habit of crawling in with Davis after his father was asleep, making himself as small as possible on the far side of the bed.

And so one morning when Thos awoke to find his father not on the bed but on the floor, already turning an other-worldly color, he was overwhelmed. But then he remembered. His heart had attacked him after all, thought Thos, who envisioned a great, pulsating heart turning in fury upon his father, grasping him and squeezing him to death. He was a victim, not of the hawk the children had heard so much about, but of his own heart.

Thos climbed out of bed, stepped warily over Davis, and crept down the stairs and over to the chairs by the woodstove where Miles and Clara were sleeping, and tapped them awake.

"He's dead," whispered Thos, as if there were anyone else to disturb. "At least, I'm pretty sure he is. He's not moving."

The Hardwick Market hadn't opened when they arrived, and so they rode their bikes around and around in little circles and made designs in the dirt while they waited for Eldon.

Spec was reading the newspaper when the phone rang. The children knew where he lived, because they'd heard him tell their father when he and Trudy visited Hardwick, and Eldon had gotten the number from Information. Half an hour later he and Trudy were ready to leave for New Jersey, Trudy in a borrowed Jeep and Spec in the pickup. If they drove down separately, she said, it would be simpler when it was time to come back. He'd have to stay and deal with the house and the funeral home, and then go through the piles and ship the furniture they, or she, anyway, wanted in Massachusetts. She knew she didn't want Davis's leather chairs. She couldn't see bringing him into their house like that, she said. As for the rest of it, "Bring the best of what there is. I'll leave it up to you." Mighty magnanimous of you, Spec thought, but he kept it to himself.

"What do you propose we do with everything that'll be coming on the truck?" he asked. "Just where do you expect to put it?"

"Oh, we'll get rid of all our stuff," Trudy replied airily. "I've had enough make-do furniture to last me a lifetime. We'll take it to the dump. It's perfectly good. Somebody will pick it up."

Spec nodded absently. And then it was time to leave. He was so preoccupied he half-expected her to climb up onto the seat beside him. He would have no memory of the long ride to Hardwick.

"This place is the center of fucking chaos," said Spec aloud as he pulled in and parked, unintentionally crushing pieces of the children's game of Society. Trudy pulled in behind him. It was mid-afternoon. As they made their way down the path to the water, a warm April breeze blew over them, ruffling Trudy's silk scarf and Spec's flannel shirt. Eldon and Uncle Stuart were waiting with the children, as Spec knew they would be.

"Where is he?" demanded Spec, an irate customer insisting upon seeing the manager.

"At the funeral home, and they're waiting for instructions," said Eldon, his voice trembling.

"Well, here are the instructions," said Spec. "There isn't going to be any funeral. He didn't have money for a funeral, and I sure as hell don't either. He'll get buried in a nice pine box, and that's all."

Spec started back up to the house, and, as he passed Miles, he reached out and tousled the boy's hair. He drew his hand away immediately, and had to restrain himself from glancing at it for signs of infestation. He continued walking, but Miles's voice behind him made him stop and turn around.

"I want to know what's going to happen to us."

His words detached themselves from him and hung in the air. They danced and fluttered, spinning in the atmosphere, until they finally came to rest.

"Quite frankly," began Stuart, "I hadn't planned to get into this so soon, but, well, I might as well say right off that I wish we could take the children, but we can't. Gran is just too frail. She couldn't manage it."

He shifted his shoulders as if his denim jacket had become too small.

The other children had gone over to Miles, and now the three of them stood looking at the ground. They didn't move. Eldon spoke next.

"Nothing in this whole, entire world would give me more pleasure than to take these kids in. I love them like my own," he added, his words whistling through ill-fitting dentures. "But I've been thinking about it and thinking about it, since before the Doctor died, really, and see, I know the state Lucille gets herself into just cooking their Thanksgiving dinner, and to tell you the truth, there's no way I can even bring myself to ask her."

He pushed his rimless glasses up and wiped his eyes with a large, red bandanna.

Spec glanced at Trudy. He had never brought this up with her, knowing it was likely she wouldn't be on board. He didn't think he could have endured her saying no, or shaking her head, or even just turning away.

"I thought this day might come, and since we're being frank, I have to tell you I can think of things a whole lot easier than taking on an almost ten-, eleven- and twelve-year-old." He was speaking as if they weren't there—indeed, as if someone else were talking for him. "But whatever happens, wherever they go, the main thing is, well, that they don't get split up."

The children looked sidelong at each other, heads still lowered. This was something they hadn't even considered.

"And there's another thing," Spec went on. "Quarter Harbor isn't a whole lot different from Hardwick, and I really think the kids will like it there."

Stuart had the feeling he had missed something. Had Spec said he was taking the kids? He saw that Eldon had his bandanna to his eyes again, and that the children were whispering together.

And so it was decided, as are so many things, without the actual words being spoken. Miles wanted to know if they would be coming back to Hardwick, and Spec said sure they would, sure. And when would they see Uncle Stuart? He would come up to Massachusetts to visit them, Stuart said. How about Eldon? Clara wanted to know. Oh, he would write, he said, and would see them when they came back to Hardwick.

But Thos was quiet, and for the first time in many years Spec could hear his mother saying, "Never assume that because people don't say something, they aren't thinking something."

"Since we're being frank," Spec had said, knowing there was no way on earth he could be frank, say what was really on his mind. He was still, after all these years, too cool for that. What he couldn't say out loud, not to Trudy, not to anybody, could barely say to himself, was that he had to have these kids. His father's kids. His kids. If Eldon or Stuart had laid claim, he, Spec, would have fought for them, kidnapped them if necessary. He hadn't recognized it until now, but it was true.

Spec was amazed that the conversation continued around him. Apparently no one noticed anything out of the ordinary, yet it seemed to him that the need he felt was so powerful it actually appeared to ignite the air.

Eldon suggested they spend the night with him and Lucille, but Trudy looked down at her sandals and said no, she wanted the kids to get their things packed up so she could head right back to Kings Island with them, and Spec knew better than to argue with her. She wanted to get away from here as soon as possible. She'd told him that, and she'd meant it.

Spec could only guess what she thought about taking the kids to live with them. He knew she'd broken an engagement because the guy wanted kids and she didn't. He knew about her childhood, a pretty awful one, and he could see why she didn't want to have anything to do with children. But this was different. He prayed she would come to understand.

The children didn't have long to decide what they wanted to take with them, but they didn't have much anyway. They talked quietly as they brought their bikes and kites and whistles and the plastic ball and bat to be put into the Jeep, but the bikes wouldn't fit and Spec promised to bring them in the pickup. They next went to gather up the straw people from the driveway. Thos was upset when he saw the damage to Society, but Miles hushed him and said it didn't matter, they were leaving, weren't they?

The children began stacking their bricks, but Spec put his hand on Miles's shoulder and said don't worry, we have plenty of those in Quarter Harbor. They entered the house and were in the bathroom picking through the clothes when Trudy rushed in behind them.

"You'll only need a couple of things," she said. "We'll be getting you nice new clothes in Massachusetts."

That was what she said. What she was thinking was that she would burn even those few loathsome pieces as soon as she could.

Just before Trudy and the children pulled out of the driveway, Spec handed her the carved ivory box.

"Here," he said. "You take this."

"What is it?" she asked.

"Never mind. Take it," said Spec, and then, realizing she wasn't about to extend her hand, he packed it in with their things. Good, he said to himself. No cop in his right mind would stop a woman and three kids and expect her to have guns in her car. He'd given the shotgun to Eldon.

There was no one to wave good-bye. Eldon and Stuart couldn't bear to wait around until they left, and Spec was too distracted to think of anything but the job that lay before him.

Spec had asked Eldon to get a couple of men to help him, and the next morning they stood in the doorway, twins, big and brawny, wearing black T-shirts that didn't quite cover the hairy bellies that hung over their jeans. Periodically, as if by prearrangement, they yanked up their pants in unison. They had the same unshaven faces, the same hairy forearms, the same long, stringy hair, and they wore identical "Keep on Truckin'" caps and mirrored sunglasses indoors as well as out. The dumpster they'd brought stood at the end of the driveway, and the furniture truck they would be driving to Kings Island was parked by the front door.

"We'll have to back out of here," said one, by way of greeting.

Spec nodded.

"Cost you extra," said the other, and Spec nodded again.

He was tired and in no mood to argue. He had spent a sleepless night in his father's grimy bed, initially disturbed by the knowledge that his father had died in this bed, and then confused by the arousal he felt when he thought of his father making love to Frances, right here where he lay now.

Spec didn't want to spend a lot of time cleaning out, and he told the twins that all the rotted, mildewed junk could be discarded wholesale. If he could have had them throw away the windows so streaked with dirt they barely let in the light, he would have done that, too.

"Want us to come back and give her a cleaning for you, mister?" asked one of the twins.

"Yeah. Get some of this grease out of here? Some of this dirt?" asked the other.

Spec hadn't thought about doing anything like that, but he said sure, why not, that's a good idea.

For the next three days, the men dismantled the piles. There, shrouded in years of neglect, was all the furniture from Spec's grandmother's house, as well as the large mirrors and the paintings in the massive oak frames that his grandmother had favored. Water damage to the artwork was extensive, and canvases of what appeared to be family portraits had to be disposed of, but Spec figured he'd take the frames for Trudy, who was sure to want them. If she didn't, he suspected, she would sell them.

He found, too, great, hulking antique pieces that must have come from the clinic. Of course, it made perfect sense. His father never would have had a conventional waiting room, with functional metal-and-vinyl chairs and a couch covered in some practical tweed. Nor would his office have been conventional, Spec was reminded, as they freed a huge, roll-top desk.

The last thing Trudy had called to him as she and the children pulled out of the driveway was "Don't forget those Orientals!" and now he took them off the railing, rolled them up, and added them to the growing pile of things to go to Kings Island.

But they found more than furniture, more than mirrors and paintings. Desiccated mice lay beneath the couch cushions, beside a squirming nest. The aquarium remained where it was when Spec last visited.

Inside the barn in Davis's office, Spec found boxes of his father's old wallets and appointment books and reading glasses, broken microscopes, beakers and Bunsen burners and what looked to be miles of rubber tubing, and everything covered with black dust. Spec had thought of his father as a saver, but now he saw that wasn't it at all. He didn't "save" things, which would have meant actively deciding he wanted to keep them. No, it was simply that he never threw anything away. Anything. Ever.

CHAPTER TWENTY

The children gripped each other's hands as the Jeep left the driveway and picked up speed, heading for the main road, the Garden State Parkway, and the long ride north. Trudy tried to make conversation, but the three huddled silently in the back seat, and she pictured herself wearing a chauffeur's cap. Finally, there being nothing on the radio but static, she opened her window wide and let the rush of cool air whip her long hair and fill her ears with sound.

Trudy felt the tenseness leave her shoulders when she realized, somewhere in the blackness of Connecticut, that the children had fallen asleep. She had been trying not to think what it would be like to have the disruption of children living with them. She thought of a line of poetry she had read in high school, "April is the cruelest month." Well, she had to agree with that one.

She made a long stop for gas and coffee, but the children did not awaken. They slept the entire way and missed their first view of Quarter Harbor in the early morning light.

Trudy nearly forgot the children asleep on the back seat, she was so relieved to be back. She loved it here. She felt completely at home with the fishermen, carpenters, plumbers, and electricians, who lived here all year, not like the rich people in Fair Haven with their second or third homes. The gray, weathered-shingle cottages made her think of a winter sky.

As she neared the house, she caught a glimpse of the fishing boats in the harbor, and of the bluff above with its unheated fishing shacks, where she and Spec used to live. She felt a pang, but it was gone in an instant as she remembered the children, and she was overcome with rage. She was furious at Spec, who had made this major, life-altering decision without her, and then expected, assumed, she would jump in and do this thing with him. At the moment she couldn't conceive of it.

As the children discussed later, they felt as if their minds had been emptied and all of this was happening to somebody else. It had been like watching themselves on a tiny TV, Clara said, and the others agreed. The set was turned off when they dropped off to sleep, and when they awoke it was dawn, and they were pulling up to the house in Quarter Harbor.

"Don't worry about the empty bedrooms," called Trudy from the kitchen, as they peered around. She tried to keep her voice light. "I see ads for used beds in the paper all the time. And Sam, my boss at the tavern, might be willing to part with some old bunk beds I happen to know he has, because he's told me plenty of times how his boys used to fight over who would get the top. I'll borrow some sleeping bags, but tonight you can curl up in bedrolls on the floor. You won't need much. It's actually pretty warm for April."

She listened for a response but there was none. Lord, she said to herself, it's like living with a little colony of deaf-mutes, and she flicked on the radio.

As it turned out, the children spoke only to each other until Spec returned a few days later. Trudy could hear their murmuring, but the moment she approached they stopped talking. Still, she dutifully cooked meals she thought would appeal to them, and she set the table, too, but they simply helped themselves and took the food outside, where they sat on the step and ate.

Can I really stand it? she asked herself again and again. I thought I'd paid my dues when I helped Spec get sober. Now I'm supposed to do this? And she counted the hours until he came back. Four days, he'd said. Four days. She could hardly wait.

When Trudy announced it was bedtime, the three merely looked at her. At some point they went to sleep—on the couch, on the chairs, anywhere but in the sleeping bags she had gotten hold of. It dawned on her that she understood nothing about these children, including how in the world they knew to pull on shorts without being told.

That first morning on Kings Island, Miles, Thos and Clara walked to the beach and spent hours in the spring sunshine, sauntering along the shoreline with tall grasses on one side of them and ocean on the other. They couldn't get used to the sight of the expanse of water that stretched forever. Their feet were toughened by years of going barefoot, and they shuffled through the wet pebbles that mingled with the sand at the water's edge, talking about Hardwick and when they might return. They ambled to the far end of the beach, where great, jagged rocks extended out into the water.

Then, as the sunlight spilled across the wet pebbles and cast rainbows on them, Miles spied a piece of sea glass lurking among the stones. The gem-like bit of bright green glass had been worn down by the sea and the stones and the sand. Perfect for the people to use as money when they played Society, the children decided. The search for sea glass became their quest, and they discovered that green and clear glass were the most common, always difficult to find, but still the most common, and there were occasional bits of brown and aqua to be found as well.

Because Miles was the discoverer of sea glass, the others approached him with each new piece of glass, wondering if it was all right, if it was one to keep, or if, like some too-small fish, it would have to be left behind. Miles examined the piece carefully. If there was the slightest hint of a rough edge, the merest suggestion of shininess, it would have to go. "Not rutted down enough," he would declare.

Thos and Clara fell into step together, a slow dance that took them along the ridge of pebbles at the edge of the waves.

"I wonder," mused Thos, half to himself and half to his sister, "what part of your brain tells you that's not a pebble you're looking at, that's sea glass. And before you even know you've spotted it, you're bending over to pick it up."

And then he discovered the cobalt blue glass. More beautiful than the others, it was partially hidden under a black stone with a white stripe around it, and he nearly missed it. Miles saw him bend to pick something up and walked over to see what it was.

"Blue," breathed Miles, gazing at the glass. He turned to Thos, smiling as he looked into his brother's eyes. "Nice job, Thos. I think you've found something special."

Thos smiled back. All that day he held the blue glass tightly in his fist, with his hand in his pocket. He knew he would keep it with him always.

The following day a van pulled up alongside the children as they walked to the beach.

"Hey, kids, how about a ride?" The driver, a heavy-set, bearded man, with a red kerchief over his hair and a small gold ball adorning one earlobe, was already reaching back to open the door.

Looking quickly from Clara to Thos, Miles said, "Sure! Great! Look, guys, we don't have to walk to the beach!"

They climbed in and sprawled on the seat.

"The beach is it? We're on our way. Next time, stick out your thumb, like this," he said, as he jabbed the air with a beefy digit, "and someone will stop and give you a lift. Guaranteed. Nothing to it. Can't beat hitchhiking to save your feet and your pocketbook. Once I hitchhiked the entire way across the country. Folks gave me food, gave me a place to sleep, everything. When I got back, I still had the same twenty I had in my wallet when I took off. Best way to travel." A moment later, he said heartily, "Okay, here we are! You have a good one, now, you hear?"

The next day the children hitchhiked to the beach, incredulous at how easy it was to get a ride.

"Move over, Jeremy," said the woman driving the white station wagon. She laughed. "You'll have to excuse him. He's only five. Come on, Jeremy," she said, more sharply this time.

They crowded into the back seat with the young boy, who never took his eyes off of them.

A pickup truck not unlike Spec's stopped for them the following morning.

"To the beach!" called Clara, as they climbed into the open bed of the truck.

But after several minutes, she said anxiously, "This isn't the way to the beach."

"Lucky for us! We're taking a longer way!" cried Thos, opening his arms to the wind.

Miles put his arm around Clara, who relaxed against him. Soon, however, it became apparent even to Miles that they weren't headed for the beach, but he kept that thought to himself.

The truck had speeded up and Miles presumed they were being taken to the other end of the island. Then, scarcely slowing down, the truck turned sharply into a dirt road, pulled into the woods, and stopped.

The driver got out, and for the first time the children were really able to see the short, clean-shaven man. They were not used to the formality of his khaki suit, his red bow tie, his white shirt. But the suit was stained and the shirt cuffs were dirty.

He touched his dark hair nervously, then took off his jacket, folded it neatly, and laid it on the driver's seat. The children watched, transfixed, and when the man suggested they get out of the truck, they did so.

"Now," he said, "I'm going to show you something I know you're going to like."

He removed his leather belt and put that, too, on the car seat. Then very slowly he unbuttoned his pants and unzipped his fly, his eyes on the children. Suddenly he let go of the pants and they dropped to the ground, revealing a ruff of dark hair around a long, languid penis.

"Let's get out of here," said Miles, and the children took off on a run. Cries of "Shit! Oh, shit!" faded rapidly behind them.

Miles wanted to hitch home but Thos and Clara refused, so they began the long walk back to the house.

"What was *that?*" asked Clara, after a few minutes had passed.

"I have no idea!" replied Miles.

"Me neither," said Thos.

"Was it a regular person?" Clara demanded.

"How should I know?" said Miles.

Then they began to laugh. They laughed harder and harder, until their stomachs hurt so much they had to sit down.

It was afternoon when they came in, and Trudy glanced up from her magazine, looked at her watch, and went back to reading. Knowing they wouldn't answer, she didn't ask where they had been. The children stopped short, nudging one another. They saw that she had cut her hair.

When Trudy entered the kitchen that evening, Miles and Clara were watching Thos capture an insect in a glass he held against the wall. While Thos freed the bug outdoors, Trudy waited, tapping her foot rapidly. Then she dropped a postcard and a package on the kitchen counter.

"These came for you," she said, avoiding their eyes, and left the room.

The postcard was from Stuart, the first of the cards he would send faithfully each week. He always included a riddle, or a puzzle, or a joke of some sort. "Why did the moron throw the clock out the window?" said this first one. And then, in tiny little upside-down letters on the bottom, "Because he wanted to see time fly." In between was news of Philadelphia and Gran.

A note accompanied Eldon's package, and the children had to struggle with the handwriting, even though Eldon had adopted a clumsy printing for their benefit. Eventually they made out how he'd meant to write every day, really he did, but he wasn't good at writing, and besides, there wasn't anything going on in Hardwick anyway, and he hoped they'd forgive him if he sent them Yummycakes instead, so they'd know he was thinking of them. He'd done some investigating, he said, and found that you can't buy Yummycakes in New England. He missed the three of them, he said, adding that Sally Bea did, too.

This was the children's favorite of all the many treats Eldon had brought them back in Hardwick. Nonetheless, the mood was somber as they opened the box that revealed three packages of Yummycakes. The children stared at them for a long time.

At last Clara said, "Well, we might as well eat them, don't you think? Or else they'll get stale."

Miles agreed, but not Thos.

"I can't eat mine. Not yet, anyway," he said, and closed his eyes, at once shutting out the present and bringing back the past.

The mood lightened with Spec's return. The mover twins had followed Spec back, and, under his jocular command, everyone pitched in to get the old furniture out of the house and the Hardwick things in. The flood had left permanent marks, but Trudy nevertheless cleaned and polished each piece before it went inside, and knew exactly where it would go. The woman must have been planning this since that first visit to Hardwick, said Spec to himself.

Although he didn't tell her, Spec thought the house looked ridiculous, crammed as it was with dark, heavy furniture. It could've worked in Hardwick, he thought, with that two-story room. Could've looked great, as a matter of fact. But here, the couch, the grandfather clock, the huge mahogany table with its twelve chairs, conspired to overwhelm the house. The mirrors, enormous oak frames with not much reflecting glass, didn't make the house feel larger, as mirrors often do, but instead made it seem even more crowded than it actually was.

"Where's the ivory box? You know, the guns?" asked Spec.

"Gone," said Trudy. "I sold them."

"You *what?*"

"You heard me. I sold them."

"Without consulting me?"

He was very angry.

"Ha! You're a fine one to talk about 'consulting' somebody ahead of time."

Spec remembered his mother's advice to count to ten before saying something he'd regret, so he counted to twenty for good measure. He was still furious but was able to contain himself when he discovered that the Oriental rugs never made it to the floor. Trudy sold them, too.

Spec was sorry he'd brought back so much furniture. Christ almighty, he thought, I'll have to go outside to breathe.

"It's like a goddamned furniture showroom," he mumbled, when everything was in place, and Trudy, overhearing, reminded him that it had belonged to his father, his grandmother, not hers.

That was how her mind worked, just veered off, and it infuriated Spec. She couldn't seem to grasp things. It turned out that quite a lot of the furniture she'd talked about, she'd been planning to sell all along. She needed money to buy a car, she said. Jesus, he told her, it would've been cheaper to sell the stuff down there instead of paying to bring such a big truck up here.

"Why didn't you take them to buy clothes, for God's sake?" he asked now, changing the subject. "Or get them to take a shower? And how about beds? What the devil were you doing since you got back, Trudy? Taking a vacation? Spending your time at the *beauty parlor*?" he finished sarcastically.

Trudy touched the short, uneven ends of her hair, then folded her arms across her chest and narrowed her eyes. Hoping he hadn't seen her tears, she turned and went into their room, shutting the door behind her. Spec could hear the lock turn. So could the children.

Sam was certainly willing to part with the bunk beds, but he wouldn't let Trudy pay for them. Call it a welcome home present for the kids, he said, giving her a hug.

They bought a cot that went into the end bedroom for Clara. The room was so tiny it was crowded with just the bed, a small chest and a nightstand. They set up the bunk beds in the center bedroom for Miles and Thos, who were delighted with their private quarters, never mind that the room barely accommodated the beds and one chest of drawers, let alone two. Spec built shelves in their diminutive closet so they would have a place to store the sweatshirts and jeans and T-shirts and shorts he bought for them. He hung a full-length mirror in the hall outside their door.

Clara hated all of it and refused to sleep in bed.

"I don't want this old bed! I'll sleep on the couch!" she said loudly.

She knew she'd been left out because she was a girl, had to have her own room because she was a girl, and she loathed the very thought of being a girl. For as long as she could remember she had prayed every night that the next morning she'd wake up a boy, and, although she hadn't given up hope entirely, she was beginning to have her doubts that the prayers would have any effect. She hadn't even bothered to ask Spec and Trudy to call her "C" instead of Clara.

On the night that Spec came back, the children had their first shower. Clara went first. She hated being separated from Miles and Thos, as Spec talked to her through the bathroom door and gave step-by-step showering instructions. Then, while she was in her room dressing, he stripped down with the boys, responding to their stares with, "Don't worry, guys, you'll look like this too, someday," and a wink. He could not guess at the confusion they felt, seeing the fully developed male member for the second time in a week—indeed, for the second time in their lives.

Spec raced the boys to the bathroom. Laughing, he pulled first Miles, then Thos under the water and demonstrated how to lather up and wash off and how to shampoo their hair.

"What say we get you guys a haircut tomorrow?" he asked, and because of the way he said it, with a chuckle working its way up from the back of his throat, they agreed.

Clara was not happy to miss the fun and the water fight, which ended with Spec and the boys laughing and dripping their way into their rooms to get dressed. Trudy was left to mop up.

Spec had pleaded "extenuating circumstances," allowing the children to delay school until the fall. Time stretched before them, but they could not bring themselves to play "Society." Instead, when they weren't on the beach, they rode their bikes along the road and walked in the woods. Days that glinted in the sun mixed with others that were gray and shadowless, when a chill wind blew across the water and onto Kings Island. Then, almost as they watched, the branches of trees and shrubs turned the palest green, and soon wildflowers were blooming. Purple wild geraniums and white Arrowwood grew by the roadside, and red lady's slippers in the woods. Blue-eyed grass and wild roses decorated the fields, while pink Rosa rugosa lined the path to the beach. The sunlight, not yet the harsh sunlight of summer, fell on the meadows and highlighted each blade of grass. Then the wind rippled the meadows and looked to the children like thousands of tiny creatures running, running, first in one direction, then in another, as the wind shifted and reminded them of home.

Trudy had insisted they get rid of the kitchen table and chairs, since they would now be eating at the mahogany table. Because of its size, an uncomfortably large section of living room space was given over to a piece of furniture that begged for liveried servants to stand behind the chairs during dinner. That first night with Spec, dinner consisted of the hamburgers, chips and cole slaw that Trudy had prepared.

"Sorry about the meal," she said. "I didn't have time to do anything more elaborate today."

"Gee, this is more—" said Miles.

"—than we're used to getting—" continued Clara.

"—at home!" finished Thos.

It went on like that, the children finishing each other's sentences, until Trudy had to excuse herself from the table, saying she had a headache.

"Headache, my eye." The children could hear Spec's lowered voice through the thin walls that night. "What the hell's the matter with you?"

"The matter with *me*? What's the matter with *you*? I don't know who you are anymore!" Trudy was restraining herself with obvious difficulty. "And the kids! Good God, they finally talk, and I don't even know where to look! You can't tell which one's talking, they switch off so goddamned often!"

"Well you better get used to it, 'cause that's the way they talk. Be glad they're talking!"

"And the hoarse one! Every time he says something I clear my throat for him!"

After a long moment, she muttered, "I don't know what I'm hanging around for, anyway."

"Ah, don't start with that, huh?"

There was the sound of drawers opening and closing. Then it was quiet. When Spec spoke again, his voice had changed so completely that for a minute the children thought someone else had entered the room.

"You—you're not going to take off on me, are you?"

His voice was cracking. There was a pause and then Spec sounded as though he were choking.

"Please, Trudy. Please."

Then there was no mistaking it, he was sobbing, and Clara crept into the boys' room and the three of them held tight to each other. A grownup crying. A man. They couldn't believe it.

CHAPTER TWENTY - ONE

The next morning Trudy set twelve places at the mahogany table, using the china, crystal and silverware from Hardwick. She'd seen them do that in antique shops, just for show, she told Spec, who bit his tongue. At dinnertime that evening, she cleared five places and substituted paper plates and plastic utensils and they sat down to eat.

This continued for several nights, but it was uncomfortable, forbidding, a series of failed dinner parties at which none of the invited guests showed up, and so they began to help themselves from the pots on the stove.

"Quite a comedown, from dinner guests to kitchen help," Spec joked with the children.

They ate in the living room while they watched TV. Secretly, Trudy was glad they had given up eating at the table. She hated to sit and watch the children, all with the same short haircuts, as they picked food off each other's plates and ate it with their fingers, as if each plate belonged to the three of them. And Spec refused to reprimand them. She knew their Gran in Philadelphia had taught them manners that would have served them well at Buckingham Palace, but these were certainly nowhere in evidence.

———

Trudy returned to work on the day shift, but Spec decided not to go back to fishing.

"You love fishing!" Trudy protested when Spec told her. "You've told me a hundred times how you'd rather be way out there on the ocean than anywhere else! Except with me, of course," she added, nudging him playfully.

"Yeah, but it's more complicated now. You know." Spec was aware how easily sound traveled through these walls. "Besides, I'd be away an awful lot," he continued. "I talked to Charlie Williams, and it's all set. I'm going to paint houses with him. It's good money, I can be outside, and I'll just have to get used to working on dry land."

"Oh, Spec," said Trudy, with tears in her eyes. "Nobody could love those kids more. They are really lucky to have you."

———

Spec discovered that he liked to be high up on an extension ladder, scraping and painting, rather than on the ground with the other painters. Painting, like fishing, allowed his mind to roam free, and he was thankful for that.

"It's not exactly walking around the edge of a deck, but it's close enough for me," he told Trudy.

They all knew how much Spec missed fishing, even though he didn't talk about it. Whenever the children saw him sitting alone in the living room and staring at nothing at all, they were pretty sure that, in his mind, he was looking at the sea.

———————————

Early one particularly still, glistening Sunday morning, when the sun caught the water and made it crystal, Spec and the children set out for the lighthouse at the tip of Kings Island. They had watched it together from the bluff overlooking the harbor. The top story of the distant brick tower housed lamps that signaled passing ships: white, white, red, white, white, red. The endless, predictable pattern seemed, in its very monotony, to promise security. But Spec told of the time when the lights failed to save the sailors, when their ship foundered on the rocks off Kings Island and more than a hundred men went down in a single shipwreck a century before. And he told them bone-chilling accounts of the succession of lighthouse keepers and their families who had lived in the keeper's cottage—lived there and died there, mysteriously, no one knew how.

It was already hot and the pavement shimmered before them as they drove on this mid-summer morning. The flat road was bordered by shrubs that were stunted by the fierce winter winds that came off the water. Gradually the land narrowed, and they could see the ocean on one side and the sound on the other, as the waters headed toward a meeting point off the tip of the island. Then the truck went up a rise and there, in a meadow of tall grasses, was the lighthouse, soaring higher than anything they'd ever seen.

A weathered, split-rail fence surrounded the property, and the children climbed through it while Spec flung one long leg over as if mounting a horse, and dismounted on the other side. Chattering excitedly, Miles, Thos and Clara bolted past the timbers that were all that remained of the keeper's cottage and continued toward the lighthouse. Their bare feet were impervious to the stiff, rough grass.

While they waited for Spec to catch up, they looked out across the beach and the island, feeling the smooth wind that was only here, only at the lighthouse, and then they closed their eyes and tipped their faces toward the sun, stretched out their arms, and let the wind wash over them.

The creaking of the heavy door roused the children, who followed Spec into a cramped, cylindrical space, scarcely large enough to accommodate the spiral staircase that spun its way to the top of the tower.

"This is my favorite place on Kings Island," said Spec, "especially at sunset."

He saw the children trying to see up the stairs.

"Hello?" Miles called tentatively. Then louder, more boldly. "Hello?"

No response came.

Spec laughed. "No one's here," he said. "The town took it over and they leave it open so people can visit. They've got some kind of part-time caretaker, who checks up on things." He lowered his voice and said menacingly, "Not so easy to find keepers anymore."

Then, seeing the look on the children's faces, he laughed again and rumpled their hair.

They began the steep ascent. The children held tight to the railing and glanced up frequently to watch the top as they approached. When they reached the chamber with the flashing red and white lamps, they found it was hot, too hot, and Spec led them out onto the iron balcony that circled the lighthouse.

They thought they had stepped onto a cloud. From almost-flat Hardwick, many of whose residents remained convinced the earth itself was flat, they had come here, a vantage point in heaven, where the wind was stronger, the sun was brighter, and everything was clear, no matter how far away.

Spec smiled as he watched the children, their eyes closed, the wind blowing through their hair. A good day, he said to himself, and then repeated it. A good day.

He couldn't know that Miles would remember hearing louder than ever before the voice that he could never quite place, the voice that cried, "Mama! Mama!" Clara would remember the sudden, chilling sensation that she was at eye level with her father. Thos would remember his terror as he descended the narrow, winding staircase that seemed to plunge downward forever, into the very center of the earth.

"Letters!" sang Spec, entering the boys' room late one afternoon, where the three children sat together on the floor. "We get letters! We get stacks and stacks of letters!"

He waved an envelope playfully under the nose of each child in turn. They looked at him curiously, and he realized, belatedly, that of course the Perry Como Show wouldn't mean anything to them.

"Who wants to read it?" he asked.

The children gathered around and looked at the shaky handwriting.

"Can you, Spec? I don't think we're good enough readers," said Miles.

Spec opened the letter and began to read:

> *Dear Miles, Thomas (this was crossed out) Thos, and C,*
>> *Ever since your papa died and you went on up to Massachusetts, Stuart and I have been trying to make arrangements to see you. We miss you so much! Finally we got bus tickets to go up there . . .*

"Gran and Uncle Stuart are coming!" shouted Clara.

"Wait, there's more," said Spec.

> *. . . and we made all the necessary arrangements here. I even went and bought myself a pretty summer dress. No one wants to look at an old lady in her black clothes, I said to myself!*
>> *But then I took a fall, just tripped on the porch step. Maybe I got careless because I was so excited at the idea that I was going to see you again after all these months. Fortunately your Uncle Stuart was at home, and he drove me to the hospital. I thought maybe I had sprained my ankle and bruised my side, nothing more than that, but it seems I've "fractured" my hip, too. (That's doctor talk!) Right now I'm lying in bed writing this letter to you.*
>> *It broke my heart when the doctor said I wouldn't be making any trips for a long, long time. We asked if he thought I could manage without Stuart for a few days so that he, at least, could visit, but the doctor said I would need him here at home, to take care of me. It's true, I do need him. I can't do anything for myself these days, and he's a great help.*
>>> *Give each other a hug from—*
>>> *Your loving Gran*

Spec folded the letter slowly, slipped it back into its envelope, and looked at the children. He hardly recognized them. They were like three little automatons, no expression on their faces whatsoever. He left the room quietly and listened outside the door as the children spoke in low voices. He wanted to know how they felt, even if they didn't tell him directly.

"We'll never see her again, will we?" said Clara, not asking a question.

"No," said Miles, "but we can imagine how she looks, right? And we can hear her voice, right? Even though we haven't seen her in a long time? So that means we can see her whenever we want to, C. All we have to do is think about her, and she'll be right there."

"Everybody gets taken away from us!" said Thos, with unaccustomed anger.

"Nobody got 'taken away from us,'" said Miles. "People died. That's what people do, you know?"

"But doesn't it make you sad? Or mad? It doesn't seem like it," said Thos.

"Sure it does, but I have something that I don't think you have. It's kind of like I've got a little moat around me and it protects me. I don't think I feel things the way you do. When something bad happens, it has to jump over my moat to get to me, and by that time I just don't feel it so much, I guess."

"I sure wish I had a moat like that," said Thos.

"Me, too," said Clara.

There were more letters from Gran, and then there was one from Stuart, saying she'd died "peacefully" in the hospital from complications of pneumonia.

Two weeks later, he wrote again:

> *Dear Miles-Thos-C,*
>
> *I think about you a lot and I would really like to come and see you, but I hope you will understand when I tell you I am just too sad. I am sad all the time. I miss your mama, even though she died a very long time ago, and I miss Gran. I'm sure you do, too, but I lived with her and saw her every single day. When I walk around the house, I keep thinking she'll be in the next room, or the next, but of course she isn't. I am going to sell the house and try to be happier someplace else.*
>
> *You know that the company I work for once sent me to London to live for a while. Maybe you remember the sweatshirts I sent you. Anyway, I have decided to go back and work in London. Maybe I can be happier there. It is far away, but I hope that will be good for me, and maybe someday you can come over and visit me. I will probably be there for a long time.*
>
> *I haven't been a very good uncle to you, and I'm so sorry about that. I started out all right, but I was never much good after your mama died. When you came to Philadelphia to visit Gran and me, it looked like we were both taking care of you, but it was Gran. It was always Gran. She took care of all of us. I've loved you, though, and I really hope you know that.*
>
> *I will write to you when I get to London. Try to remember your Uncle Stuart, who will always love you very, very much.*

He had printed the letter with care. Tears had stained the page.

"Will we ever see him again, do you think?" asked Miles.

Spec could see the effort he was making to keep his voice steady. Thos and Clara were standing next to him, and the same question was in their faces.

"Oh, sure you will! Absolutely! May not be real soon, but what a great trip you guys will take to London one of these days! You'll get the royal treatment. Probably meet the queen and everything!"

He forced a smile.

But late that night, Spec wept as he read this latest letter to Trudy.

"My God," he said, sobbing, "aren't these kids ever going to have someone they can rely on?"

"Oh, Spec," said Trudy, cradling his head in her lap. She wet her fingertip with his tears and kissed it. "My dearest, dearest Spec," she whispered in his ear. "They have you."

Stuart was true to his word, sending postcards almost weekly. But now, instead of jokes and riddles, there was news about his tiny apartment, his job, his friends, the "fish n' chips" he had come to love, and how they were wrapped in newspaper. The postcards featured pictures of Big Ben and Westminster Abbey and the Royal Family, exactly like the ones he had sent to their mother.

"I think I know how we can make some money!" said Clara one evening as they ate supper and watched television. A commercial had come on. It was unusual for anyone to start a conversation while they ate, and the others turned to look at her.

"See," she continued, "I thought we could get some of those old lobster traps? The ones they have down at the dock?" Her voice tilted upward. "We could pay for them if we had to, but maybe someone will give them to us. Anyway, then we take one and prop it up against a tree in front of the house, not with a sign on it or anything, just kind of leave it there? I'll bet you anything some dumb tourist will want to buy it!"

She was right. All the rest of the summer, people stopped by the house and asked, embarrassed and hesitating, if they might possibly buy that lobster trap out by the tree. "I'll have to ask," Clara would say. Then she would run off and stay away for what seemed an appropriate amount of time before coming back and saying, "They said to make sure you know you can get a brand new trap down at the store? But if you really want it, okay, and they're sorry but they'll have to charge you kind of a lot, because they have to go buy another and stuff." And one more grateful tourist would press the money into her hand and leave.

Soon Miles and Thos began to take turns with Clara, and each evening they divided the day's take three ways. Miles and Clara bought bells and baskets for their bikes, as well as caps and T-shirts that said "Kings Island—Ya Gotta Love It," but Thos kept his money in a box and never spent any of it. He was saving it for when they were back in Hardwick, he said.

"Here's something you guys might want to look at," said Spec, tossing a burlap sack to Miles one morning before he left for work. Miles pulled open the drawstring and peered inside.

"I kind of grabbed it before I left," continued Spec. "Actually I meant to give it to you as soon as I got back, but things were pretty hectic, and, well, I sort of forgot."

"Where did you find it?" asked Miles.

"In the 'office'." He couldn't keep the sarcasm entirely out of his voice, but Miles apparently missed it.

"Oh, the office. Right." Miles's voice trailed off and his eyes misted.

"Hey—you guys okay?" Spec's brow was furrowed.

"We're fine." Clara answered for them, and Spec, looking concerned, left for work.

Trudy had gone off early to help Sam do a major cleaning at the tavern, and the house was quiet. Miles carried the sack outside and sat on the step in the June sunshine; Thos and Clara perched on either side of him. He extracted a small pile of black and white composition books that someone had numbered.

"Like Sally Bea sells," breathed Thos.

Miles opened the first notebook and saw it contained family pictures. They had not remembered their father taking a single photograph of any of them.

"Let's wash our hands," said Miles.

Somehow this gesture seemed right and they headed for the kitchen, letting the screen door slam behind them. They poured dishwashing soap into their palms and took a long time washing.

"Good," said Miles at last, satisfied, and together they dried their hands on a dishtowel. His voice cracking, he added, "I'll bet that's how he washed his hands when he was a doctor at the hospital."

Thos and Clara nodded. It was the first time any of them had mentioned their father.

They went outside and sat again on the step. This time when Miles opened the composition book, he did so warily, as if afraid the pages might turn to dust. The book was bound tightly, too tightly for the cardboard cover to lie flat, so Thos and Clara each held down one side. The black-and-white pictures had been glued neatly into the book, positioned along the thin, blue lines so they would be perfectly straight, but the glue had rumpled the paper, and the pages made sounds of resistance when they were turned. Every photograph was meticulously labeled in a tiny, careful hand.

"That's not his writing. He didn't write this," said Miles.

"So it must be . . ." Thos stopped in mid-sentence.

"Mama," said Miles, finishing for him. "We called her Mama."

He heard it often in his head, but it had been a long time since he'd said it aloud.

The children were quiet as they peered at the first photograph, of a dark-haired young girl, enveloped in a man's cardigan sweater. They recognized her from the pictures on Gran's piano. Below the picture were the words "Frances. 1967. Hardwick."

The next was labeled "Frances and Miles. 1968. Hardwick." Frances, in a shapeless, sleeveless dress, stood in the driveway cradling a tiny Miles in her arms, hugging him so tightly and kissing his cheek so fiercely that his head was forced away.

The initial pages contained photos from Miles's first year. In each he was with Frances: Miles examining a banana as Frances lay on the grass next to him; Miles sitting on her lap while they looked at a book; Frances breast feeding him; Frances holding him on her hip and smiling down at him as he watched something out of camera range; Frances changing his diaper, looking up with a hint of annoyance at the distraction of having her picture taken.

Then Thos was born and there were pictures of Frances with Thos, and of the boys together, solid Miles and slight Thos. Not until

Clara came along did Davis take pictures of one child alone. Here was Clara with the black pocketbook she used to attack her brothers; Clara playing with a dandelion; Clara sitting, posing, gazing steadily into the camera, her lips pursed ever so slightly, the merest hint of a whistle. Her eyes were wide and dark, fringed with black lashes that contrasted with her light hair and the pale softness of her skin. Like the boys, she was invariably naked. Unlike them, she did not seem to mind sitting still to be photographed.

And every picture with its label, even though the cast of characters was very small and the place was always the same. Hardwick.

"She was holding these same books, you know?" said Thos, as his finger traced the words she had written. And he started to cry.

"It's okay," said Miles. "Don't worry, Thos. It's all okay."

In none of the notebooks did the children find a picture of Eldon or Hank. There was only one of their father, who was sitting on the front step with his arms folded and his pipe in his mouth. A shadow fell across his face, but it was clear that he was looking squarely into the camera.

Thos kept the composition books next to his bed. While Miles and Clara went for bike rides, or for walks, or, if the weather was bad, stayed in and watched television, Thos sat on his bed and leafed slowly through the pages, over and over again, examining each photograph as if to memorize its every detail.

One afternoon when Thos was alone in the house, the telephone rang. He walked over to it and waited while it rang twice more, hesitated, then picked it up. It was the first time he had ever spoken on the phone.

"Hello?" he said warily. A disembodied voice was asking if his father was at home. Thos was confused for a moment and almost replied that his father was dead, but then he realized the voice wanted to talk to Spec. "He's not my father," he said. "He's my—he's kind of my brother. Yeah, my brother," and Thos hung up the phone.

He had finished telling Miles and Clara about the phone call when Miles suggested they go to the beach, but Thos, who was looking at the photo album across his lap, shook his head without raising his eyes.

"Thos doesn't want to do anything but look at those old pictures of us with Mama," said Miles, as he and Clara prepared to mount their bikes.

"Have you noticed he doesn't talk to Spec and Trudy anymore? Just us?" asked Clara.

Miles, who was pushing off, stopped abruptly. He frowned. "No-o," he said slowly, "I haven't noticed that. Not at all. Are you sure?"

"Well, sometimes when we're at dinner? And Spec or Trudy asks us something? You and I are the only ones to answer. Thos never does. And if he wants to know anything? He asks you or me. Then if we don't know, we ask, but he doesn't."

"Since when, C?"

"Around when Spec gave us the pictures, I guess."

"Why didn't you say anything before?"

"I don't know. I guess I thought you must've noticed, too."

"How about Spec? Do you think he has?"

"I'm not sure, but probably not."

CHAPTER TWENTY - TWO

Clara was wrong. Spec had indeed observed that Thos was no longer speaking to anyone but Miles and Clara, and he, too, dated this behavior from the morning he gave the photographs to the children. When he'd mentioned the situation to Trudy, she'd rolled her eyes and said how can you tell the difference anyway, and he hadn't brought it up again.

I wonder if Trudy is in this with me or not, Spec thought to himself, as he did so often these days. I can't really blame her if she's not. Kids won't give her the time of day. It's like she isn't even here. It occurred to him that they didn't have much experience with a woman in the house.

Without being able to discuss it with Trudy, Spec had decided to take the three children to the doctor. Chances were good they'd never had their shots, and Miles could be checked to make sure the hoarseness was just part of his makeup. As for Thos—Spec figured while the boy was up on the examining table, well, Spec could casually ask the doctor a few questions.

Dean Campbell had an opening the following week, the receptionist said when Spec called, and he told his boss he'd have to take that afternoon off. Family business, he said, and his boss nodded and said no problem. Hope everything's okay.

Spec hadn't known quite how to break it to the children that they were going to the doctor, and so that morning, before he left for work, he told them to stay around because he had somewhere to take them in the afternoon. Then later, as they climbed into the pickup, the words were there.

"You know your father was a doctor, right?" Spec could never seem to bring himself to say "our father." "And that he helped people? Well, there's a really nice doctor not too far from here, Dr. Campbell, and he likes to help kids, make sure they stay healthy and everything. He's going to like you guys. He's going to like you a whole lot."

And he smiled at the three of them in the back of the pickup.

Spec sat at the wheel in the rigid, unmoving way he had, with his right hand on the gearshift and his left on top of the steering wheel, and greeted those he passed by opening his hand without removing his palm from the wheel. They left Quarter Harbor, skirted Fair Haven, and drove over the causeway to the mainland. Thos and Clara shouted to each other in the truck bed as the wind played with their voices. Miles laughed and gestured along with them, knowing he couldn't possibly make himself heard.

They had been on the mainland for a short time when they turned into Oak Lane, a quiet street neatly lined with white clapboard houses. Spec drove past Dean Campbell's small shingle without seeing it, made a U-turn, and cruised back up the street so slowly that he saw a neighbor pull her curtains slightly apart and peer out at him. Old biddy probably thinks I'm driving around collecting kids, thought Spec, and was on the verge of ringing her doorbell to ask if she had any for sale when he spotted the sign, DEAN

CAMPBELL, M.D., PRACTICE LIMITED TO INFANTS AND CHILDREN.

Spec parked, led the children up the path, and rang the office doorbell. He noted there was a second bell for an upstairs "residence." Nice commute, he thought.

A starched-white figure, the nurse-receptionist, greeted them. She was an imposing woman, whose high, stiff, gray hair was trapped unwillingly under a nurse's cap. As she bustled them in, another woman, slight and attractive, came down the stairs, slipped past them, and disappeared out the door. Spec, who had guessed her to be about his own age, was startled when the nurse called after her, "Good-bye, Mrs. Campbell!" He had assumed Dr. Campbell would be older, the counterpart to this nurse, the kind of pediatrician Spec remembered from his youth. He hadn't thought about it before, but now it came to him that he counted on a doctor being considerably older than his own thirty-six years. Older and therefore wiser.

He needn't have worried. Dr. Campbell was a large, white-haired man with a ruddy, comfortable face and the requisite wire-rimmed glasses. Even his office had the smell of stale peppermints that Spec remembered.

Good for you, Doc, said Spec to himself, as Dr. Campbell's hand swallowed his own in a handshake, and he flushed to find himself imagining the doctor and his pretty wife making passionate love.

"Well, and hello to you!" Dr. Campbell was saying to the children as he bent over, hands on his knees, looking like an umpire ready to call the first pitch. His immaculate white coat hung open, revealing a rumpled blue work shirt unbuttoned at the neck. "Now let's see. I'll bet you're Miles," he said, touching Miles's hair. "And you're Thos, and you're—let me see—Araminta?"

Clara shook her head and was about to correct him when Dr. Campbell tried once more.

"Matilda?"

Clara shook her head again, but she was beginning to see that this was a joke.

"Ophelia? Bettina? Loretta? Minerva? Jordana? Prunella?"

"No, no, no, no, no, no!" said Clara delightedly, shaking her head and laughing.

"Well, if it isn't any of those, it must be Clara!"

"That's right! It is!" she squealed, as the boys looked on uncertainly.

Patting Clara's hair and still smiling at their joke, Dr. Campbell addressed the children together. "Well, Miles, Thos and Clara, I hear your father was a doctor, just like me."

The children seemed not to have heard, or didn't realize a response was indicated.

"Did he see patients in an office at home?"

Spec checked a derisive snort.

"Actually," said Clara, the unexpected sound of her voice surprising them, "he kind of brought them along the path to the couch outside the kitchen? And then cleared the stuff away to make room for them to sit down?"

Spec was relieved to hear Clara's words, glad she was bringing things into the open, but at the same time he was distracted by her way of speaking. He found it difficult to listen to her without becoming disoriented by the upward lilt at the end of her sentences, which made everything she said seem like a question that begged for a nod or some other form of assent. The occasional "uh-huh" that he might ordinarily interject seemed oddly misplaced and mistimed.

If Dean Campbell was surprised by anything Clara mentioned, he didn't let on. Nor did he indicate he had noticed that, as the other children warmed to him, Thos seemed to withdraw. But he departed from his usual practice of examining one child at a time, and instead seated the three of them on the edge of the examining table and checked, assembly-line style, their throats, their noses and their ears, and listened to their chests and backs. Each had a turn lying face up on the table while Dr. Campbell probed and prodded and tickled in such a way that even Thos gave a quick, reluctant laugh. When it came time for their shots, he lined them up by the tall window, through which the sun and the hot air poured in.

"Look outside and tell me how many birds you can see on the feeder over there."

"We can't count very well," offered Clara.

"Well, you do the best you can. Now don't turn around, but let me know if you think a bee flies in and stings you on the behind." He pronounced it "*bee*-hind," and Clara giggled.

Before the children left the examining room so that, as Dr. Campbell told them, "Nurse can tell you how to pee into a cup," he drew blood from each of them. Thos was first. He uttered a faint, high-pitched cry that lasted while Miles and Clara had their blood taken as well. The cry lingered in the air when the children left the room and Spec stayed behind to talk with Dr. Campbell.

Although Trudy didn't ask about the visit, he described everything, the two doorbells, the starched nurse, the doctor himself, the examinations, everything but the doctor's young wife, although he wasn't sure why this was. He told Trudy that Dr. Campbell had said the children were extremely small for their ages, smaller than he'd ever seen in forty-five years of practice, but there were no other signs of malnourishment. And Miles's vocal chords were fine, no polyps or anything. "That's his God-given voice," Dr. Campbell had said. He told Trudy the doctor had asked if the children were aware they would be starting school in a few weeks, and Spec had admitted they were not. And then he told her that Thos was in a deep depression. He could still see the concern on the doctor's face.

"He needs help," the doctor said.

"Okay, fine, but I'll be the one to help him. What should I do?"

The doctor was quiet for a long time.

"I can't tell you that."

"Why are the other children fine?"

"Maybe they are and maybe they aren't. Time will tell."

"What will happen to Thos?"

"We'll have to wait and see," said Dr. Campbell.

They didn't have long to wait.

Trudy was awakened by the crash. "Spec, wake up! Spec!" she hissed, unable to move. "Something's in the hall!" And then she thought the crash might have been part of her dream.

But Spec had heard it too. He was on his feet immediately, stopping to pull a shirt and pants over himself, an act he would often wonder at in the weeks to come. Seconds later he was in the hallway, trying to make sense of the scene before him.

He didn't know where to look first. Glass from the mirror was everywhere, and blood, and there was Thos. Spec's throat closed against a dry swallow.

Miles and Clara appeared, holding hands tightly.

"Is he dead?" asked Miles softly.

"No, no, he'll be okay," said Spec, hoping this was true. A mirror was replaceable, but not Thos. Never Thos.

"What happened?" Thos asked groggily, as if expecting news of anyone but himself.

"You tell me," answered Spec, exulting over the fact that Thos was speaking to him again. He looked at the cuts that covered Thos's arms and legs, but they were deepest on his chest.

"I don't know. I must have been walking in my sleep. I thought I saw the river behind our house in Hardwick, and it looked beautiful, the way it used to. And then—and then—I jumped in, like always." Tears coursed down his cheeks, but he made no weeping sounds.

"Oh, Thos," whispered Clara. "You're right. It was so beautiful."

"What's going on?" called Trudy from the doorway.

"Thos tried to go swimming. In the mirror."

"Just what we need," she muttered. "Seven years of bad luck." She turned and went back into the room, hoping no one had heard her.

Spec caressed Thos's face and quietly thanked God that it had been spared. He knew there would be scars all over his chest for the rest of his life, but not on his perfect face.

"What do you say, Thos? Should we get this taken care of over at the hospital? You tell me."

Thos inhaled in a series of short breaths, as if breathing was painful. "Yeah. Yeah, I guess we better." He made no attempt to rise. "Thanks, Spec."

Spec gathered up the slender, naked figure, lighter even than Spec would have dreamed. He wrapped the boy in the down sleeping bag that had lived in all his pickups, and he knew this was its last duty. It would be soaked with blood by the time they got to the hospital.

———

Trudy and the children were waiting in the late-day sun when they drove up. Spec carried Thos inside and laid him carefully on his bunk bed. The boy wore a white hospital gown over the layers of gauze thickening his girth.

The chest wounds had required a great many stitches.

"Gee," said Trudy, poking her head into the bedroom, "I guess we're keeping you in stitches!" She waited for Thos to say something, but he didn't. "See," she added, "that's a way of saying you're laughing." She knew her smile was too bright and she let it fade.

"Oh," said Thos politely. "Thank you. I didn't know that."

Trudy walked into the room and set a dish of ice cream on the nightstand. A cookie, poked into the center, stood at attention. She tried to think of something to sustain the conversation, although she didn't particularly want to stand there talking to Thos.

"Did you ever have stitches before?" she asked.

"One time, I—Miles and I—see, there was a flood, and we—" For a minute he seemed unable to go on, then said simply, "Yeah, once. I did once."

Thos would have to be kept quiet for a while, the emergency room doctor said, and Spec knew this would not be difficult. He would talk to Miles and Clara, explain about Thos. As it turned out, without any prompting from Spec they elected to stay quiet with their brother. There was no mention of bikes or beach, and the children spent long hours imagining what it would be like when they returned to Hardwick.

It wasn't easy to get Thos alone, but Spec managed it a few days later. Thos was propped up on the bottom bunk, and Spec, hunched forward, sat on the edge of it.

"So," he began, not at all sure where this was going, "what was with the human cannonball act?" He glanced at Thos, whose T-shirt had ridden up slightly, revealing the dressing.

Thos looked at him, confused. Spec began again.

"Why the swan dive into the mirror?"

The words were more blunt than he had intended, and he wished he could call them back.

Thos forced himself into a sitting position.

"I was asleep! I didn't do it on purpose! I told you! I thought it was the river!" His voice was high and strained.

"Sure, sure, I know that," said Spec kindly, pushing up his sleeves in an effort to cool off. Thos settled back uncertainly against the pillow.

Spec was uncomfortable in the role of therapist to begin with and had a sinking feeling that he was going about this all wrong. Better than nothing, though, he said to himself. The kid sure as hell isn't going to any bullshit so-called professional who gets paid good money to fake an interest in people.

He tried again. "Look, you were asleep, but something inside you made you get up, walk into the hall, look in a mirror and think it was a river, and then try to swim in it. I thought maybe we could figure out together what that something was."

He was having trouble keeping his voice even.

Thos was looking at his bent knees, bare below his shorts. Spec, watching him, was aware of how thin Thos's ankles were. He could picture himself touching a thumb and middle finger around each one.

Spec took a deep breath and blew it out through his mouth like cigarette smoke from his long-ago habit.

"How about we both give this a little thought and talk about it another time," he said, more a statement than a question. He got up slowly and walked to the door.

"Sometimes I feel like all inside me it's black," said Thos in a voice so low Spec wasn't sure he'd really heard it. He turned and walked back to the bed.

"If you cut open my head, it would be all black. Inside my neck and my chest and my stomach and my arms and my legs and my fingers and my toes is black, black, black. Black."

The words pierced Spec. Thos was still looking at his knees.

Spec nearly let himself put his arms around Thos, draw him close, and tell him that he, too, felt black inside sometimes, less often now than he used to. Instead he forced his hands deeper into the pockets of his jeans and sat down again on the bed. He cleared his throat and tried to speak, then cleared it once more before he was able to say, "Yeah, I know. I know about the black."

"Thank you for coming, Mr. Davis," began Miss Marie Conover, principal of Branford Regional School, before Spec had fully settled himself in the chair across from her desk. She made it sound as if he had come at her request, when in fact it was he who had asked for this appointment to discuss the children before school opened, a follow-up to the letter he had sent her.

He was anxious to look around, see if a principal's office had changed since he was in school, but Miss Conover obviously put a great deal of stock in eye contact, and he was afraid to look away. She sat forward in her seat, back perfectly straight, and Spec didn't know why she bothered with an upholstered desk chair when a wooden stool would have served the purpose. He took in the plain, faintly disapproving face, no makeup, no effort to hide the years, which bespoke a vintage that explained "Miss" instead of "Ms." Except that she wore a suit and blouse, she reminded Spec of his mother. He wondered if he should have borrowed a tie and jacket.

She reached for a tissue, and Spec took that brief opportunity to glance around. He could see that the desktop was devoid of anything not deemed absolutely necessary. Next to Miss Conover's carefully folded hands were a black telephone, a jar of newly-sharpened pencils, and a pad of white paper neatly aligned with the edge of the desk. A calendar for the month lay in front of Miss Conover like an oversized placemat.

"As I am sure you are aware," she said, her eyes again meeting his, "we are a K-12 school . . . ." Spec let his mind, if not his eyes, wander as she went through her set speech. K-12, said Spec to himself, that must be—kindergarten through twelfth grade! Jesus, of all people you'd think these guys would speak English.

At some point it occurred to Spec that Miss Conover didn't use contractions and that she had a fondness for '60s slang. The slang, an attempt to be cool that backfired repeatedly, froze her in time, and Spec realized that, if she had been using slang back in the '60s, she was considerably younger than she looked, a member of his own generation. Because she refused to use contractions, her conversation was stilted in a way that, Spec was pretty sure, would be off-putting for kids.

"I want to tell it like it is," she was saying in her broad Massachusetts accent, and talked candidly about the biases and prejudices of the local people, and why it might be a while before the other children accepted Miles, Thos and Clara. She described the school population as "a mixed bag," and said later, "But after all, a school is where it is at."

'Where it is at'? Spec almost laughed out loud. She couldn't make one small-but-essential exception to her anal-retentive refusal to use contractions?

She explained that his children, because they could read ("though not on grade level, I expect"), would be placed in the fifth, sixth and seventh grades, as would any other ten-, eleven- and twelve-year-old. "They will then be tested and provided with remediation as necessary. Their teachers have been made aware of the situation." She paused briefly. "Under the circumstances, I am taking it upon myself to waive the paperwork that we normally require of those entering school for the first time." Miss Conover smiled demurely. "I thought it was the very least I could do."

Wow, thought Spec. I'll bet she's proud to call herself an "educator."

She sounded to him like a stewardess, emphasizing the unexpected word so that he found it hard to focus on what she was saying.

"Now let me be clear. They lived *with* their father after their mother—died." She added this last word delicately. "They did not *go* to school." Soft drinks *are* available, he imagined her saying, then blinked and shook his head slightly.

"No? I am incorrect?"

"No, no, sorry, that's right, that's absolutely right. Listen, I have a question."

"Yes, go on."

"See, I haven't exactly told the kids they're going to school, and I was wondering how to . . ." Spec stopped when Miss Conover raised her eyebrows.

"Am I to understand you have not yet advised these children that they will be attending school? Which commences, I might add, in precisely eleven days, the third Monday of September?" Even from his upside-down vantage point, Spec could see the date clearly marked on the desk calendar.

He was back in another principal's office, and he could hear Miss Dewey saying, in the accusing manner he had come to despise, "Am I to understand you have been tardy every day this week?" Tardy. He really hated the word tardy. Besides, why the question? She had the facts. He'd have detention.

"May I ask why you have chosen to delay until this late date, Mr. Davis?"

"F." She had given him an "F." He stood up. "Thank you, Miss Conover. Thank you for seeing me."

She, too, stood up. She offered him her hand and a strained smile. "I strongly suggest you bring the children in one day next week, prior to the opening of school. You might wish to tour the building with them, and I should like to meet them."

She tucked a stray bit of hair into its hairpin. She appeared to have something else to say.

"Thank you for coming, Mr. Davis," she said at last, and he left, wondering if she always began and ended meetings this way.

CHAPTER TWENTY-THREE

Spec followed Miss Conover's suggestion and drove the children over to mainland Branford Regional a week later, explaining that this time he was giving them VIP treatment, but that they would be taking the bus when school started. As it turned out, the children had known all along they'd be attending school. They just didn't know when during the year it was "held," as they put it.

Spec parked the pickup in the nearly empty parking lot and they walked to the Lower School entrance, located at the rear of the old stone building. Clara sprinted ahead but found she needed help opening the doors, and Spec thought of the double doors at Philly High, a subject of much joking. You went through them hundreds of times, maybe thousands, and every single time you'd push the door on the right before you'd remember it was locked and that you had to use the one on the left.

The children followed Spec soundlessly down the deserted, classroom-lined hallway that led to the principal's office. Teachers had been readying their rooms, he noticed, and "Welcome Back, Students" signs had been tacked to the walls along the hallway next to other, permanent, ones that read "NO RUNNING IN THE HALLS!" and "SH-H-H! LESS NOISE, PLEASE!" Everywhere was the familiar smell of paste mingled with pine-scented disinfectant, and a wave of sadness he couldn't understand came over Spec.

They passed a lighted display case that he figured had been there since the building opened, probably more than fifty years earlier. A faded sign in spidery script read "Birds of Prey," and was positioned above the assortment of glass-eyed stuffed owls, eagles, falcons and hawks perched on branches. The birds, protected by their glass enclosure, had nevertheless managed to accumulate a fair amount of dust, Spec observed. They also looked damn scary for an elementary school display. He peered at the hawk and wondered if this was what Davis's hawk had looked like.

Across from the principal's office, a low table held a number of propped-open library books that stood straight and tall and proud, the librarian's signal to passing children that young readers would surely be as straight and tall and proud as these books.

Biographies were featured: Henry Ford, Eleanor Roosevelt, Thomas Edison, Amelia Earhart, for every male there was a female; no one could say she, Agnes Merriman, was behind the times. Soon the biographies would be replaced by stories of Halloween, then Thanksgiving, Christmas (the one true December holiday), then a lull when Mrs. Merriman's ingenuity was truly taxed until, mercifully, Valentine's Day and the presidents' birthdays again gave her something to work with.

Spec thought of his elementary school librarian, who kept a supply of bright yellow bookmarks on her desk that were printed with a poem Spec still remembered:

> Books are guides to lands of pleasure,
> Books are keys to wisdom's treasure,
> Books are paths that upward lead,
> Books are friends! Come, let us READ!

The principal was not in, and Spec, more than a little relieved, left word with her secretary that he and the children had stopped by to have a look around. The secretary, who prided herself on her ability to judge children's ages, made a mental note to check the files on these three. She was quite certain that Marie had told her fifth, sixth and seventh, but that wasn't possible. There had to be a mistake someplace. Good looking, though, she'd give them that. Especially the boy, the thin one. Beautiful, really. And eyes to knock you out.

Spec and the children wandered through the Lower School wing looking like a little marching band. Spec led the way, and Miles, Thos and Clara, three abreast, followed him. They did not, however, follow him into any of the rooms, but preferred to watch from the doorway and listen to his improvised tour-guide chatter, which was facilitated by the hand-lettered signs posted at each door: "Mrs. Bradley's Third Grade," "Mrs. Dixon's Fourth Grade." Not a guy in the bunch, thought Spec. "Learning Center." What the hell was *that*? Isn't the whole goddamned place supposed to be a learning center? And the "All-Purpose Room/Cafetorium." Cafetorium? He almost gagged. Christ almighty, some genius combined cafeteria and auditorium to make a new word.

He said none of this aloud, merely explained that, when he went to school, there were different rooms for everything. There was even a nature room, and a nature teacher who liked to demonstrate his ability to eat live red ants by biting off their heads. The children said they hoped they would have a teacher like that.

Miles and Thos were not looking forward to giving up their freedom, but Clara was getting bored following the same routine every day. Even the business of using lobster traps to lure the tourists was becoming old hat.

Now, besides the change she was looking forward to, Clara was secretly anticipating having friends her own age to play with. The kids on TV were always bringing other kids home from school and having a great time, and she wanted that, too.

The closest she'd come was earlier in the summer, when she was approached on the beach by a girl whose family had chosen Quarter Harbor rather than Fair Haven to moor their yacht for a couple of days. She was seven years old and, being the same size as Clara, assumed Clara, too, was seven. After she introduced herself, she began to describe her yacht.

"We have a little kitchen where my mom makes bouillabaisse and stuff, and we have this really neat TV that gets pretty good reception, but not as good as in Newport, and my mom and dad have this big double bed, and my bed gets made out of the upholstered benches in the living area. We have this little flag with a martini glass on it that my dad hoists at cocktail time, and then he and my mom sit out on these chairs that swivel all around, and you use them when you fish. I like to play on them and pretend I'm at an amusement park. Usually I do that with Jody, he's my brother, but this year he went to summer camp, so it's only me. I kind of miss him, but I get more room and he doesn't bother my stuff. Want to come see?"

Clara reported that evening, "She has this head that she can put makeup on? And do the hair?" Trudy was about to breathe a contented sigh, when Clara added, "Can you imagine anything so stupid?"

And so it was that she approached the first day of school with more excitement than trepidation. Meanwhile, the boys treated each day as if it were just one more in summer's never-ending stream.

On that first day of school, Trudy got up early and made a batch of pancakes, but Clara was too excited to eat, and Miles and Thos said they weren't hungry.

Spec and Trudy watched from the front doorway as the children waited for the school bus, holding the lunch boxes Spec had bought for them and packed with their favorite sandwiches.

"I used to spend ages planning what I would wear the first day," Trudy said. "Doesn't look like it's a problem for these kids, does it?"

Indeed, when the children had come into the kitchen that morning, dressed in the same shorts and T-shirts they'd worn for the last few days, she had outright lied to them, said it was a school rule that you wear clean clothes, especially the first day. For his part, Spec was silently hoping no one would make fun of the casualness with which they had obviously dressed. He was relieved there was no outward hint of the thin dressing Thos wore under his T-shirt and jeans. The wounds were healing well, Dr. Campbell had said, but warned that the angry marks on his slight chest, which appeared to have been raked by a gigantic claw, would not fade for a long time.

As soon as the bus was in sight, Trudy went back to bed, but Spec waited while the children climbed on. Then he watched, a lump in his throat, until the bus disappeared, leaving a lengthening cloud from the dusty road between him and the children.

"How come we're the only kids on the bus?" said Clara in a hushed voice, when they were safely past the driver's hearty greeting.

"We're the first stop. It'll be okay," said Miles, who was disappointed that their "bus" was really a van. He had pictured a load of rowdy kids, laughing and shouting and tossing their lunch boxes back and forth. Instead here they were, the three of them in one seat.

There were two more stops in Quarter Harbor and none at all in Fair Haven. At the first, three boys waited, smoking cigarettes. They started up the steps.

"Okay, okay, hold on there," said the driver. "You guys know darn well you can't bring those things on the bus."

"Bus? You call this a bus?" said the tallest of the three, even as he made a big show of dropping the butt on the ground and grinding it out with his heel. His companions mirrored his actions after a split-second delay. Then they boarded, looking at each other and snickering, winners always. They scuffed their shoes as they walked to the back. The tall boy loudly tapped a pencil on the metal edges of the seat backs. The three sat down in unison with enough force to rock the van.

The driver consulted a clipboard. "Says here there's supposed to be a girl at this stop."

The leader of the pack spoke again. "Yeah, my sister. She's not coming to school. Got herself knocked up and says she's never leaving the house again." He laughed crudely.

As if by common consent, the children did not turn around to look at him.

At the last stop, two little girls climbed on. Their mothers helped them up the first step, handed them their lunch boxes, and waved good-bye as the bus pulled away and continued down the street.

They look like the little kids in Sally Bea's Sears catalogue, said Miles to himself, as they nestled into the seat across from him with their heads together, whispering earnestly. Miles did not take his eyes off of them, but they appeared not to notice.

Twenty minutes later theirs was one of several buses arriving at school, and then the children were off the bus and enveloped in a confusion of shouted greetings and instructions as teachers' aides directed students to the proper classrooms.

Clara was excited, Miles was resigned, Thos was terrified. He watched his sister and brother go down different hallways, both turning back and waving at him.

"Good luck!" called Clara. "You'll be fine!"

But Thos didn't think he would ever be fine. He was surrounded by people he didn't know, who didn't know him. He wanted to vanish. He thought that might be possible. He saw a magician make a woman vanish on TV.

Except for the trips to Philadelphia when Davis wouldn't let them all go at once, it was the first time in their entire lives that they had been separated.

That evening Spec was reminded of the story of the blind men and the elephant, each of whom had touched a different part of the animal and therefore had his own version of what it looked like.

Clara already had an invitation to a birthday party that was to be held the following week. She referred to "my friends," as if she had known her classmates for years, and, laughing, told of how they took turns picking her up, carrying her around, and calling her their mascot.

"I'm the smallest in the whole, entire class? So I get to be the very first in line, *all the time?* It's really neat!"

Slowly Spec let out a relieved breath. His heart lifted with the upward turn of her voice, and all at once he understood why she spoke that way. He knew how tentative she felt in a confusing world, how a nod or murmur of affirmation meant everything to her.

As far as Spec could tell, Thos hadn't said one word at school. "Nobody to talk to," he mumbled.

"Did you talk to the teacher?" asked Trudy, who had come into the kitchen, where the others had gathered.

"No, was I supposed to?" Thos asked in dismay. Then, "She gave us homework. I think I better go do it now." He started for his room.

"What kind of homework?" asked Spec.

"We have to read something. American History. Anyway, I know all that stuff. Washington, Adams, Jefferson, Madison, Monroe. He made us memorize all of them, when they served, who their vice presidents were and their cabinets and everything."

He went into the room he shared with Miles, shutting the door quietly behind him, and Spec knew that Thos had spent the day missing Miles and Clara.

"Who was Monroe's vice president?" Spec asked.

"Daniel Tompkins!" Clara rushed to answer first.

"How about his secretary of state?" This time Spec looked at Miles.

"John Quincy Adams," he said, without hesitation.

Spec knew he'd gone far enough already, probably too far, but he couldn't seem to stop himself.

"Who was Millard Fillmore's vice president?"

"Trick question! Trick question!" crowed Clara. "Millard Fillmore was Zachary Taylor's vice president? And when President Taylor died, he became president? He has the best name of all the presidents." She chanted it several times: "Millard Fillmore, Millard Fillmore, Millard Fillmore," and added, "I know *his* secretary of state. Daniel Webster!"

"But not for the whole term," interjected Miles. "Remember, C? Halfway through, Edward Everett came in."

Edward Everett? Jesus Christ, who in hell was Edward Everett? Spec felt a certain discomfort and a strong desire to change the subject. He asked Miles what he'd thought of his first day at school.

"I tried to make friends, but it didn't work out so well, not like it did for C. I did everything I could think of. I shook hands and introduced myself, told jokes, did cartwheels down the corridor, but nothing worked. And they made fun of my voice."

Spec thought of his own seventh grade year. He was one of the lucky ones, tall already and starting to fill out, so he was accepted, because that was the standard. How you looked. He hadn't yet hit what he came to think of as his "outsider" period.

And here was Miles, tiny Miles. Spec could still see little Bobby Lewis, standing on tiptoe at the edge of the group talking in the hall, making the supreme effort to fit in. But he didn't, of course. Never did, in fact, and Spec found himself wondering what had become of him. Probably a CEO now, million bucks a year, knockout wife, Porsche convertible, weekend place in the country. Hell, said Spec to himself, whatever the guy's got, he deserves it.

CHAPTER TWENTY - FOUR

Spec's second visit with Marie Conover was at her suggestion. "Would you be good enough to come around to see me? Perhaps next Tuesday, after the close of the school day?" was how she'd put it when she'd called, sounding to Spec like some elderly, bedridden aunt who had watched "Masterpiece Theatre" once too often. He took it for what it was, not a legitimate question but a command performance, and he made an appointment with her secretary, who came on the line.

Had Trudy shown any interest at all he would have asked her to go along, but she seemed preoccupied lately and made it clear that the children were his family and therefore his responsibility.

"I have enough to deal with," she said, a statement that stunned him, since she did little these days but sleep and go to work. She had stopped even the pretense of cooking, leaving Spec to cope with getting food into the house and onto the table. "Don't worry about me. I'll pick up something at the tavern," was her standard reply when he invited her, begged her, to join them for a meal.

Things were changing, no question about that. On the infrequent occasions when they made love, Spec's mind drifted to Dr. Campbell's wife, and he was saved from calling her name by the fact that he hadn't the slightest idea what it was.

Once again, then, Spec found himself in the principal's office.

"I feel it is time for a three-month assessment," began Miss Conover, the formalities over. Spec saw that she'd colored her hair and changed the style to one that featured the kind of finger waves popular decades before. Her blouse, peeping out from the pink wool suit, was frillier than the severe one she'd worn last time. He wondered if she was having an affair. He glanced down at his worn work boots and blue jeans, at his faded plaid flannel shirt, and smiled at the contrast.

"The children's teachers have told me that you stop by their classrooms on an informal basis, in order to have a word with them about the children," she was saying. "Naturally, teachers appreciate this sort of parental, well, this sort of interest a great deal. I thought perhaps you might tell me the kind of progress you feel the children are making."

"Actually," said Spec, and coughed, "actually, I'd feel better if *you'd* tell *me* how they're doing. That's from your point of view, naturally." He was aware that he was using as many contractions as possible in an effort to see if he could get her to slip.

"Yes. Well, overall I feel they are quite remarkable, considering they are presently experiencing formal education for the first time. They are anxious to learn, which is, of course, pleasing as well as rewarding to our teachers. All three children have fine problem-solving skills, which have facilitated rapid improvement in their mathematics proficiency."

It appeared to Spec that Miss Conover was reciting a report from memory.

"Mathematics comes less easily to Thomas. They have a sound foundation in the sciences, no doubt attributable to their father and his professional interests. The girl, Clara, shows genuine artistic promise.

Her drawings are—but I am certain this is not unfamiliar to you, Mr. Davis."

Spec nodded, thinking of Clara's drawings that he had taped to the refrigerator door.

"The children use the spoken language well. Their writing skills, however, continue to need remediation, and tutoring will remain a feature of their school day."

Spec thought now of the curiosity that played a definite if unacknowledged role; so many teachers had volunteered to tutor the children. Small town gossip had come his way, and he knew they were referred to as "the little savages" until school opened and the term turned out to be entirely inappropriate. He knew, too, there were some townspeople who were disappointed that such was the case.

"The children are extremely polite," Miss Conover was saying. "I do not mind telling you that I was initially quite apprehensive, thinking that, given their unusual background, they would be completely lacking in self-discipline, that they would be running in the corridors, shouting, perhaps, and generally disrupting the life of the school. None of this, happily, came to pass. The children have come to us equipped with respect for others. In addition, they care for one another in a way I have never seen before, not in my twen—" she stumbled "—not in all the years I have been in this school." She was flushed, Spec noted, and he realized that she'd gotten herself dressed up for him. Sorry, lady, you're not my type, he thought.

"Miles has taken it upon himself to meet with Thomas's and Clara's teachers from time to time for the express purpose of reviewing the progress being made by his brother and sister. He wishes to be certain they are keeping to a high standard, and he is quite serious about this.

I assure you, Mr. Davis, I find that very impressive, very impressive indeed.

"As to their physical education, Miles and Clara are gifted athletes, and will, in all probability, have numerous opportunities to represent the school in athletic events. Thomas is not so blessed, but he is willing to work extremely hard, and that is commendable.

"They have not as yet chosen to avail themselves of the many opportunities for extracurricular participation, but perhaps a desire to do so will come in due course. At this time, they apparently prefer to return to the 'haven of home'"—she smiled quickly—"once the school day has drawn to a close.

"Nonetheless, as must by now be obvious, the children are faring extraordinarily well. What is more, it seems to have been something of a relief to them to know precisely what is expected of them, to be in a highly structured environment in which goals are set, tasks are performed, goals are met."

Spec thought the sentiment was probably embroidered on a pillow in her living room.

He noticed that Miss Conover was now hesitating, as if she'd forgotten the next line. He waited, enjoying her momentary discomfort. And then she abandoned her script altogether.

"I would be remiss if I did not voice some concern about their social skills. To be precise, they have none, none at all. As for Clara, Mr. Davis, to put it bluntly, she will do anything to make the other children like her. It has come to my attention that she lets them undress her and examine her—her—her body. One of our teachers witnessed such an episode, and later, when she confronted Clara, the child denied it so vehemently that Miss Matthews began to doubt her own eyes. But there have since been other reports, and I have no reason to question their veracity."

Spec felt he was suffocating. He wanted to hold up his hand, call a halt, but he couldn't move, and Miss Conover went on, relentlessly.

"Miles, too, is extremely anxious to be liked by his classmates. I understand he frequently talks about a former girlfriend. Winnie, I think was her name? Perhaps this is an effort to be accepted. Unfortunately, he is perceived as something of a buffoon by the other children. It is a shame, really. He is a nice boy, a kind boy, and he has all the best intentions, but he prances about and makes animal sounds in order to draw attention to himself, and in the process, he drives the other children away. I know. I have seen it for myself."

In her clear-eyed manner, Miss Conover had been looking steadily, unwaveringly at Spec, and he thought surely she could see his discomfort, but she scarcely paused in giving her report. He could stand it no longer.

"Excuse me, Miss Conover, but may I have a glass of water? Please?" His heart was beating furiously and his head was pounding.

Miss Conover, clever, perceptive Miss Conover, did not see this for the ploy that it was. She merely nodded absently and rang her secretary, asked her to fetch a glass of water, and continued to speak, not pausing while the door opened, while the water was delivered, while Spec whispered his thanks.

"It is of Thomas, however, that I wish to speak," she declared, and Spec understood that this was the big one, the one she'd been saving up for.

"I do not know how much you have observed, Mr. Davis, but our teachers are trained to observe, and observe they do."

Okay, okay, enough about observing, Spec wanted to shout. Let's get going and get it over with, for Christ's sake!

"What they, and I, have observed is that Thomas, unlike his brother and sister, has no interest in making friends. Indeed, he keeps entirely to himself, and does not interact at all with his classmates. Perhaps you are already aware of this, Mr. Davis, but on the second day of school, Thomas walked out of the classroom, sat down on the front steps outside the building, and refused to return. I was summoned. It seems that Thomas's class had been reprimanded for not completing the homework assignment, and Thomas was confused and upset at being chided when he had, in fact, fulfilled his obligation. It developed that he did not understand the concept of a teacher speaking to an entire class, rather than to him as an individual. In his experience, whenever he has heard the voice of an authority figure, that voice has always been speaking to him."

That figured, thought Spec. Davis was the voice of authority if ever there was one, and he would've spoken to the kids together, as if they were one person. But Spec was far more concerned about the fact that he hadn't known any of this. He remembered the first day of school, when Thos came home and went into his room to do his homework. It had become a pattern, and Thos's diligence, far from worrying Spec, had impressed him. Sure, he had asked the boy about friends, but Thos had replied that he had no time for them, he was too busy, he had too much homework, and Spec admired him and let it go at that. The boy never reported anything, certainly not anything like Miss Conover was describing. It crossed his mind that she was making all of this up, about all of them, maybe writing a psychology book and wanted to see how he would react. Jesus, if only that were true.

Miss Conover was saying, "None of this about Thomas would in itself necessarily be worrisome, but there is something else."

She waited a moment, apparently to collect her thoughts, and this time it was Spec who silently urged her on. He was under the impression there was a great deal more to come, but she said simply, "Have you ever really *watched* Thomas, Mr. Davis? Have you looked into his eyes? Do so, please. I implore you."

And that was it. Miss Conover stood up, Spec did likewise, she thanked him for coming, and class was dismissed.

When Spec left the house for his late-day meeting with Miss Conover, the children were busy with their homework. In the disappearing gray half-light of the mid-December afternoon, Miles and Thos were on their beds as usual, and Clara sat on the floor, leaning against Thos's bunk. They talked quietly to each other as they worked, and their low, steady conversation was a familiar and comforting background hum that enhanced rather than hindered their concentration. They talked of Eldon and the Yummycakes that were coming less often now; of Uncle Stuart's most recent postcard in which he said he missed them and wished he could see them, but London was too far away for that; and of Hardwick, and their plans to return one day.

When by mutual agreement they closed their books, Miles climbed down to join Thos and Clara, and the three stretched out on the floor, hands behind their heads. Their feet were bare, and they wore the T-shirts and shorts they put on each day after school, whatever the weather. They could have been lying in a Hardwick meadow on a summer afternoon, watching the clouds. No one said anything for a long time.

Then Thos, his voice scarcely audible, said, "I have dreams that take place in that house. I dream that I'm—that I'm—screaming. Screaming and screaming and I don't know why, but so loud it seems like my throat hurts, and it wakes me up. The bed is all wet and cold and it smells and I feel like a baby and I hide the sheets and wash them when nobody's home. And I'm so sure I was screaming that when I look over at you, Miles, I don't know why I didn't wake you, it's so, so real. You know?" he finished weakly. Then he began to shiver, violently, as though the room had grown much colder.

"It's okay," said Clara softly, putting her slight arm around his shoulders. "Everything will be okay. Don't worry."

But Thos continued to shake and his teeth began to chatter. Miles pulled the blanket off his bed and wrapped it around his brother. As the children sat huddled in a circle, Miles and Clara each slipped an arm around Thos. He would have looked, to someone entering the room, like a tiny tribal chieftain, and they sat in silence until Thos gradually calmed down. Miles and Clara released their hold on him, and as they watched he began to sway, slowly at first, then faster and faster, and a hoarse wail issued from deep within him. His wailing defeated their calming words, and Spec could hear it from the driveway as he pulled up in his truck. When he entered the room, Miles and Clara watched in silence as Spec gathered Thos and the blanket in his arms and sank to the floor, rocking him and weeping.

Trudy returned from the tavern that night to find Spec and the children asleep on the floor of the boys' room. They were leaving her behind, the four of them. She didn't know how to follow them to this place they were going. They were a family, and she wasn't part of it. She should have been happy. From the beginning she hadn't wanted to be part of a family, but that wasn't true anymore. She wanted desperately to be one of them, but she wasn't, and she never would be. She went to bed, and when she awoke the next morning, Spec had already left for work, and the children for school.

Trudy stood before the hall mirror and gazed at herself. Her hair was growing in, but it would be some time before it was long and smooth and even again. Lines were beginning to crease her forehead, and her eyes had long since lost their shine. She looked pale, fragile, old. And sad.

House painting has a lot in common with fishing, thought Spec as he primed a window, feeling the weak, winter sun warm on his back. You've got your hands busy and your mind free, maybe too free, he admitted to himself as he reviewed the events of the previous day. Then, as if changing a channel on a television set, switching off a program too distasteful to watch in favor of one more palatable, he found himself thinking about Lydia Campbell.

Lydia. He'd learned her name by following the mail truck to Oak Lane one morning and hastily, furtively, perusing the letters in the box at the curb, most of which were addressed to Dr. and Mrs. Dean Campbell, or simply to Dean Campbell, M.D. Then he saw the pale green envelope with the elegant script, from her mother, Spec had figured, or maybe her grandmother, and there it was: "Lydia B. Campbell." He considered what the initial might stand for and compiled a list in his mind, from Baldwin to Bennett to Brown, from Black to Booth to Butler. Nothing fancy. That wouldn't suit her somehow. He'd tried each one out, exploring the sound of it and imagining her introducing herself to him. The day would be breezy, he thought, warm, and he saw her approach in a pale green silk dress, long and blowing against the curves of her body. Her dark hair was piled on top of her head, but pieces escaped from their fastener and played around her face. "Lydia Bond Campbell," he could hear her say, as she extended her hand and smiled slightly. Her voice was low, a natural invitation to him to incline his head toward hers, and he thought he could smell her dark red lipstick. He wondered if lipstick ever had any smell.

The following day, as soon as the children left for school, Spec went to the diner for breakfast and used the pay phone to call his boss and say he wouldn't be in today.

When he parked across the street from the Oak Lane house, it was still early and quite cold, but he was afraid if he kept the motor running it would attract attention. He sipped coffee from a cardboard cup, wishing he'd worn his heavy jacket instead of the windbreaker he had grabbed on the way out of the house. He tried to read the newspaper but couldn't concentrate, so for a while he listened to '50s music on the radio. Then he started to worry that he would run down the battery, and so he sat unmoving in the cold, quiet cab of the truck, breathing warmth onto his hands.

All morning he watched as cars pulled up outside the doctor's office and mothers extracted small children from them, then held their hands and led the way inside. Some of the children cried when they went in, others when they came out, he noted idly.

He was wishing he'd brought along something to eat and almost missed the small, black sedan backing out of the driveway, but finally there she was, Lydia Campbell, and Spec Davis turned on the ignition and pulled out several car lengths behind her. He followed her for about fifteen minutes, keeping a discreet distance, fairly certain she didn't realize she was being followed. For the first time Spec allowed himself to think what he would say when he confronted her, and tried to decide whether it was best to pretend they happened to run into each other, wherever it might be that she was headed at this moment, or whether he should simply confess the extent to which she was on his mind.

He doubted there would need to be any kind of courtship. He assumed she must be used to this sort of adventure, considering how much older Dr. Campbell was, but for Spec it was a new experience. "Old Faithful," he had dubbed himself for staying faithful to Trudy. Still, the rush of anticipation was familiar somehow, and then he remembered his drinking days, and the anticipation he'd felt every rainy morning all summer. It seemed very long ago that he'd savored the prospect of going to the movies on rainy afternoons, where he would drink and doze into the evening, until the theater closed and he had to leave.

Spec now realized he had simply assumed Lydia would be on her way to a public place like the supermarket, maybe, or the dry cleaner. He never considered the possibility that she would be going to visit someone, but they were driving through a neighborhood of large, stone houses. The street lamps were graceful, wrought iron posts that supported elegant glass spheres. The streets were wide, the lawns were well tended, the trees were immense. And here she was, pulling up in front of one of these imposing dwellings. He was about to get out and catch up with her, speak to her, but something held him back. He watched as she emerged from her car, wrapping her black, fur-trimmed coat tightly around her, and walked up the path to the front door. Someone was expecting her, because the door opened before she'd had a chance to raise the polished brass knocker, and Spec saw a tall, dark-haired man smile as he let her in. He was wearing a bathrobe.

Spec was shivering, not from the cold, he knew, because the engine was still running and the cab was warm. Don't jump to conclusions, he told himself. It could be legitimate. She didn't try to hide her car, did she? Maybe she's a physical therapist, maybe she's delivering something for the doctor, maybe she's here to see the guy's wife. He was to make a hundred such excuses for her but he never attempted to see her again, and that night, when he made love to Trudy, he was thinking of Lydia.

CHAPTER TWENTY - FIVE

It had been a long time since Spec had wanted a drink that badly. He'd driven away from the house into which Lydia Campbell had disappeared and gone directly to the tavern. The place was practically empty, with a few patrons sitting by themselves. Sam looked up from the glasses he was drying.

"Hey, Spec! Good to see you, buddy! Been a long time. Too damn long, matter of fact! How's it going? Everything okay? You look beat. Trudy's in the back. I'll get her," he said in his rapid-fire manner, and snapped the dishtowel smartly before flipping it over his shoulder.

"Actually, Sam, I'm here for a drink."

Spec slid wearily onto a stool. Sam, already on his way to get Trudy, turned to look at him.

"Spec? Aw, come on, guy. You sure you want to do this?"

"Do what? What? Something the matter with my money? Give me a Wild Turkey."

Sam glanced at the door that led to the back room, as if willing Trudy to walk in and rescue him.

"Sam? How about it?" Spec was drumming his fingers.

"You're the boss, Mr. Davis," sighed Sam finally as he poured the bourbon.

For several minutes Spec looked at the glass. At first he could feel Sam watching him from the end of the bar, but then his mind drifted away and his thoughts grew confused, mingling Tuesday's visit with Miss Conover, Thos's pain, the Lydia Campbell fiasco this morning, and the great sadness that lay beneath everything. Other drinking temptations flitted across his memory, the times when he'd nearly given in, but the horror of coming off it kept him from lapsing. Then it was the thought of Trudy that kept him clean. Today, none of this could dissuade him, and he picked up the glass. He held it to his lips and inhaled the bourbon's fragrance, forcing himself to postpone the delicious, inevitable forgetting.

But now it was the unexpected kaleidoscope of Miles, of Thos, of Clara, of the distress signals they were sending, that appropriated Spec's thoughts. He heard Trudy's voice saying, "They have you." This was out of his hands now, he knew, not his choice anymore, and he pushed the untouched drink away and left the tavern. Sam didn't say anything to Trudy, and she never knew he was there.

Later Spec would wonder if he had seen it coming. Over the last year, since the children arrived, Trudy had begun to look different, harder. Even her hair looked different. Dull.

And then everything broke apart. One night she came home from work and said, "I can't do this, Spec. I'm sorry. I'm not like you. I'm not in the business of saving people. I saved you, and one's my limit."

Then she turned and walked, floated, into the living room, picked up her coat and pocketbook from the couch, and left the house without closing the door. Spec stood watching from the kitchen doorway as the winter wind entered the house. He heard her car pull away.

Over the next weeks Spec tried to find her. Sam knew nothing, and Spec had nobody else to call. If Trudy had any friends, or even acquaintances, he didn't have any idea who they were. He filed a missing person's report with the police.

"Face it, Spec," said his boss. "If there's no foul play, the police lose interest real fast. She knew what she was doing. She walked out, plain and simple. If she wants to stay gone, she'll stay gone, and you'll never find her. Let her go, guy."

He patted Spec's shoulder, and then patted it again.

Trudy had disappeared. She never returned to Kings Island, never sent for her things. Spec realized only now that he didn't even have a picture of her. Sometimes he believed she had never existed at all.

The children had heard everything, of course. Although Trudy's leaving was of no real concern to them, they worried how Spec would take it, but as it turned out, if indeed he was upset, he hid the fact from the children. Then one day the four of them, roughhousing together, fell laughing on Spec's bed, and the children saw that the closet had been emptied of her clothes. The wire hangers hung lifeless, separate and still. Miles, Thos and Clara pretended not to have noticed, and Spec pretended along with them.

When Spec had stopped fishing, he'd willed himself to stop thinking about it, but lately he found himself thinking about it a great deal.

"You know," he said to the children one evening as they sat once again at the great dining table that dwarfed them all, eating a supper of canned spaghetti and meatballs flanked by salad and rolls, "if you sat down and told somebody that you're going someplace far from home, no telephones or anything, and you're going to spend all your time with one or two other guys, not talking, 'cause the less talk there is on a boat, the more money you can make, and you're going to be drenched, working maybe 18 hours a day, and the place where you'll be working is going to be in motion all the time, it's never going to be stable, they'd think you were crazy to do it."

He smiled, and the children smiled back at him. As it happened, his eyes were on Thos, whose glorious, beatific smile was palpable. The boy is truly beautiful, thought Spec. Then, while he was watching, Spec saw the boy's smile fall away and his eyes go dark. They reminded Spec of the deep tea color of the Hardwick River, whose reflection hid everything that lay beneath the surface. He'd never noticed this change before.

Miss Conover's words, which Spec had forgotten until this moment, came rushing back: "Have you ever really *watched* Thomas, Mr. Davis? Have you looked into his eyes? Do so, please. I implore you." Thos was no longer there with the rest of them, Spec knew.

"Thos?" said Spec after a moment, and with an almost imperceptible shudder the boy was back, his smile in place, his eyes shining.

"Tell us some more about fishing, Spec," he said, as if on cue, as if he had prepared the sentence ahead of time, to use in such an eventuality.

And Spec, still seeing those dark, hollow pools in his mind, forced himself back to fishing.

"Well," he began, "did I ever tell you about fishing for hake?"

The children shook their heads.

"It's just the two of us on the boat at that point, Trimble and me. Fishing had been so bad we couldn't afford another guy. I'm running the deck and the winches and dressing the fish and everything. All he's got to do is drive the boat. So we're out there and I get thinking."

The children had stopped eating. They sat motionless, their mouths slightly open, ready to receive the food that was on its way to their mouths, except that their forks were at a standstill. Spec laughed to himself, thinking they looked like characters in a science fiction movie whose movements have been frozen by a ray gun.

"I was thinking about fish prices, and I realize that with hake at nine cents a pound, and we're paying a truck driver twelve cents, why in hell are we bringing them to the wharf? All we're doing is supporting the truck driver. So this thought occurs to me, out in the middle of dressing a bunch of fish, and I just start throwing hake over the side. I take the cod and throw it into the hold. Then I come to the hake and it goes overboard. Well hake, when they come up from depth, they get something like the bends. Their swim bladders blow up because of the change of pressure, and they float when you throw them overboard. They go belly up, see, and they have these great big white bellies. So all this beautiful sunny day, trailing behind the boat are these floating hake, reflecting the sunlight. And Trimble looks out of the wheelhouse for the first time in an hour or something, and he sees this and he comes out and he says, 'DAVIS,' he says, 'WHAT THE HELL ARE YOU DOING?'"

Spec had pitched his voice high and spoke in an exaggerated Massachusetts accent. The children laughed.

"So I gave him a lecture on economics. Told him I was through supporting truck drivers, and if he wanted to cut the hake, he could go ahead and do it, but I'd be goddamned if I was going to."

The children stamped their feet and clapped appreciatively. Spec stood up and took a bow.

He sat down and resumed eating as the cheering subsided. There was a lull, and when Spec spoke again, he seemed to be thinking aloud.

"I got pretty good at walking around the edge of the deck with the boat going up and down in a stiff wind, hauling gear and everything, the same way you'd walk down the street. Didn't even think about it. Somehow you get so you don't have to pay attention to keeping your balance anymore." Then, sensing that he was responsible for the now-somber mood, he forced a chuckle and said, "Guess I would've been a lot more careful if I'd thought about sharks."

A moment passed. Then Clara leaned toward him and said, "Why don't you start fishing again, Spec? If you love it so much and everything?"

Spec stroked her hair. "Oh, kids," he sighed, looking at each in turn. "Now it's too late. 'Life intervenes,' as my mother used to say. Besides, who would stay with you guys? Anyway, it's too unpredictable, money-wise. Working on houses is a whole hell of a lot more reliable, and we can all get by on that. Plus Sam's little 'stipend,' as he likes to call it."

Indeed, Trudy's boss had arranged for a monthly check to be deposited in Spec's bank account, an amount roughly equivalent to what he'd been paying Trudy. He'd never forgiven her for taking off, he said, adding that he could well afford to do it because business was booming. "Nothing like liquor sales. People will cut out everything else before they'll stop buying their booze. May not be society's greatest asset, but it sure is mine!"

It hadn't taken long for the news of Trudy's departure to spread, and soon it had moved from gossip tree to family dinner tables and, finally, to school.

"Heard your mother walked out on you and your dad," taunted one of Thos's classmates during recess. Thos, who was sitting on the step doing the following day's homework, looked up with interest, not because of what the boy was saying, but because people rarely spoke directly to him. Word had it that Thos Davis didn't talk to anybody.

"My mother? She's not my mother," he said now, turning back to his work.

It happened that the boy lived with his father and the latest in a succession of girlfriends, and thought he understood. He felt a momentary bond with Thos, even though his own father, unlike Spec, never came to school. Spec, on the other hand, attended every parent-teacher conference and P.T.A. meeting, plus every sporting event, play, concert, and anything else the school had to offer, sitting in the stands with his children.

"Not so good when they leave your dad in charge, is it?"

Thos looked up a second time. "He's not my dad." Seeing the quizzical expression on the boy's face, he added, "He's my brother."

Thos didn't think there was anyone left in school who did not know this, but he simply dropped the subject. He didn't feel like explaining that yes, you could have a really, really old brother, old enough to be your dad.

That night he told Miles and Clara of the exchange, and the three agreed that "the kids around here don't know shit." And they said again how much smarter the people were back in Hardwick.

—————

Clara's teacher, Mrs. Eldridge, selected with great care the last book she would read aloud before school closed for summer vacation. She wanted to be sure, she told the class, that she would have time to finish it.

"There's nothing worse than starting something you can't finish. It doesn't matter whether it's your dinner, or your homework, or a book. Anything worth starting is worth finishing. You remember that, all right? Someday, when you're all grown up and you start to read a book you decide you don't like, think about what Mrs. Eldridge told you back in the fifth grade, and FINISH IT!"

Clara noticed little beads of sweat had appeared on Mrs. Eldridge's forehead. Apparently the teacher had noticed it too, because she removed her large, black handbag from the bottom drawer of her desk, set it on her lap, and rummaged through it until she found a pink flowered handkerchief, which she used to pat her forehead and mouth. She seemed to be taking extra time to catch her breath.

She laid her handbag back in the drawer and closed it, then opened another and took out a book. She was smiling now.

"The book I will read to you is called *Charlotte's Web*, and it was written by a man named E.B. White. The initials stand for Elwyn Brooks, so you can see why he used E.B."

Mrs. Eldridge sniggered.

Clara had stopped listening when she heard the words "Charlotte's Web," remembering their Charlotte, who had astounded them all by turning mean. Clara could see her now, lying dead in the road. It was more than that, though, more than the name Charlotte. She remembered the book's title, too. Something about the title. But she couldn't quite remember what it was.

———

Clara could hardly wait until story time each day. She loved Fern the girl, she loved Wilbur the pig, and she hoped some day she would meet a spider as smart as Charlotte. While Clara listened, she illustrated the story. Her favorite drawing was of the web, the one in which Charlotte had spun the words "SOME PIG." Every night at dinner Clara showed her pictures and recounted the latest installment to Spec and her brothers, who enjoyed her re-telling.

One evening, while Clara was in the midst of her recitation, Miles stopped eating and turned pale.

"Oh my God," he whispered. "I just thought of something. I don't know why I didn't think of it before."

He didn't say anything for a while. Finally Spec laid his hand lightly on Miles's arm.

"What is it, buddy? What's the matter?"

Miles closed his eyes, as if he had to shut something down in order to be able to talk about what had come alive in his memory.

"A long time ago, before Mama died," he swallowed hard and went on, "one of our father's patients gave us a baby pig."

"Sure, that was Charlotte," said Thos. "Remember when it chased me and he had to shoot it?"

"Sh-h-h," said Clara. "There's something else."

His eyes still closed, Miles continued. "Right when the pig first came to our house, Mama told him we should name it Charlotte. She said when she was a little girl, she read a story about a pig and the book was called *Charlotte's Web*, so we should call this pig Charlotte, too. He said okay."

Spec didn't think he had ever seen so much pain in a face. Thos and Clara, too, had gone white, he saw, though Spec himself still did not get the full import of what Miles was saying.

"Jesus," said Thos. "Jesus Christ. She gave it the wrong name. Charlotte was a spider, not a pig."

Spec still didn't get it, couldn't see what the big deal was.

Miles opened his eyes. "He knew it, too. I know he did, sure as I'm sitting here right now. And he didn't tell her. That would be just like him, to let her make a mistake knowing some day we'd find out and think Mama was stupid or something. Well, we don't. He was wrong. He was the one, not Mama."

Thos and Clara were nodding, nodding, and Spec finally understood everything.

"Got a surprise for you," said Spec to the children, one rainy Saturday afternoon in early spring. They scrambled to their feet, leaving their unfinished game of Monopoly on the kitchen floor.

"A *birthday* surprise?" asked Thos, grinning.

"As a matter of fact . . ."

"I'm going to be twelve!" shouted Clara.

"Thirteen!" chimed in Thos.

"Fourteen for me!" finished Miles.

"As a matter of fact," repeated Spec with a laugh, "it *is* a birthday surprise. See if you can guess what it is. Twenty questions."

The children loved to play Twenty Questions.

"Have we ever done it before?" asked Miles.

"One. Good question, and the answer is No."

"So how do we know what it is? If we've never done it before?" complained Clara.

"Two and three. You'll just have to figure it out!"

This was followed by cries of "Hey, no fair!" "That doesn't count!" "She was just talking! That wasn't part of the game!"

"Okay, okay! You guys are tough! One question so far."

"Is it a place we drive to?" asked Thos.

"Two. Yes, we have to drive there."

"Is it an inside place?" asked Clara.

"Three. Yes, inside."

"Will we be the only people there?" asked Thos.

"Four. No, we won't."

"So there will be other people there?" demanded Clara.

"Five. Yes, there will."

"Time out! Conference!" said Miles, turning to his brother and sister. "C, that was a wasted question. If we aren't the only people there, obviously there are other people. Right?" His voice was kind.

Clara looked contrite.

"It's okay," Thos said, patting her hand. "So what's our strategy?"

CHAPTER TWENTY - SIX

The children's second summer was not as lazy as their first. Spec had informed them they would have to work if they hoped to have spending money, and Jake, who owned a fish store in Quarter Harbor, took them on at Spec's request.

All summer long they cleaned fish, chopped ice, hosed down the floor, tended the display cases, and prepared foods for the freezer. In addition, they sold the colorful hats and T-shirts that bore Jake's logo, a curved swordfish under which were the words "Jake's of Quarter Harbor."

Miles was the only one who could get the hang of opening clams and oysters for the raw bar, so he was put in charge of that. But they all agreed that selling fish was the best, standing on the platform Jake had built behind the counter so the children and the customers could see each other properly. There were plenty of customers, too. The Fair Haven crowd made the trip to Quarter Harbor to buy fish, believing the very freshest fish would be found in the town where the boats came in, and Jake's was the most popular fish store.

Clara offered to make signs advertising the daily specials, and Jake told her to give it a try. He provided her with colored pens and paper, and she, in turn, provided him with fish drawings and lettering so with extra whipped cream and two cherries, while Spec had black coffee.

"I knew it would be a whole lot bigger than TV, but I never thought it would be this huge!" said Miles, and he opened his arms wide and laughed.

"And it was so dark! It was like being outside when there's no moon or anything, but then there was this movie!" said Clara.

Miles and Clara were interested in the running, too, particularly how hard the athletes had to train for the Olympics. But Thos, other than to order his sundae, hadn't said a word since they'd left the Rialto. Spec took note, but he also knew Thos's eyes hadn't strayed from the screen during the movie. When he did speak, the others immediately stopped talking and turned to look at him.

"You know, that's something I could do. I can't play sports like Miles and Clara, 'cause I can't catch balls and stuff, but I can run. I can run fast." He turned to his brother and sister. "Remember when I outran Charlotte? She was really, really fast, don't you think?"

They smiled in agreement and Thos smiled back. He didn't say another word the rest of the evening, but the next day and the next and every day thereafter, he ran, regardless of the weather. When Spec drove the route in his truck, he realized the boy had worked up to five miles, and at a good clip, too.

"How about going out for the track team?" Spec asked him once, but Thos said no, this isn't for anything like that, it's for me.

eye-catching that customers began asking to be put on a list of those who wanted the signs when Jake was finished with them.

Jake was delighted with his three employees. It was nice to have help that didn't complain for a change. It was a wet job, a messy job, what with the lobster tank and the ice and the hosing down, and on a cool, damp day, wind whipped right through the shop, in the front door and out the back. Jake insisted the doors be left open all the time to keep the place aired out.

Jake liked the fact that the children were not only reliable and conscientious, but small, too, so they didn't get in his, or each other's, way. Then, too, they were something of a novelty. Customers were under the impression that much younger children were waiting on them, and began giving them tips. "Get yourself an ice cream," they'd say, pressing a dollar into Clara's hand. "Maybe you'd like to get a nice kite," to Miles or Thos. Finally Jake simply put out a jar for their tips, and it filled quickly each day.

Beach walks were in the evenings now, after the store closed, or on Sundays, their day off, and Thos often didn't get home from his running until long after dark. Still, the children were as pleased with the arrangement as Jake was, and it became their steady job for all the summers they lived on Kings Island.

Fall came, and the children, now in ninth, tenth and eleventh grades, continued to do well in their schoolwork, in most cases far surpassing their classmates. Thos, however, was having his usual trouble with math, although this year he finally had a teacher he liked, a Mr. Darnell.

"There's something so safe about him," he said to Spec during one of their talks, looking everywhere but at Spec, as was his habit. "He stands at the blackboard, holding his chalk, and he takes a problem that has absolutely no hope for a solution, I can't even figure out how to begin, and step by step he solves it. He gives me the feeling I could do that too, I could solve *any* problem, but then he goes on to the next one and the same thing happens all over again."

At parent-teacher conferences, Spec was told that Miles and Clara had settled in and were not trying so hard, which was a "positive sign," according to the teachers. However, they added, the children appeared to have lost interest in making friends. They were comfortable with each other and with their brother, and now seemed to view their classmates as something of an intrusion.

As for Miss Conover, she wondered if perhaps the other children had disappointed Miles and Clara in some way. She had hoped that athletics would foster friendships, but she reported that the Davis children kept to themselves. Although they seemed to enjoy their regular gym classes, they did not care to try out for school teams, and they continued their habit of taking the early bus home after school each day.

Thos, noted Miss Conover, could have made the track team with ease, but he, like Miles and Clara, "elected not to represent Branford Regional as a team member." Her voice was at once disappointed and disapproving.

Hell, if having no friends doesn't bother the kids, no reason it should bother me, said Spec to himself, though not to Miss Conover. They seem happy enough. In fact, he realized later, it made things a lot easier on him. He was hearing all kinds of stories about boys stealing cars, drinking, doing drugs, knocking up girls.

As far as he was concerned, Clara was one of the boys. She seemed to like it that way, and besides, he didn't have to buy her any special clothes, which he couldn't afford anyway.

Do they know the facts of life? he wondered. Probably, yeah, by now they must, thank the good Lord. Save me the embarrassment. Now, Clara, she'd be bleeding pretty soon. There's got to be some kind of class in school about that. Make my taxes go for something worthwhile for a change.

Spec was right about one thing. There was indeed a class about it in school, but his timetable was slightly off. She had already started menstruating.

Oh, SHIT, was Clara's reaction when she saw the blood. She understood what was happening, all right. She knew a period when she saw one, not like the supreme jerks in those confusion-followed-by-blessed-relief pamphlets they gave you to read in Health class. "You and Your Body." Please. And as if blood wasn't enough, she was getting breasts, for God's sake, and from the look of things they were going to be pretty good-sized, too. Well, that was that. She thought about all the times she'd prayed to be a boy, and she shook her head in disbelief.

One day, as Miles was reading on his bed, Clara entered the room.

"Do me a huge favor? I left my school bag in the living room. Mind bringing me my homework assignment? I'm so so so so comfortable."

Clara smiled and went to find the assignment. As she was looking through his school papers, she came across a handwritten page. She read silently:

> *When I was five years old, I watched my mother kill herself. She didn't know I had followed her into the bathroom and saw her put the gun next to her heart. All of a sudden she was on the floor. I don't remember seeing her fall, and there was hardly any blood.*
>
> *When she saw me, she kept saying, "I'm sorry, I'm so sorry." I didn't know why she said that, but when she died, I knew. Making yourself die is worth an apology, all right.*
>
> *I've read that you don't remember something terrible that happens when you're little. You just think you do, because you've heard people talking about it. Well, I was five then, and I'm almost seventeen now. That's nearly twelve years, and in all that time, no one has ever really talked about what happened to Mama.*

She went back into the bedroom and found Thos standing by the bed, talking to Miles.

"What's this?" she asked, handing the paper to Miles.

"Oh, something I wrote. Nothing, really." He handed it back to Clara.

Thos moved next to her and they held the page together, like two singers in the choir sharing sheet music. Thos looked up when he'd finished reading and met Clara's gaze.

It was the kind of thing they would have liked to talk over with Spec, but they'd been trained long ago to turn away from ugliness, pretend it wasn't there. By now all the children had become expert in this art. Besides, Miles's words scared them, and so Thos and Clara simply let the matter drop and didn't even discuss it with each other.

All that year Spec had been teaching Miles to drive. Can't make it in this world without knowing how to drive, he'd said. Then, cautioning Miles to be careful backing out of the driveway, Spec had told him to get behind the wheel of the pickup. You'll be seventeen in the spring, old enough to get a license in Massachusetts, he'd said when they were on their way, and Miles had grinned without looking away from the road, as he gripped the wheel tightly with both hands. He was just tall enough to reach the pedals without a strain.

It was nearly spring now, and Miles had become a pretty damn good driver, Spec thought. He'd taken the half-assed Driver's Ed course in school, so he didn't have to wait until he was eighteen to get a license. He was cautious, didn't take stupid chances. He could shift smoothly, too, although he sometimes stalled when he had to go slowly.

Spec realized that, for the license, they'd need a copy of Miles's birth certificate. Deciding that he might as well get Thos's and Clara's at the same time, he wrote to the Bureau of Vital Statistics in Trenton, New Jersey. He called to find out about the fee and enclosed a check for twelve dollars. He knew that Miles had been born on May 1, 1967, Thos the same day a year later, and Clara sometime in June of 1969. If it turned out he needed the date, he could probably get hold of Stuart. Uncle Stuart should know.

Spec's letter to the Bureau of Vital Statistics was returned. Not the check, though, he noticed. At the bottom of the page someone had stamped the words "We are unable to fulfill your request for the following reason(s):" and there was an "X" in the box marked

"Searched all indexes. No record(s) of the event(s)." There was also a sheet of instructions on how to have a birth recorded. "Delayed report of birth," the form was called.

Holy shit, said Spec to himself. He couldn't even bother to register the births of his own children? Spec was glad he hadn't mentioned anything to the kids. He'd get this straightened out. But it hit him that, even at this late date, he was in the protection business, although at this point he wasn't sure whether he was protecting his father or the kids.

Miles had his driver's license. He'd had no problems with the written test, knew how many car lengths to allow for every 10 miles per hour of travel speed, knew what to do when a traffic light was red but a cop waved him through. Then, as Spec looked on, he had taken the driving test. He had come to a full stop at a stop sign, signaled for a right turn, and, while Spec held his breath, backed into a parking place without stalling.

That night they all went for pizza to celebrate. Miles drove.

Late in the afternoon on the last day of school, the children greeted Spec at the door when he came in from work. They hadn't decided how to break the news that they were going back to Hardwick, and in the end Thos blurted it out.

"When?" was all Spec said.

"Tonight," said Miles. "No sense waiting. We came here in the night. We might as well go back in the night."

"Please, you understand that we have to go, don't you, Spec?" begged Clara. "We left in such a hurry, and it was our whole *life* we left. We've talked about it and talked about it, and we have to know what it was we left. Really, we do."

Spec nodded. He couldn't seem to make his voice work.

They made supper in silence and sat down to eat, but no one was hungry.

Finally the words came.

"Would you like me to come with you?" asked Spec.

The children looked at each other. Then Miles said, "We knew you'd say that, Spec. It's a hard offer to turn down, but this is something we have to do by ourselves."

"I figured all along I had you on loan, and one day you'd go back. I just didn't know how long it would be before you left. At least I got you for a few years."

Everything seemed to move slowly and he couldn't think clearly. He felt as if he were deep-sea diving and his air supply had been cut off.

"But we're not, we're not . . ."

"We're not going forever!"

"We'll be back by the time school starts again!" chorused the children.

"Spec," said Clara, her eyes filling with tears, "we love you!"

She managed a faint smile. Spec could breathe again.

"You know," Clara was saying, "if he hadn't died, we wouldn't be talking about 'going back to school.' We never would have gone to school at all. But he would have insisted we all go to fancy colleges. If he hadn't died. I'm absolutely sure of that."

Spec had noted with relief some time before that Clara no longer felt the need to pose every sentence as a question.

There was silence for a long moment.

"Any idea what you guys will do in Hardwick?"

Spec's way of asking how they planned to bring in money. He was hoping they wouldn't have to use their summer savings.

The children looked at each other once more. Without turning back to Spec, Miles said, "Hank taught us how to fix a lot of stuff. We could do that."

"I think I'm pretty good at drawing, at least that's what people say, and maybe I could earn some money doing that."

"Sounds good, sounds good," said Spec. "But is it okay if big brother lends a hand?"

He still couldn't recognize his own voice. He knew he would miss them desperately.

The children turned to Spec, nodding. He knew they were doing him a favor, not the other way around.

Spec's gaze lingered on each of the children in turn.

"Jesus," he said, "I feel like I should give you something, some kind of going away present."

"You already did," said Miles. "Where would we be now if it wasn't for you? You rescued us, Spec."

He knew it was the children who had rescued him.

"Go back to fishing," said Clara unexpectedly. "You could give us that."

"Yeah," added Thos. "You won't have us to worry about now!" He forced himself to sound enthusiastic.

"Anyway, I want to picture you out there on the ocean, walking around the edge of the boat like you were walking down the street," said Clara, smiling.

"We'll see. You never know."

Spec was hoping he wouldn't cry. He'd hate like hell to have the kids see him crying.

"Say," said Spec, a thought having struck him, "how do you plan to get to New Jersey?"

"Hitchhike," they said in unison.

"No way. You're taking the truck," Spec announced flatly.

They began to protest, but he put up his hand and raised his voice over theirs.

"No, please." His voice had turned imploring. "Please. Take the truck," and the children didn't argue further.

And then it was time.

They stood by the truck, and Spec hugged each of them, wishing he could hold on forever. They threw their things in the back and climbed into the cab, Miles behind the wheel, Clara on the other side, and Thos settling in between them.

Resting his hands on the window frame, Spec slammed Clara's door, but he didn't let go.

"There are a bunch of maps under the seat. And let me know where I can send a check if I get in the mood."

Talk of specifics made him feel better. Something to do. A goal.

For a long moment he gazed at each of the children in turn, as if etching their images into his memory. They'd always be small, Spec knew. They had their father's miserable care to thank for that.

Miles and Thos were the same height, but Thos's features were more carved, more delicate. Thos had developed muscle since he'd started running, but he would stay thinner, lighter than Miles. And Clara, who would always look like she'd been brought in on a sunbeam. They were smart, he thought, smart as hell. Besides, Miles was clever, Thos was handsome, and Clara was artistic. It was like a fairy tale, the gifts of the good witch who had attended their births. He prayed she was still around and would watch over them now.

"Safe trip," he said abruptly, without adding "be careful backing out," his usual admonition when Miles went out of the driveway. He slapped the truck once and moved away, hands already in his pockets. He called good-bye but couldn't bring himself to return their waves as he watched them drive off.

Spec went into the house, into his room, and began rummaging in the closet through his clothes. At last he found Trudy's blue silk dress, the one she wore to their wedding, the only thing of hers he had saved. He buried his face in it, imagining, even after all this time, that her smell lingered.

Then he went out to the lighthouse, more than an hour's walk, and stood on a patch of impossibly green grass and watched the sun go down. At first it was too bright to look at straight on, but at some point it turned the color of sunsets and he was able to see it as a ball hovering over the horizon, poised to drop, he thought, like the glittering one in Times Square on New Year's Eve. The sun hung there for what seemed a long time before balancing on the line that separated the sea and the sky, then allowed itself to be bisected, and finally slid out of sight. Spec stood in the wind, watching, until the last tiny dot of light was gone.

CHAPTER TWENTY - SEVEN

Thos and Clara were too excited to sleep on the way back to Hardwick, and they talked with Miles about playing in the river, about the game of "Society," about Hank and Eldon and Sally Bea. They didn't mention their father, or their mother.

It was still dark when they arrived, and the three decided to pull over and wait for daylight before actually entering Hardwick. And so the sky was beginning to brighten when they drove through town. Five years had passed since they'd left, and it hadn't changed as far as they could tell. It all looked exactly the same—the gas station and the laundromat, the antique shop and the Hardwick Market. They'd come back later and surprise Eldon and Sally Bea.

Thos fingered the piece of blue sea glass in his pocket as they approached the house. Miles went as slowly as he could without stalling. He pulled into the driveway, even more grown over than they remembered, and turned off the engine. They sat in silence, waiting. Everywhere they saw ghosts of their younger selves.

"We didn't make it up, did we?" whispered Miles. Then, "Let's go in."

Thos and Clara followed him into the house. All three stopped short once they stepped inside.

"Where is everything?" asked Thos.

They knew Spec had brought lots of the furniture back to Kings Island, but somehow they hadn't realized this meant the piles had been dismantled.

The men who had helped Spec clean out, who had followed him to Kings Island with a truckload, had kept their word. They had come back and done a thorough cleaning, ridding the house of the dirt and grease, the dead mice and dried feces. A thick layer of dust had accumulated in their place.

What furniture there was had been lined up along the wall. Some of it they recognized and some they didn't, and they knew it had been stored in the piles. Without speaking, the children went directly to the leather chairs and together they dragged them over to the woodstove and arranged them as they knew they had to be.

"It doesn't look like home," said Thos as they worked.

"No, but we'll get used to it," said Miles practically, brushing a cobweb from the back of one of the chairs. "Besides, it's as close to home as we're going to get while we're here."

The children brought in their things from the truck, little piles of shorts and T-shirts and jeans, and took them upstairs. Then, as if remembering there was more to the house than what they'd seen, they went down to look at the bathroom, and at the kitchen, and knew the memory of what this place used to be would never leave them.

They walked over and peered out the window where, years before, they had stood with their mother and father and watched the river waters rise.

"The trees have gotten so thick you can hardly see the river from here," said Miles softly.

"Well, I'll be!" shrieked Sally Bea delightedly. "If it isn't Miles and Thos and little Clary, back from the dead!"

Nothing would do but that they tell her all about Kings Island, what was it like, what did they do there, how was it different from Hardwick, what was the story on Spec and his, what's her name? Oh, yes, Trudy. How were they?

It was some time before Miles was able to ask the question on all their minds.

"Where's Eldon?"

"Eldon? You didn't hear? Guess you wouldn't have, come to think about it. See, he couldn't stand this place without you kids and that doctor father of yours. 'Course he never said that right out, but I knew. Anyway, he and his Lucille, they moved on down to Florida to live with her sister. But Eldon, he goes and gets himself a stroke and all he does is sit all day, Lucille says, kind of looking into space, but not really, if you know what I mean. I get a card from her every once in a while, has palm trees or oranges on it, something like that."

"But the Yummycakes! He sends us Yummycakes!" said Thos.

"Well, now, when they first got to Florida, Eldon calls me in a panic. 'Sally Bea!' he says, real upset. 'There aren't any Yummycakes down here! You'll have to send them for me, you hear?' So that's me sending them. Still taste good though, don't they?" She laughed her crackly laugh.

"I got some extra help in the market," said Sally Bea, as if they'd asked. "Tried to do it with the one clerk, but it was too much, with my shop and everything. But I'm making do just fine."

The children chatted a while longer, bought a few groceries, and turned to leave.

"See you soon, Sally Bea," said Thos.

"Probably see you every day," added Miles.

"Every day," echoed Clara, but her voice sounded hollow even to herself.

Hardwick without Eldon. It didn't seem possible.

From force of old, old habit they had walked into town, never thinking to take the truck. Now, on their way back to the house, they passed the road to the cemetery.

"Let's go visit Mama," said Miles. "We haven't been to see her in a long time."

"He'll probably be there too, don't you think?" asked Thos.

"I guess so," said Clara. "He has to be somewhere."

"Valhalla" came into all of their minds, but no one said it aloud.

Two surprises awaited them at the cemetery. The first was that their mother's grave had a stone marker: "FRANCES TAYLOR DAVIS," it said in letters too large for the small stone. "BORN NOVEMBER 2, 1945. DIED NOVEMBER 16, 1972." Underneath, in smaller letters, were the words "Our blessed daughter, sister, and mother." The children spent a long time talking to her, telling her about Spec and about their life on Kings Island.

The second surprise was that there was no sign of their father's grave. They knew he'd had no funeral, Spec's words forever fresh in their minds: "Well, here are the instructions. There isn't going to be any funeral."

"Even if there's no funeral, I'm pretty sure they have to do something with the body," said Thos.

"Do you think they burned him up?" asked Clara.

"Cremated him, you mean?" said Miles. "Maybe, but he could still be buried. I wonder if that funeral place is still there. Where we went for Mama. They could probably tell us."

They walked on to the house, put the groceries away, and got into the truck.

"We'll have to ask Sally Bea how to get there," said Miles, before turning on the ignition. "I can sort of picture the inside of the place, but I don't really know where it is."

"Think we're dressed okay?" asked Thos a few minutes later as they headed for the funeral home, armed with directions from Sally Bea.

"It's not like we've got ties and jackets back at the house, you know. Jeans and T-shirts will have to do," said Miles.

The funeral home was a small, tacky, shingled building that looked as if a good wind would carry it away. A sign on the door said "Welcome to all who are in pain," and they let themselves in, setting off a tinkling bell as the door opened.

"Hello, and what can I do for you young people?" inquired the portly man who seemed to have been lying in wait. He looked them over carefully.

To Clara, he appeared to have been dipped in oil. His hair, his suit, his shoes, even his voice had a greasy shine.

Clara and Thos looked expectantly at Miles.

"We'd like some information regarding the whereabouts of our father's remains."

Now Clara and Thos looked at each other. Where had he learned to talk like this?

"Certainly. You are members of the family, I presume?" His heavy sarcasm was not lost on the children.

"'Our father,' I said." Miles was keeping his temper with difficulty. "Yes, we are 'members of the family,' if children are considered 'members of the family.'" That one was too good to pass up, he thought.

"Of course," said the man. He drew the words out slowly, so that their original meaning slipped away. "Now, what was the name of the deceased?"

He had produced a gold pen and a small notebook, and a pair of reading glasses had landed on his nose.

"The name of the deceased *is*," Miles paused for emphasis, "Leslie Davis. He 'passed on' on April 23, 1979." This sucker would faint if I said "died," he thought.

"Let me look that up. I'll be with you in a moment."

Clara watched him slide out of the room on his own personal oil slick.

He returned sooner than they expected. He was holding a large volume and reading from it.

"Leslie Davis. Here it is. 'Transported to Philadelphia.' That means the deceased was taken to Philadelphia for burial at a cemetery there." He glanced up. "I suppose you would like me to provide you with that information as well?"

He blinked rapidly several times.

"That would be very nice. We would appreciate it," said Miles, resisting the urge to blink rapidly in turn.

The man left the room again, and the children expected him to come back with Volume Two, but instead he held a piece of paper, which he handed to Miles.

"Here you are, Mr. Davis," he said. "This is the name of the cemetery as well as its address, should you wish to pay your respects. It is a very prestigious resting place, let me assure you. Undoubtedly, your father is highly honored to be interred there."

"Yes, well, thank you so much for your time," said Miles, smiling a sudden, chilly smile, which he let drop almost immediately.

They closed the door and hoped the man couldn't hear their violent giggling.

Thos was the first to catch his breath. "How in the world did you know to talk like that?"

"TV," said Miles. "You know, you can learn a lot from TV."

With the aid of Spec's maps they drove an hour to Philadelphia, where they pulled into a gas station and asked directions to the cemetery. A few minutes later they were following a narrow driveway that led through iron gates and up a rather steep hill. At the top was a sign that said "Buildings and Grounds," with an arrow pointing to the right.

"This must be it," said Miles, as he parked the truck.

They climbed out and started toward the door when Thos spoke.

"I'm a little bit scared," he said. "How about you?"

He looked at Miles and then at Clara.

"Scared?" said Miles. "No, not scared. Excited, I think. Curious."

Clara took Thos's hand.

"I know why you're scared. It's 'cause you feel like he's near here. It's okay."

She gave him a quick kiss on the hand.

Thos looked at her and then at Miles.

"Okay," he said, "I guess we should go in."

They entered a stone building with a long corridor lined on either side with offices. There were small signs beside each door, and, having read them all, they settled on "Caretaker."

A thin, gray-haired man wearing a black turtleneck sweater sat behind a counter. He badly needed a shave.

"Can I help you?" he asked, already making his way over to them.

"We're looking for our father's grave," said Miles.

No more fancy talk. This was the real thing, he thought. We're almost there.

"Name?"

"Leslie Davis. He died on—"

"Nope, don't need that. The name is all."

He went to a file cabinet and appeared to be rehearsing the alphabet before pulling open a drawer. Then he closed it and opened the one right below, and took out a document.

"Wait a minute, I'll make you a copy of this," said the man, and turned on the copying machine behind him. They didn't speak while it warmed up. The copy came through and the man set it down on the counter so it faced the children.

"Here you go." Reading upside down, the man explained the map of the burial plots and drew a line along the path they should follow.

TV, Miles had said, and now Clara remembered a commercial she'd seen that showed a car rental agent drawing the route on an upside-down map so his customer could better follow the driving instructions. Then this scene deviated from the television script.

"Know what?" said the man, crumpling the paper and tossing it into a trash basket. "I'm going over that way now. Come on with me."

Once outside, he hurried ahead, his long strides making it difficult for the children to keep up. Every once in a while they had to run a few steps.

"Well, this is it," said their guide after a time, and led them into a small grove with a view that opened onto the city. "Nicest location we have. What do you think?"

Without waiting for an answer, he showed them to a very large, marble headstone and there they were, standing at their father's grave. "LESLIE DAVIS, M.D. MARCH 5, 1914 - APRIL 23, 1979." That was all. Except that underneath there was a space for another name and pair of dates.

Miles looked questioningly at the man, who shrugged in reply.

"Got me. I can tell you the stone was what we call 'pre-need.' He ordered it for himself. Guess he knew what he was doing, don't you suppose? His stone and all?"

CHAPTER TWENTY - EIGHT

The children stood silently, looking down at the stone, unaware that their guide had said good-bye and left.

"Do you think we should say something to him?" asked Clara.

"Like what?" said Miles.

"Oh, maybe tell him how we're doing?"

"Good idea," said Thos. "We can tell him how much better things are for us now, how great Spec is, how we don't miss him at all."

He turned to Clara.

"Is that what you meant?"

"Something like that," she replied, and started to laugh. Miles and Thos laughed too.

Then Miles said, "Maybe we should leave. Anybody who sees us here, three kids standing over a grave and laughing—well, it might not look so good."

They grew quiet again.

"Good-bye, sir," said Miles after a moment.

"Good-bye, sir," chorused Thos and Clara.

And they went back to the truck.

They drove slowly out through the iron gates and there, directly in front of them, was Philadelphia Founders Hospital, an enormous, gray building. Trees had been planted along the front, but they were struggling and did not seem to have been well tended. A large sign with an arrow and the word "Parking" was propped against a telephone pole.

"It's his hospital," breathed Clara.

"It looks like a jail," said Thos.

"Yeah," agreed Miles. "It sure does."

They sat looking at it for a long time.

It was early evening when they got back to the house.

"Can we go to Shoreline and get something to eat?" asked Clara. "I'm hungry! We haven't had anything since those hot dogs on the way down here!"

"Don't forget the potato chips," said Thos, touching her lightly on the chin.

"Oh, how could I forget the potato chips?" laughed Clara.

"We'll go to Shoreline after Thos goes running," said Miles. He turned to his brother. "*Are* you going running?"

Thos nodded.

"Would it be so terrible if you missed a day? One day?" demanded Clara.

He smiled. "It would."

But by the time he returned they were too tired to go out and made do with some canned soup and a few crackers. Then they went upstairs to the bare foam mattresses that remained on the floor of their bedroom. Covered by only a thin blanket, they fell asleep quickly and slept dreamlessly until morning.

They awoke early, warmed by the sunlight that came through the window, but aware that the air had turned much colder. Miles, his eyes still closed, spoke first.

"What do you say we check out the office this morning?"

"Would anything still be in there, do you think?" asked Thos.

"It seems like everything that came up to Kings Island was from the house. I don't remember any stuff from the office," said Clara.

Slipping on their sweatshirts, they went downstairs and past the kitchen. Miles stopped.

"Anybody hungry?" he asked.

The others shook their heads.

"Better not risk using the toilet," he said, glancing into the bathroom. "But I'll bet Thos and I can fix it. For now we can go outside. Like old times." And he forced a laugh.

Outdoors the sun highlighted the tangle of thorny catbrier vines winding around, then up the trees. Dozens of inkberry bushes, fighting for space, had grown into a single mass. The office was no longer visible from the house.

They walked out the driveway and along the road, their sneakers making dust rise from the sandy soil, and there it was, exactly as they remembered it.

The door, which had been left ajar, creaked loudly as they forced it open. They stepped inside and felt keenly the vastness of the space and the memory of Johnny Johnson working on his cars. In the sunlight they could see dust motes hanging in the air, which mingled with the tiny clouds of their breath.

An inner door opened into the office. Here they walked around warily, avoiding the many boxes of X-rays, and peered into carton after carton filled with lab equipment. They didn't touch anything for fear their father would somehow appear and reprimand them.

They found the boxes of personal possessions that Spec had been unable to cope with and simply left where he'd found them. They stared at these items that had once been their father's, in his pockets, in his hands.

They talked very little, remarking only on something one of them found and wanted to draw to the attention of the others.

Thos found the journals.

"Look at these," he said. "These are those books he was always writing in."

He lifted the journals out of their carton and the children counted them, twelve in all. Each was dated, the first 1967 and the last 1978.

"He would have been working on 1979, I guess," said Thos. "That's why it's not here with the others."

They carried the notebooks outside, hoping to be warmer in the sun, but the air was still cool. They sat down on the grass and shivered as they began to read. It was slow going. Davis had used numerous abbreviations and a private shorthand. Still, they were able to understand a good part of what they found, which included Miles and the mouse traps, "Society," and Thos's tears following the incident with Charlotte. The children had thought they'd kept the weeping a secret from their father.

Clara picked up "1972" and opened to November 16th.

"Listen to this," she said, and read, "'F. died today. Used wadcutter!'"

"That's it?" asked Miles.

"That's it," replied Clara.

The children searched the other books but that was the last mention of their mother.

They stacked the notebooks in the carton and put it back where they had found it. They were unable to shake the feeling that they were someplace where they shouldn't be, that someone would find out they'd been there and they would be in trouble. And yet they couldn't seem to leave, and they continued to poke around.

Miles sat down at his father's desk and began opening the drawers. The small, top drawer was practically empty, with just some pipe tobacco and a tape dispenser. The other drawers were crammed with medical journals and scientific papers of various kinds. They were so heavy Miles could hardly get them open. When he pulled the bottom drawer, the largest and heaviest, it kept coming until it fell onto the floor, spilling its contents.

"Shit," said Miles, and began to pick up the papers. Which was how he happened to come across a large manila envelope with the word "Frances" printed in the upper left-hand corner.

"C, Thos, I think you better come see this." He hadn't opened the envelope or taken his eyes off of it. He waited until they stood by him.

Miles withdrew the contents of the envelope, three items, which he laid on the desk. The first was their mother's death certificate. "Occupation: Housewife," he read.

The second was an X-ray. Stapled to it was a typed note, dated 11/7/66: "Twenty-one-year-old female. Fetal development approximately twelve weeks. X-ray reveals presence of twins."

"Oh Jesus oh Jesus oh Jesus," whispered Clara. "You don't think she knew, do you?" She was crying.

The third item was a letter, folded several times. It had been written in ink on a piece of white paper torn neatly from a tablet, and the script was small and precise, identical to the labels in the books of photos Spec had brought with him to Kings Island.

Miles, furiously wiping his eyes, began to read it aloud, but he could not continue and finally they huddled together, reading silently:

> *My baby—*
>
>   *I don't even know if you were a girl or a boy, but I do know you would have been the twin of my little Miles, and I would have loved you so much!*
>
>   *Your father thought we should keep you from coming into the world. I thought we were sinning against God, but now, my sweet, sweet baby, I know he was right. This world is a very sad place, and you were the lucky one. But I will always, always miss you.*
>
>   *I kiss you and I love you.*
>
>   *Your Mama*

They read the letter again and again, their tears falling on the paper and blurring the words. At last Miles looked at Clara and at Thos.

"For as long as I can remember," he said softly, "I've felt like I lost something. Someone. It's hard to explain. I used to think it was Mama, but then when we started going to visit Gran and Uncle Stuart in Philadelphia, I knew that wasn't it. I mean, sure, I lost Mama. We all lost Mama. But I—I was a twin. There were two of me. And you guys lost a brother or a sister. There should have been four of us, you know?"

After a moment, Miles went on in his hoarse voice that faded in and out of a whisper.

"I'm not sure why, but this makes me feel better. Well, better about me, because I didn't make it up. But I feel worse about him. Much, much worse about him."

Thos and Clara nodded.

"She was a good mother, wasn't she?" said Clara. "Even for a little while. You know, I'll bet she hated to leave us. I'll bet she really loved being our mother."

They gathered the things together and put them carefully back into the envelope.

"Can I keep this stuff?" asked Miles. "I mean, I know it's not really mine. It's not really anybody's, I guess. But if I could look at it whenever I felt like it . . . ."

And then they were crying again and hugging each other.

The next morning there was a knock at the door. All three went to answer it, as if the task required that. A tall woman stood before them.

"Hello," she said. She was smiling but her eyes were sad. "I wondered how long it would be before you'd come back. I've been waiting for you. You probably don't remember me, but I was your mother's friend. There are so many things she wanted me to tell you."

Dorothy stepped inside and Miles closed the door behind her. It was the first time she had been in the house.

She continued, "You were so young when she—left. Just three, four and five." She looked from Clara to Thos to Miles. "Do you know that she thought she was the luckiest person in the world, because she got to be your mother? That she called you her three 'lucky charms'?"

Dorothy knew she was talking too much, talking too fast, but she couldn't seem to stop herself. She saw that the children were looking at her as if trying to place her.

"But if we were her lucky charms, why did she have to die?" said Thos suddenly. "Why couldn't our luck save her?" The words tumbled out.

"Oh, my dears," said Dorothy gently. "Sometimes luck just isn't in charge. Sometimes it isn't even invited to the party."

Dorothy stayed most of the day. The children showed her around the house and tried to describe it as it was when they lived there. They couldn't know that their mother had described it before them. Then Dorothy, Miles, Thos and Clara took a walk along the dirt road. When they passed the site of Hank's cabin, Miles exchanged glances with his sister and brother.

As they walked, Dorothy asked them, "Do you remember the rhyming game your mother made up for you?"

They shook their heads.

"You would say, 'Hard,' and then she would say, 'Card,' or 'Lard,' and you would say, 'That rhymes!' Then you would say, 'Wick,' and she would say, 'Brick,' or 'Quick,' or 'Thick,' and you would scream, 'That rhymes!'"

Miles, Thos and Clara looked at each other and smiled.

Everywhere along the road there were blossom-covered bushes—blue huckleberry, pink and white mountain laurel and dewberry. The vegetation had grown higher, fuller, more dramatic. But the houses they passed had not changed.

"We thought Hardwick would look different," said Miles.

"It does seem kind of frozen in time, doesn't it?" said Dorothy. "People don't seem to move away from here, and new people don't come very often. I guess everybody likes things the way they are. Nothing gets built, nothing gets torn down. That could be Hardwick's motto."

She looked at the children and tried to read their faces.

"How did you think it would look?"

"I don't know. When I imagined it all the time we were in Quarter Harbor, this is what I saw. But something doesn't feel right." Miles shifted his gaze from Dorothy to the ground.

"It feels that way to me, too," said Thos.

"Me, too," said Clara. "I guess we changed but Hardwick didn't." She frowned slightly as she spoke.

Dorothy smiled. "Do you miss Hardwick?"

Clara stopped walking and closed her eyes. The others stopped and looked at her.

"I was sad here. I don't think I knew it then, but now I do. Anyway, everything I love came with me to Quarter Harbor. Except for Sally Bea and Eldon. I used to pretend that they moved there, too, and they opened a market just like the one here. And Spec . . . ."

She opened her eyes. They were filled with tears.

When Dorothy and the children got back to the house, the four stood awkwardly outside the door.

"Would you like to stay for supper?" asked Clara politely. "We don't have anything fancy, but if that's okay with you . . ."

Dorothy looked down at their tired, anxious faces.

"Your mother would have been so proud of you. She said she could picture you grown up, how beautiful you would be, how glad the world would be to have you here."

Once more she smiled her sad smile.

"Thank you for the invitation. I'd love to do it some other time, but I think I should go now."

As she turned toward her car, Miles demanded,

"How do you know so much about us? I mean, even after Mama died?"

Dorothy turned back and looked from one to the other.

"Oh, I know you. Until the day you left Hardwick, I watched you when you came into town. I used to take my paints and work at the market, over in the corner, so I'd be sure not to miss you. You never noticed me. There was no need for you to notice me. And Eldon. Eldon told me things." Her voice trailed off. "You know," she said then, "we have much, much more to talk about. I'll see you tomorrow."

She wanted to hug them but it was too soon.

As soon as she'd gone, Thos looked at Miles and then at Clara, and the three of them knew they had to go tell their mother about the visit. They drove to the cemetery and sat around her tombstone, talking together, finishing each other's sentences. The sun was beginning to set when they climbed into the truck.

They drove back toward the house, but suddenly Miles made a right turn; Thos and Clara looked at him questioningly. Then they understood, and smiles played around their lips.

When they got to Gravity Hill, Miles put the truck in neutral and shut off the engine. With the heat off, the cab quickly turned cold, and they sank down into their sweatshirts. Already they could feel themselves being pulled forward, slowly, slowly, up the hill, and they looked out the window until the warmth of their breath clouded the view.

ACKNOWLEDGMENTS

Twenty-one years is a long time to work on a book, and more people than I can possibly thank have helped me along the way. It takes a village, and I owe every single member of this particular village a debt of gratitude: The readers, who read draft after draft, people like Leslie Newman, who made perceptive, intelligent observations, and my mother, Julia Rosenwald, who, though in her 90's, remains the most literate, literary person I know; my writers group, Marge Dwyer, Mary Jane Aklonis, and Areta Parlé, who read the manuscript and worked through countless obstacles with me; and the many experts who helped me understand what it would mean to live in a kingdom of madness.

My greatest thanks go to Areta Parlé, who began as a fellow member of the writers group and became my editor. She is gifted and wonderful, filled with insight and humor. Besides deciding to write this book, my best idea was to ask Areta to be by my side over these last two years. If words could describe what she has done for me, I would write them here.

And finally, I thank my family—my husband, Paul, who is my support in every way, including tech, and our children, Jeff, Deb and Tim, all of whom may have doubted that this day would ever come, but who never stopped cheering me on.

Edwards Brothers,Inc!
Thorofare, NJ 08086
28 September, 2010
BA2010271